WRECK ME

BECKETT BROTHERS
BOOK 1

L A GALLAGHER

Copyright © L A Gallagher 2024

All Rights Reserved

All rights reserved. No part of this publication may be reproduced, stored in a retrieval system or transmitted in any forms or by any means, without the prior permission in writing of the publisher, nor to be otherwise circulated in any form of binding or cover other than that in which it is published.

All the characters in this book are fictitious. Any resemblance to any actual persons, living or dead, is purely coincidental.

ASIN: B0CMXG4KXQ

For those of you who long to be seen...

Chapter One
JAMES

I look.

But I never touch.

I love women, but I never pay for sex. It's a matter of principle. It's not because some silly society magazine voted me Ireland's most eligible billionaire three years running.

Even if the sheer carnality of being surrounded by stunning, half-naked women, while I sip whiskey with my brothers appeals to the caveman in me. Which is precisely why I've scheduled tonight's family meeting in the Luxor Lounge, Dublin's most exclusive gentlemen's club. We're the wealthiest family in the city, but we're usually only gentlemen when our mother is around.

The club is only a stones' throw from the opulent Grafton Street headquarters of our family business, Beckett Enterprises. The dancers employed at the Luxor Lounge are privately educated, intelligent, and stunning. Many of them are also willing to provide additional services in the sultry confines of one of the numerous private rooms flanking the main stage, for the right price.

But I have no interest.

Never have.

Never will.

I like a woman to take my cock because she *wants* to take it, not because she's being paid. Perhaps I'm more gentlemanly than I thought? A small scoff catches in my throat as I approach the door. The name of the Luxor Lounge is scrawled in a rich gold italic font across tinted glass.

Two burly guys in black Armani tuxedos greet me with a curt nod. They could pass for wedding guests instead of security guards, which is why I'm certain they're my brother Killian's men.

Beckett's Whiskey was founded by my grandfather and is the original source of our family's wealth. Over time, we've acquired a number of lucrative subsidiaries, each different division run by a different brother.

Killian runs one of the country's most prominent security companies, catering to high-profile clients and venues, providing everything from high-end security systems to highly trained men. And his employees are always immaculately dressed, discreet, and deadly – just like Killian himself.

'Good evening, Mr Beckett.' One of the bouncers holds open the door.

As I step inside the dimly lit lounge, tucking my hands casually into my suit pockets, the familiar scent of orchids and jasmine fills my nostrils. I bet Christopher Cole, the club's sycophantic owner, paid some expensive perfumer to create this signature scent. It's the kind of egotistical bullshit he'd get off on. *Eau de Sleaze*.

Cole was two years ahead of me at school. He golfs with my father and the rest of Dublin's elite, ruthlessly exploiting eighteen holes to ass kiss anyone he thinks can help him slither up the social ladder, like a snake gliding through the grass. It could be a hundred degrees outside and I still wouldn't warm to him.

Mind you, I don't warm to many people outside of my family. My brothers are my best friends. We feel like killing each other at times, but we always have each other's backs. Blood is thicker than water, and everything in between.

As I enter the main lounge, the beat of a loud bass thuds through my body, heavy and sensual. My eyes are drawn to taut, tanned flesh, expensive scraps of strategically placed lace, and the subtle contours of what lies beneath.

Even if I refuse to pay for sex, my dick can't deny the lasciviousness of the scene in front of me.

Dancers dot the room, some on elevated platforms, hips swaying, fingers grazing over slick, sweat-misted skin. Others linger at tables, drinking champagne, perching on laps, and subtly gyrating their hips in time to the beat.

Strategically placed lilac lighting lines the low-coved ceilings. Spotlights illuminate an elevated circular platform which forms the main stage, punctuated with a gleaming chrome pole. A slender dancer wearing a silver silk thong and sky-high stilettos swings gracefully around it, bending, contorting and exposing herself in a slow seductive show.

Giselle, the manager, approaches. In a tailored pencil dress and suit jacket she looks more suited to the managerial role of a hotel than a high-end strip club.

'Mr Beckett, it's lovely to see you again.' She points to my brothers, sprawled across a private booth to the left of the stage. A bottle of whiskey sits on the table between them.

Fucking O'Connor's Whiskey, of all things.

The O'Connors are our bitter rivals. The feud between our family spans decades. I swear Cole stocks it just to piss me off.

'The girls will be with you immediately.' Giselle pats her chignon. 'If you need anything, don't hesitate to ask.'

I stride across the polished concrete floor. Every eye

burns on my back as the crowd parts in front of me like I'm Moses and they're the Red Sea.

I'm used to scrutiny. As the CEO of Beckett Enterprises, I'm permanently in the public eye. In under a year, I've steered the business to the forefront of the global whiskey market, doubling our net worth. My name is featured as regularly in the Financial Times, as it is in the society pages.

Unfortunately, today, I'm on the front page of The Irish Insider, one of the less reputable papers.

Once again, I'm at the centre of a sex scandal.

I've spent the day defending my actions to my PA, the press and even my mother, and I'm expecting a summons from The Board sometime very soon.

Which is precisely why I called this family meeting.

Because I have a plan.

Chapter Two
SCARLETT

Stunning women of all descriptions flit around the changing rooms in various stages of undress. I shift on the thick velvet stool and readjust the gleaming platinum wig framing my face. I barely recognise the woman in the gilded oval mirror. Huge kohl-lined eyes, expertly contoured cheekbones, and thick dark lashes. Full lips outlined in a rich, sultry shade of crimson match the decadent lingerie sculpting my skin.

If you can call it lingerie.

Two lace scraps cover my nipples and a matching triangle nestles between my legs and ass cheeks. It's the tiniest outfit I've ever worn, but undoubtably the most expensive, thanks to the Luxor Lounge's limitless account at Belle de Nuit, Dublin's most exclusive lingerie store.

'Sister, you look smoking,' my best friend, Avery, declares in her distinguished private-school accent. She might be a glorified stripper, but she's also six months off graduating from Trinity, Dublin's most desirable college, with a doctorate in psychology. We were roommates in the first year. We lived together, ate together, studied together, and now she's finally convinced me to work with her, too.

Avery perches on the vanity station in front of me and places a bottle of open champagne between us. In a two-piece silk ensemble that cost more than my monthly rent, Avery looks pretty fucking smoking herself. Her ability to move her body gracefully and shamelessly is pretty dang attractive too.

My eyes return to the mirror. 'I don't know if I can do it,' I confess.

'Course you can.' Avery reaches out, stroking the back of my arm. 'You were born to perform.'

'Naked?' I motion to inch after inch of exposed skin.

'Trust me. The sensation of being watched, being admired, desired, and fought over and sought after by the wealthiest, most powerful men in this country is almost as exhilarating as having one of them between your legs.'

I wouldn't know.

I've never had any man between my legs.

At the age of twenty three, I've barely been kissed.

What happened to my mother was enough to put me off men for a long time. Both her marriages were miserable. The second one literally killed her. My fingers instinctively reach for the dainty silver cross lodged in the hollow of my neck. It's the only item I own that belonged to her. I never take it off.

What would she think if she could see me now?

Would she be horrified?

Probably not. Carlotta Fitzgerald was the most liberated person to walk the planet. She used to say, 'If you've got it, flaunt it.' And she had it. She was beautiful. Dark hair and piercing eyes, although her most attractive quality was undoubtably her heart.

Avery touches my bare shoulder, dragging me back to the present.

'Like I'd know.' I pull a face. Avery is well aware my

virginity is a burden I haven't been brave enough to shake. Not because I'm afraid of the pain. Not physically, anyway.

'Trust me, Scarlett, being on that stage is enthralling. The seductive thrum of the beat. The weight of every wanting stare. The power you hold with every deliberate flick of your hips. You'll never feel as alive.' She grabs two champagne flutes and holds them up to inspect them, before filling them.

'I'll take your word for it.' There's no way on this earth I'd contemplate dancing at the Luxor Lounge if I wasn't desperate. With less than a hundred euros in my current account, forty thousand euro of debt on various credit cards, and about a tenner in my purse, I'm out of other options.

Especially now my money-grabbing landlord has increased my rent with immediate effect.

The college pole-dancing classes we started in our first year were supposed to be for fitness, but Avery quickly learned to harness them in more lucrative ways.

'Drink this.' Avery thrusts a glass under my face. 'It'll help.'

I take three huge mouthfuls then place the half empty glass on the marble table. 'What if they don't like me? What if I fall flat on my face?'

Avery's low throaty laugh isn't unkind. 'Honey, you are the most stunning woman to pass through those fancy tinted glass doors.' She gestures towards my olive skin. 'You radiate an innocence that no amount of money can buy. And you won't fall.' She takes a sip from her glass. 'Not unless it's head over heels in love with a rich, sexy banker, of course.'

I scoff. 'No chance.'

Love isn't a part of my plans. I've seen the destruction it causes. My plan is to graduate with a masters in finance and travel the world. Finally escape the city where I've been hiding in plain sight. Romance is for books and movies. Not real life. And certainly not for me.

'Never say never.' Avery crosses her long legs, her features pinching into a knowing look. 'I've seen you ogling the society pages. Don't think I don't know you have a relentless crush on James Beckett.' She taps her nose conspicuously.

He might be Ireland's most eligible bachelor, but she has no idea I was raised to despise him.

I dab a trace of mascara away from under my eye. 'Doesn't every woman with a pulse have a crush on him?'

'I suppose I wouldn't kick him out of bed for eating crisps.' Avery likes her men the way she likes her martinis— dirty. And James has a reputation for doing dirty deeds.

Avery lifts her glass to her lips but pauses before taking a sip. 'You do know he's a member here, right?'

'No way!' My brows skyrocket.

'He is, but he never pays for anything other than the whiskey, if you know what I mean.' She waggles her elegant eyebrows.

Even if he did, I'm not for sale. I'm here to dance. Nothing more.

Two suited security guys duck into the changing rooms to escort the next set of dancers to the podiums.

Including me.

I'm in the next set.

I down the contents of my glass.

'You've got this.' Avery winks and stands to escort me. 'Think of the money.'

I swallow back the bile rising in my throat.

The money. That's why I'm here. Two thousand euro a night plus tips. I can do this. It's just a few dances. Albeit, almost naked.

Shoving the stool back with my legs, I stand, nod at my friend and swivel on my six-inch gold stilettos.

'It's just a dance. Owen and Tristan will make sure no one

touches you.' Avery gestures to the two broad security guards. 'Unless you want them to, that is...' She winks lasciviously.

I suck in a breath, straighten my spine and follow Owen and Tristan along a wide, carpeted corridor to the main lounge. Avery falls into step beside me. She takes my hand and gives it a fleeting, reassuring squeeze.

As we approach the main lounge, the sensual beat reverberates through every cell in my body. The aircon whips cold air across my bare ass cheeks, a reminder of my near nakedness. Then Owen places a hand on the small of my back, motioning me up onto the stage. I crane my neck, looking up at him, desperate.

It's my first night. Surely one of the side stages or smaller podiums would be more suitable?

My heart hammers like a war drum. I glance at Avery. She shoos me up the small flight of steps with her pink painted fingers.

'You aced your audition.' She shrugs and nods towards the manager, Giselle, who's standing at the bar in a power suit and wearing an earpiece, surveying her surroundings like she's in charge of a military operation, not a glorified strip club.

Men fill the lounge, flank the bar, and congregate on low leather couches.

I swallow thickly, and mount the steps.

Chapter Three
JAMES

'Finally, he graces us with his presence,' Rian, my youngest brother, drawls. He reclines in the leather booth seat and flashes a cocky smile.

Rian is on the cusp of launching his own nightclub chain, turning his passion for partying into a career. At least that's his plan, anyway. One thing's for sure, his establishments won't be stocking O'Connor's Whiskey.

'Show a bit of respect to your elders.' Caelon kicks Rian under the table but his tone is playful.

At thirty-three, I'm the oldest. Caelon's next, followed by Killian, Sean and Rian. We have a sister, Zara, but she's too young to attend family meetings yet, even the ones that aren't in high-end clubs with mediocre whiskey.

I slide into the seat next to Killian, my nose crinkling with distaste at the sight of the half-empty bottle of liquor. 'Why doesn't the most opulent gentlemen's club in Dublin stock our whiskey? I thought this was supposed to be a classy establishment.'

'Shouldn't you know that?' Caelon pipes up, lifting his

glass to his lips. 'Given you're the CEO and father's prize protégé.' His eyes glow with amusement.

'You won't be either of those things for much longer if you don't turn things around.' Sean pours me a double from the bottle.

'It was a bit of bad press, that's all.' I take a swig of whiskey and wince.

'Bad press? It's a sex scandal.' Caelon swirls his drink around his glass. 'You were caught with your cock out with three members of your own staff for christ's sake.'

I blow out a breath. 'They were willing participants in a consensual act.'

'You're the fucking CEO, James. You pay their wages.' Killian annunciates every word gruffly.

'I had no idea who they were. I've never met anyone in the UK marketing division.' I inhale sharply. 'We were simply celebrating the new year in style in Dubai.'

'On the company jet!' Irritation blazes in Sean's black eyes. 'And then you invited them on to the company yacht for an orgy. You didn't even attempt to be discreet.'

'Is it technically an orgy if there's only two people having intercourse?' I force my lips to kick up in a smile, though truly, there's nothing funny about the situation.

I fucked up. I blame the alcohol. And boredom. And, let's be honest, I was lonely. Not that I'm looking for a relationship or anything serious. Hell, no! The last time I let a woman into my heart, as well as my bed, she didn't just break it, she snapped it clean in half. I'm not taking that risk again.

But a man has needs. He can't live on water, or whiskey alone. And that's the root of the problem. I seem to have developed this reputation as some kind of playboy. Which sounds fun, until it impacts the business. I have a nasty feeling that unless I turn things around, everything's going to come crashing down around my ears.

'When your other two employees are drinking company whiskey and watching you fuck whilst touching themselves, then yes it's an orgy.' Killian interjects.

Killian, of all my brothers, says the least, so his frustration speaks volumes.

'What did you expect?' Sean splutters. 'You were on the top deck of a multimillion euro yacht with our family fucking name emblazoned on the side. In case you forgot, Dubai is a Muslim country. You were blatantly disrespectful and bang out of order.'

'We expect that sort of behaviour from him,' Caelon nods towards a smirking Rian, 'but not from you. Even he keeps his dick in his pants in public, at least.'

'Okay, it wasn't my finest moment.' The truth is, New Year's Eve is my least favourite night of the year. All that fresh start bullshit. Blah blah blah.

I have everything a man could want in life; a high-powered career, more money than I could spend in several lifetimes, a family who cares deeply about me, but sometimes... sometimes I wonder about the point of it all.

My life has been mapped out for me from the day I was born.

Where's the fun in that?

'What has my little indiscretion got to do with you lot anyway?' I palm the stubble dotting my jawline.

Caelon dusts off some imaginary lint from his immaculately tailored suit. 'All of our businesses bear the Beckett name and your behaviour is making a fucking mockery of it.'

Candice, one of the servers, approaches the table dressed in transparent chiffon lingerie. She brandishes a bottle of Dom Perignon and five champagne flutes. 'A welcome gift from Christopher.'

Huh. More ass-kissing from that creep.

Rian beams at the bottle of champagne like it's his fucking birthday.

'Can I offer you anything else?' Candice leans across the table to place the bottle in the centre, pushing her tits up higher. Three sets of eyes follow as her breasts almost burst from beneath the flimsy fabric. 'Some company perhaps?'

I say three sets of eyes because Caelon never looks. He's ridiculously happily married to his childhood sweetheart, Isabella. Even after fifteen years, he only has eyes for her.

And I have zero interest in Candice. As elegant and eloquent as she is, she's probably fucked half the men here.

Rian might not care, but I don't share.

'That will be all, thank you,' I clear my throat and turn to Rian. 'You can play when we've talked.'

Candice pouts and turns on her heels. 'Come find me later,' she says to Rian, shimmying her hips before strutting away.

'She is gagging for it.' Rian exhales a low whistle and readjusts his suit pants. His expensive education appears to have been utterly wasted. Our parents should have sent him to finishing school.

'It's her job to pretend she's gagging for it, you fucking fool.' Killian glowers at him.

'If you've finished berating me, perhaps we can get down to business?' I lock eyes with each of my brothers in turn.

Their enthusiasm is far from fervid. They might buck up when they hear what I've got to say. 'There are rumours circulating that the Imperial Winery Group is in trouble. It could be ripe for the picking. It would certainly be an interesting subsidiary to our portfolio.'

Killian straightens himself. 'I heard the whispers.'

'They're based in France, right?' Caelon says. I can practically see the cogs turning in his brain.

'Provence. And there's land, so scope to expand all of our businesses.'

'I'm in,' Rian blurts, his gaze still intently focussed elsewhere.

Sean's eyes flare. 'How much land are we talking?' As head of property acquisition, naturally he's interested.

'The estate has multiple vineyards totalling thousands of acres.' My eyes flick to Caelon. 'There's potential for two, maybe three new hotels. Maybe a luxury glamping site or whatever the fuck is popular these days.'

While Sean is all about acquiring property, Caelon oversees the chain of boutique hotels our father acquired during his time as CEO.

'It seems like a deal that could be beneficial for all of us.' Sean clasps his hands together on his lap.

'Exactly. So, if we're in agreement I'll draw up a proposal and put it to the board.' A lucrative takeover might be just what I need to distract them from the Dubai scandal, and enable me to retain my position as CEO.

'Agreed.' Killian nods.

I glance round the table. 'Agreed,' my brothers mutter in unison.

I top up their drinks before helping myself to another measure . 'I'll draw up a proposal over the next couple of days.'

'Hoping it'll save your bacon?' Rian smirks. 'Never mind the board, Dad is gunning for you.'

'I hope your dick doesn't shoot off as quickly as your mouth.' Killian folds his arms across his muscular chest. 'Or Candice is going to be highly disappointed.'

Caelon and Sean snort but Killian doesn't even crack a smile.

My phone vibrates in my pocket with an incoming text. I pluck it out and squint at the screen.

Dad.

> Your presence is required in the boardroom. 8am sharp. After yesterday's front page yacht porn, the governors are on the warpath. And so am I. For fuck's sake, pull yourself together, son.

I blow out a lungful of air. Looks like I'll need to draw up that proposal sooner rather than later.

'Rian's right.' I hold up my phone. 'I've been summoned.'

Rian exhales a low whistle but he's not looking at my mobile. His beady eyes are transfixed on the main stage. 'Fuck. Me.'

I follow his gaze. Something hot and sharp ignites in my gut.

Even if I wasn't a regular, it's obvious the woman taking to the stage is new. There's something unique about her. Something untouched. Unscathed. Untarnished.

Innocent. The word pops into my head like a wayward champagne cork.

Her olive skin radiates a luminosity that makes my fingers itch to touch it. Long, toned legs are only emphasised by the sky-high stilettos supporting her feet. Her full, round breasts are concealed by another couple of tiny scraps, but there's no hiding the twin pebbles beneath. A tiny scrap of scarlet lace forms a triangle between her legs, showcasing the subtle contours of what lies beneath.

A long neck leads up to the face of a fucking angel. She's even wearing a tiny silver cross. Her features are feminine, doe-like and dainty but that mouth– it was made for sin. Plump, perfect lips that could lead God himself into temptation.

My teeth scrape over my lower lip. Damn, she is something else.

A hushed silence hijacks the room.

Thick dark eyelashes flutter closed for a split second, like she's praying to a God I don't believe in.

But for some strange reason, I will her prayers to be answered.

And mine too.

Because the second she leaves that stage, I want, no, I *need* to know everything about her.

Chapter Four
SCARLETT

My body is ravaged with nerves. I close my eyes briefly, trying to shut out the world, what I'm doing here, then force my eyelids open. Talk about a baptism of fire. Hundreds of eyes stare back at me, but only one set catches my attention.

James Beckett. In the flesh.

No, that's not right.

James doesn't catch my attention— he commands it.

He was handsome in photographs, but they don't capture the sheer presence he radiates across the room.

Thoughtful chocolate eyes peruse every inch of my exposed flesh like a caress. His pupils glint as his focus returns to my face. Our eyes lock and a hot burst of electricity pierces the air between us, firing and flaming and igniting sensations that I've only ever read about in romance novels.

Every inch of my skin prickles and it takes all my will to break our stare. And when I do, I feel the heat of his for a long time afterwards.

I sashay across the stage under the spotlight with more confidence than I feel inside. A wolf whistle sounds from behind me and I know without a shadow of a doubt it's Avery.

My eyes home in on the chrome pole in front of me. I don't look, can't look, at anyone or anything else.

The atmosphere is charged with expectation as the weight of a hundred eyes burn my body. None heavier than from the table immediately in front of the stage where James Beckett sits.

I curl my fingers around the pole, gripping the cold metal like my life depends on it, and sway seductively for a few seconds, before hoisting myself up in one swift movement. My biceps flex and tighten as I swing around it.

A murmur of appreciation is audible even over the rhythmic beat.

My thighs tense as I twist and twirl. After years of practice at the college gym, the movements come with grace and ease. The pole is a familiar anchor in a sea of uncertainty. Being up on stage is strange but... Avery was right, it's oddly euphoric.

I cling to the cool chrome, arching my back and elevating my breasts in a slow, seductive dance. The beat seeps into my blood, dictating every minor muscle movement like an invisible conductor until I'm lost in the music, bending, contorting and gyrating. Butterflies crusade through my stomach and lower, excitement eradicating any trace of nerves.

I roll my hips and grind the thin lace against the pole and shiver. Low whistles of appreciation echo from the front of the stage sending a deep sense of satisfaction soaring through my soul.

It hits me then like a shot of heroin. I've spent the last five years deliberately not drawing attention to myself. Hiding in plain sight.

And now I'm finally under the spotlight, it's liberating.

As an educated woman, almost anyway, this entire scenario should be utterly degrading. Being objectified so sexually should be debasing, but after years of hiding, the rush of being watched so intently floods my flesh.

It is empowering.

Enthralling.

Addictive.

I understand what Avery meant. The hedonistic draw of being desired. The weight of all those eyes.

The champagne cruising through my veins makes me brave. I flick my wig from my shoulder and let my fingers linger on my collarbone for a second before trailing them across my clavicle and between my slick breasts. Hundred euro notes fly through the air from every direction. Then the music changes. That's my cue. My slot is almost up.

Time for my party piece.

The grand finale.

I stretch my legs as wide as I can until they're in the splits position, giving everyone in the audience a direct view of the lace barely sheathing the junction between my thighs as I slide down the pole. Applause sounds like thunder from every direction.

I chance a final glance around the lilac-lit room as my stiletto meets the polished marble.

Those deep brown eyes remain fixated on my body, stoking a fire I have no idea how to put out.

Chapter Five
JAMES

Half the men in here would give their right arm for a piece of her.

Who am I kidding?

Every man except Caelon would give both arms for a night with this mysterious stunner.

Hell, I've never paid for it in my life but even I'm seriously reconsidering. Which is worrying on so many levels.

This place is renowned for employing beautiful women, but she is something else. And the way she swayed against that pole was like watching poetry in motion.

Where the hell did Christopher Cole find her?

Who is she?

Her eyes snap towards the bottom of the steps, as if someone has called her name. Something sharp twists in my stomach as my focus follows the flimsy scrap of material slick between her granite-sculpted ass cheeks as she exits the stage.

Where's she going? Who's she going with? There are more than twenty men already making a beeline for her with fistfuls of cash, and no doubt propositions for private dances. My stomach twists with something unexpected– jealousy.

'Where are you going?' Caelon eyes me with surprise, as I rise to my feet, intent on following the woman from the stage.

'Nowhere.' I watch as Avery, one of Luxor's most coveted dancers grabs the new girl's hand. She drags her away from the main stage, in the direction of the changing rooms and thankfully away from the private rooms spanning in the other direction.

Relief rushes through my blood.

What the actual fuck?

I sink back into the leather. 'I thought I saw someone I recognised.' I lift my glass from the table. The whiskey burning my throat has nothing on the flames licking over my skin.

It's ridiculously hot in here. Did the aircon break? I readjust the collar of my crisp white shirt and slide off my silk tie.

'Well, if you know that piece of ass, you might give me her number.' Rian exhales a dramatic breath and gestures towards my dancer.

My dancer.

One shared glance doesn't make her mine.

Besides, I don't do 'mine'. Not for more than a night, at least.

I swallow down the urge to punch my youngest brother. 'Candice not enough for you?'

'If you can take three in your ripe old age,' Rian shoots a smirk in my direction, 'I'm pretty sure I could manage two.' He reaches for the bottle of champagne in the centre of the table.

'Dude, you couldn't keep up with one woman, let alone two.' Caelon shakes his head and elbows Rian in the ribs.

'What would you know about it?' Rian's head whips to Caelon. 'You've only fucked one woman in your entire life.'

'And she's only fucked me, so I must be doing something right.' Caelon's chest puffs out like a fucking pigeon.

I'm no romantic, but knowing you're the only man to ever have been inside your wife must be sublimely satisfying.

'Earth to James,' Sean shouts across the table. He nods towards the stage. 'Incoming.'

The next dancer has nothing on her predecessor. Sure, she's stunning, if you're into botox and silicone. But she lacks class. And intrigue.

Candice approaches the table again. Rian grabs her by the hips and drags her onto his lap.

'How's my favourite dancer?' he purrs, and I roll my eyes.

'Better now.' She shimmies her ass and Rian exhales, happier than a pig in shit.

Before I can think better of it, I lean forwards and ask casually. 'Candice, who's the new girl?'

Candice's hips pause from rolling over my brother's crotch and her face angles towards mine. 'That's Scarlett. She goes to college with Avery.'

Of course she's still in college. She has to be at least twenty-one, though. Christopher won't employ any dancers younger than that.

'Did Mr-I-Won't-Pay-For-It finally spot something he *will* pay for?' Candice picks up Rian's champagne glass and takes a mouthful.

'Not all the dancers feel the need to go above and beyond for their paying customers. What makes you think she will?' She doesn't strike me as the type. And I'm an excellent judge of character.

'I overheard Christopher himself telling Giselle he'd give Scarlett ten grand for an hour of her time. Who'd turn that down? Though, I'm sure you could afford to double that figure.' Candice eyeballs me.

'James doesn't pay for it.' Rian reaches around to Candice's stomach, splaying his fingers across her tiny waist and grazing a thumb beneath her breast. 'But I do. So get your sexy ass to one of those rooms so I can fuck you into next week.' His hips thrust hard enough to propel her into the air, and she squeals.

I sink back into my seat as Candice leads Rian away from the table, her fingers entwined with his like they're on a fucking date. I'm not judging my little brother. It's his life to live, but where's the challenge when you know it's a sure thing?

Where's the fun in the conquest?

Where's the meaning in it?

The yacht scandal was fun, but I can't help envy what Caelon and Isabella have. A relationship that transcends all others. But relationships like that are impossible to find. I had one once, or so I thought, but Cynthia Van Darwin turned out to be a liar and a cheat. When we broke up, I promised myself I'd never allow myself to get hurt again. Which is why I never sleep with the same woman twice. No danger of catching feelings that way.

'I'm heading.' Caelon downs the remainder of the whiskey in his glass and stands.

None of us are surprised. Caelon always returns to Isabella the moment his business meetings are concluded.

'Stay,' I urge him, motioning to the whiskey.

'Hmm. Let me think about it.' He pushes his floppy hair from his face. 'Stay with my brooding big brother, or go home and fuck my stunning wife?'

Looks like everyone's getting laid tonight.

Everyone but me.

I have a phone full of willing contacts but my mind's

stuck on Scarlett, the goddess who graced the stage and captivated my senses. I scan the room, silently searching for her. I'd pay a hundred grand to watch her dance again. And a hundred more to prevent her being tarnished by Christopher Cole's slimy touch.

The urge to speak to her consumes me.

'I'll call you tomorrow.' Caelon interrupts my thoughts. 'Good luck with the Board.'

'Safe home,' Killian says with a solemn stare.

A flash of platinum materialises in my periphery.

Scarlett.

She's with Avery and they're striding towards our table. I snatch a breath.

Sean opens his mouth to speak but I lift a hand to silence him, my entire attention focused on wordlessly willing over the most alluring woman in the room.

As if Scarlett hears my silent subconscious plea, her face whips in my direction. She leans into Avery and whispers something into her ear.

Avery's eyes land on mine and I beckon her over with one long finger.

Chapter Six
SCARLETT

'Holy hell, he's beckoning us over,' Avery hisses in my ear.

I don't need to ask who. I'm surrounded by men but my body is intrinsically in tune to the minute movements of just one.

The same one I was programmed to hate but instead, passionately pined after. It was his face at the forefront of my mind the first time I pushed a vibrator inside myself, not that I would *ever* admit that out loud.

'I've worked here for almost three years and he's never once showed a remote bit of interest,' Avery squeals, 'which can only mean it's you he wants.'

I swallow thickly, allowing Avery to steer me towards his table. Every atom in my body hums with nerves. The sensual rhythmic beat is loud enough to drown out the clacking of my heels, but nothing can drown out the blood roaring through my ears.

Rich espresso-coloured eyes rake over the expanse of my body, then bore unwaveringly into mine as I close the distance between us.

He's even more gorgeous up close. More formidable.

More *male*. His open suit jacket reveals a pristine white shirt. A hint of dark hair peeps from the open top button. Dark stubble dusts his razor-sharp jawline and lines the column of his throat.

He rises slowly as we approach the booth. As he stands, he readjusts his suit pants and my gaze is drawn to his crotch. I catch myself, heat flooding my face as I avert my eyes back to his.

He arches a single thick eyebrow in my direction, his pupils flickering with amusement.

'And there was me thinking I pay a hefty membership fee to eye *your* crotch.' His velvety voice slides beneath my skin, making it too tight, too hot, despite the goosebumps rippling across it.

My mouth opens. Then closes. Then opens again.

Avery nudges me. 'Mr Beckett, it's a pleasure to formally meet you. I'm Avery, and this is Scarlett.' Her hand sweeps in front of me like she's presenting me in a ballgown, not three decadent lace triangles.

'Call me James, please.' He's talking to Avery but his eyes don't stray from mine. We're locked in a crazy, intensely potent stare. Lifting a hand, he motions us to join them in the booth. 'A glass of champagne, perhaps?'

I glance at Avery.

A low chuckle rumbles from James's throat. 'Don't worry, I don't bite.'

His companions, his brothers, judging by their remarkable similarity, glance up, halting their conversation. Avery slides into the booth opposite James, leaving the only free seat directly next to him.

I slip into it, the leather dipping beneath my bare ass cheeks.

James has barely said two sentences, and the tiny scrap of material covering my modesty is already saturated. I might be a virgin, but I've fantasised about this man since it dawned on me that my vagina had more than one purpose. Not only is he devastatingly attractive, but ogling my former family's biggest rival seemed like the ultimate *fuck you*.

Avery turns to the other two men and introduces herself while James studies me like I'm some sort of endangered species.

'Scarlett is a beautiful name.' He reaches for the champagne bottle and pours two glasses.

He hands one to Avery and places the other in my hand. Thick tanned fingers graze fleetingly against mine and electricity sparks between us. His eyebrows skyrocket for a second before he composes himself. 'Is it your real name?' He inches closer to be heard over the music.

I nod and raise the glass to my lips, just to do something with my hands. I thought dancing on a stage in front of a room full of men was unnerving, but it had nothing on meeting James Beckett in the flesh. I've never seen a dick in my life, but even I can tell he oozes big dick energy.

The question is, what does he want with me?

'How did it feel up there, knowing you had the attention of every man in the room?' The creases at the corner of his eyes hint at a wealth of experience. I feel like a child in comparison, yet more woman than I've felt in my entire life.

'*Every* man?' Those two little words slide past my lips like a question, and he chuckles.

'Every man,' he repeats in a gravelly tone.

My fingers skim over the tops of my thigh and his eyes fall, following the motion. 'It was intoxicating.' *Almost as intoxicating as sitting here, with you.*

'Intoxicating.' He turns the word over as if he's contemplating it. 'I'd have to agree.' He shifts slightly in his seat and a muscular thigh rests against mine.

'So, Scarlett,' James draws out my name in a way that

makes it sound sensual, 'when did you start at the Luxor Lounge?' He picks up his drink and swirls it thoughtfuly around the crystal glass.

'This is my first shift.'

Surprise lights up his eyes. 'So you're a Luxor virgin, so to speak?'

I feel my face flush. Is it that obvious? Or is his choice of words coincidental?

'I guess you could say that.'

'Well, you were,' he glances at the chunky timepiece on his wrist, 'until about fifteen minutes ago.' His lips lift in a grin and his eyes crinkle at the corners. 'You absolutely nailed it.'

I take a large mouthful of champagne. 'Thank you.'

'What's a nice girl like you doing working in a place like this?'

I shrug. 'I need the money.'

'What for?' His tone is one of genuine curiosity.

'Forty grand of student loans. I'm on a scholarship but it only covers my tuition. Rent is extortionate and my landlord just increased it.'

Twisting his torso towards me, he leans forwards. 'Which college do you attend?'

'Trinity.' I exhale a shaky breath. College is a safe subject. Safer than my virginity, of any kind. 'Less than six months until graduation.'

'That's remarkable. Scholarships to Trinity are like gold dust.' His thumb roams over his stubble again. 'I graduated from Oxford. Economics and Finance.'

'Really? I'm studying for a masters in finance too.' I'm not familiar with his academic credentials. His personal life is much more juicy, if the tabloids are anything to go by.

James Beckett and three women on a yacht.

I press my thighs together tighter and fight the urge to squirm.

'If you need some extra tuition with your upcoming finals, perhaps I could help.' He eyes me over the rim of the glass.

My pulse spikes as my mind wanders to the gutter, imagining a different type of tuition.

A low laugh purrs from his lips like he can read my mind. 'Rest assured, you're safe. I know my reputation somewhat precedes me, but I don't indulge in *extra* activities with dancers.' He heavily accentuates the last word.

For some inexplicable reason this feels like a test. But in what subject?

My integrity?

My morals?

Indignation flares in my chest.

Just because I dance, it doesn't mean I'll sell my body. Or my soul.

I don't have a lot. I don't have money, or family anymore, or a billion-euro empire, but I do have my pride. I know my worth. I paid for every damn ounce of it in blood, sweat and tears.

'You too are safe, Mr Beckett.' I mimic his tone, 'It would appear that the reputation of others in my profession precedes *me*. But rest assured, I neither require any extra tuition, or offer any *extra* activities– of any description.'

'Is that right?' James straightens his spine and inclines forwards. The rich scent of his citrus cologne, tinged with a potent manliness, envelops me. 'So if I offered you a million euro tonight for,' he muses, '"extra activities," sex say, for example,' torrid flames ignite his irises, 'you'd turn me down?'

I down the remainder of my champagne and run my tongue over my lower lip before answering. 'When I have sex, it will be entirely because I want to, not for money. It might be hard for a man like you to understand, Mr Beckett, but there are some things money can't buy.'

He's so close we're sharing the same breath.

'Like what?' he whispers.

I brush my lips over his right ear and whisper two words that I never dreamed I'd voice out loud. 'My virginity.'

I stand, place the glass on the table and shoot James my widest smile.

That square jaw almost hits the floor as his pupils devour his irises.

I march back towards the dressing room to change into another decadent ensemble before I'm called back to the podium.

Chapter Seven
JAMES

The Beckett headquarters is based in a five-storey Georgian building a stone's throw from Grafton Street. Its grand façade boasts symmetrical proportions, intricate stonework, and tall windows overlooking the city. Over the grand entrance, framed by towering Corinthian columns, the Beckett family crest is on proud display.

Two immaculately dressed receptionists bid me good morning as I step into the palatial foyer. Pushing the button for the lift, I stare at the enormous portrait of my grandfather, Benjamin Beckett. Stern, dark eyes glare back at me.

'Don't give me that look,' I mutter. 'As if you never went drinking on a school night.'

An image of Scarlett's silky skin rises to the forefront of my mind for the hundredth time this morning and I've been awake less than an hour.

'My virginity.'

Those two fucking words have haunted me all night, her flawless olive flesh forever imprinted in my subconscious. Every time I close my eyes, it's all I can see.

No woman has ever walked away from me, not like she did last night. She might not have experience, but she has buckets of sass. She didn't even so much as glance my way as she strode off. It didn't stop me leaving a five grand tip for her time.

How has a woman with looks like hers hung on to her hymen?

It's implausible.

An image of her laid out naked across my four-poster bed has burned its way into my brain and I can't for the fucking life of me erase it.

The lift doors slide open with a soft ping that brings me back to the present as I'm about to lose the run of myself completely.

My office is on the top floor, along with the main boardroom and several large, opulent meeting rooms. Each of my brothers' businesses occupy a different level. Rian has the ground floor, which he perpetually curses, but as the youngest, and last in the door, he has no choice but to suck it up.

I'm the first of the Becketts in this morning. Work hard, play hard has always been my motto. I played hard last night, but today, I need to get some sort of proposal drawn up for the Board.

Now I have my brothers' backing, I'm determined to execute this takeover.

I stride into my office, hang my coat on the back of the solid mahogany wood door, and slide into the burgundy leather chair. My desk is the same mahogany as the door and the wood panelled walls. Everything looks archaic, but our technology is state of the art.

I've just about finished preparing my initial presentation when my PA, Chantel, sticks her head around the door. 'They're ready for you.'

Chantel is short, blonde, and bolshy. She has no qualms about pulling me up on my shortcomings, both personally and professionally, and I've come to respect the bluntness that initially irritated me.

'You've got this.' Chantel marches in, nodding vehemently, which sets her ponytail swinging. 'Just tell them you're taking a vow of celibacy, a vow of sobriety, and vow to squeeze the damn grapes one by one if it means getting the go-ahead.'

'Thanks, Chantel.' I appreciate her support. Especially as there's a possibility it's the only support I'll receive this morning. 'How's Miles getting on?'

Chantel's son, Miles, was born three years ago, eight weeks premature, with a life-threatening congenital heart defect.

Chantel grins at the mention of her only child. 'He's great, thanks to you.'

'Not thanks to me.' I stand, preparing to face the music. 'I didn't perform the surgery.'

'You paid for it though, and all his aftercare.' A wistful look sweeps over her face as she tucks a stray strand of hair behind her ear.

'It was nothing. I'm glad he's doing well.'

'Shout if you need anything. I'll send in tea and scones shortly.'

'I might need whiskey and stitches.' I sigh. 'You know they're all gunning for me, right?'

'Don't worry, I'm a dab hand with a needle,' she jokes, flexing her fingers as she accompanies me out of the office. 'Good luck.'

'I'm going to need it.' With my laptop tucked under my arm, I strut down the wide corridor towards the boardroom. A nervous tension settles on my sternum as I open the heavy door and step in.

The twelve board members flank a huge oval table. My

father sits at the head. My mother forced him to retire when he suffered a heart attack two years ago, but he's still a major shareholder. Despite her best efforts, my mother can't keep him away from this place.

The weak winter sunrise casts an orange glow across the table, like a physical manifestation of the ring of fire I'm stepping into. I stride across the room to the only free seat, purposefully confident. Hell, if I don't believe in myself, how the hell am I going to convince this lot?

'Good morning.' Instead of sitting, I remain standing, deliberately meeting the eye of each and every person in the room, before finally locking eyes with my father.

Alexander Beckett is ruthless in business, but he is a wonderful father.

Strict—yes.

Stern—absolutely.

But he has always been stoically invested in his wife and sons too. He's not hard on us for the sake of it. He's hard because he loves us. He loves this family. Which is why I'm determined to take our business to the next level. To make him proud. To be worthy of the Beckett name.

'James.' My father acknowledges me publicly as if I'm not his own flesh and blood, but he'd never deny me either.

At almost seventy, he could pass for sixty. His once dark hair is peppered with grey speckles at the temple, but the old fucker is aging like George fucking Clooney. He's a handsome man, even with a four-inch scar indenting his left cheek, courtesy of the O'Connors. I told you the rivalry between our families is ruthless.

'Well, that's certainly one way to court publicity, James. I think we've all seen the lurid headlines regarding your behaviour on the company yacht on New Year's Eve.' He raises a wiry eyebrow and gives me a hard stare. 'Employees?

What the hell were you thinking? I think it's only right you provide an explanation. And of course, a full and frank apology.'

'Absolutely.' I nod and arrange my features into a solemn expression. 'I sincerely apologise for my indiscretion and misuse of company property. I will explain in depth, but while we're all together, I have a proposition I'd like to present.' Distraction is my only defence. And if the Imperial Winery Group acquisition isn't enough to distract them, then nothing will.

'Begin,' my father commands.

My presentation flows smoothly. From the encouraging murmurs and rustling papers, it would appear the acquisition is a welcome one. Adding Imperial Winery Group to the Beckett portfolio will diversify our business and reduce reliance on existing revenue streams, plus Imperial's brand reputation and prestige align with the company's existing luxury brand and create synergies and cross-selling opportunities. Financial projections look good. The members agree it fits with our brand. There's serious long-term growth potential. It all looks positive.

The chairman, Julian Jones, shuffles his papers and stands. The room falls silent. 'It looks like you've done your homework, Mr Beckett.'

I bow my head. 'I believe this takeover has enormous potential.'

'I'd have to agree.' Pudgy, wrinkled fingers push thick-rimmed glasses higher on to his large nose. 'My concern is not with the acquisition, it's with you.'

'I'll draft a statement issuing a public apology for any offence caused. It'll be released this afternoon.' My jaw ticks. 'I made a mistake. For which I am deeply sorry, and I can assure you, it won't happen again.'

'How can we be certain?' Julian's thick, white eyebrows pull together in a frown. 'The reputation of this company is a very serious matter. The investors are jittery.'

I pause for a beat, trying to articulate an answer that will provide the reassurance the Board requires.

'You can be certain because James has decided it's time to settle down.' My father's eyes narrow in a warning look as my mouth falls open. 'Before the year is out, he will take a wife. Someone from a suitable background. Someone who also believes in the morals and values of the Beckett businesses. The public will get behind a wedding. Everyone loves a happy ever after. It will calm him down and offer the company the stability it needs to thrive under his leadership.'

He cannot be fucking serious. My eyes bulge and my throat tightens.

I'm not sure I even believe in marriage.

A highly inappropriate image of Scarlett in a virginal white wedding dress bursts into my brain.

Where the fuck did that come from?

My father continues, oblivious or indifferent to my shock. 'If James struggles to find a suitable match, I will arrange one for him. Many successful marriages are founded this way. There's no shame in it.'

A tightness twists my chest. It's a battle to beat my frown into submission.

The room falls silent as the members of the board exchange curious glances.

Finally the chairman nods. 'Very well. And perhaps if Mr Beckett can provide an heir for this company, it may prevent him from running its reputation into the ground entirely. We'll reconvene next month for an update.' Julian pushes his chair back, signalling this meeting is over.

Does he mean on the acquisition or my relationship status?

I shake hands with each member as they file out of the room, until there's only me and my father left.

'What the fuck was that?' I rake my fingers through my hair as I pace the plush carpet.

'Don't take that tone with me, son.' Dad buttons up his immaculacy tailored suit jacket. 'It was a necessary evil. Eight members personally requested your removal from the company. It was the only way.'

'You want me to get married?' I slow to a stop, perch on the table and sigh. 'Seriously?'

'I've never been more serious in my life.' My father folds his arms across his chest. 'I've emailed Chantel a list of suitable possibilities. Women from appropriate backgrounds. She's arranging dates for you as we speak.'

'Dates? I don't date. I don't have time to date.' My voice cracks.

'No, that's right.' My father angles his head, his tone dripping with sarcasm. 'But you do have time to swan off with three Beckett employees and fuck them in plain sight.'

I close my eyes and count to five before reopening them. 'I didn't realise they were employees.'

'Whatever. Your poor mother thought the days where she'd have to cop an eyeful of your cock were well and truly behind her,' he scoffs. 'If you want to keep your position as CEO of this company, you'll take this on the chin. You're going to have to settle down at some point. You're not getting any younger.' His voice softens slightly. 'Besides, your mother and I want more grandkids while we're still young enough to enjoy them.'

'But Dad, I'm not even dating. How do you expect me to lock down a suitable wife in a year?' It's madness. Total fucking madness.

'I told you, Chantel is making arrangements as we speak.'

His eyes, the same shade as mine, flash with a brief twinkle. 'You never know. You might even have fun.'

Doubtful.

Unless one of my dates is a high-class virgin pole dancer.

Fuck's sake.

Chapter Eight
SCARLETT

Today's lecture on securing a work placement is particularly dull, but Professor Buckley has one of those monotone voices which makes it easy to zone out on. Instead of paying attention, I'm replaying my encounter with James Beckett in my head for the millionth time. He hasn't been back to the club in two weeks, but that hasn't stopped me obsessing about our brief conversation, day and night.

Even now, it galls me that he thought he could pay his way into my panties. Then again, he's not the only man to make that assumption. The past couple of weeks have presented plenty of lucrative proposals—all of which I've politely declined.

Even my boss, Christopher Cole asked if I'd given any consideration to offering any 'additional services' as his bright eyes lingered on my lingerie. My answer was a resounding *no*. Though to some men, especially wealthy, powerful men, the word *no* is a foreign concept. It only serves to drive them harder. And as the days blur into weeks, it's becoming increasingly obvious that Christopher Cole is one of those men.

But, as I told James, some things aren't for sale. Another image of his onyx-like eyes claws its way into my brain. I thrum my pen on the desk.

Professor Buckley pauses his pacing at the front of the room, halts mid-sentence and turns his attention to me. His gaze narrows. 'Ms Fitzgerald. Is there a problem?'

'No, sir. Not at all.' I sink into my seat, willing the floor to crack open and let me slide through. I've spent the last five years doing everything and anything not to be noticed. Flying just under the radar. It would be a shame to fail now the finishing line is in sight. Even under the stage spotlights at the club, the wigs and make-up are so extreme that I feel hidden even when I'm almost fully exposed.

'Given your blasé attitude, I assume you've organised your work placement already.' Sarcasm drips from each word as every head in the rooms swivels in my direction.

Oh, the shame.

I clear my throat and straighten myself in the plastic chair. 'Er, not yet.'

'Well if you have a hope in hell of finding one, kindly use that pen to write down the criteria for said placement, instead of playing the bongos on the desk,' Professor Buckley's forehead ripples with frown lines.

The guy in the seat adjacent fires me a knowing grin. 'If you like, you can copy my notes this evening,' he whispers. Shane Stenson is the college football captain, and son of a former Irish politician. He has his pick of the women. With his sunny disposition, dirty blonde hair, and a drop-your-panties smile, it's not hard to see why.

Which is precisely why I was shocked when he sought me out in the campus nightclub six months ago, and kissed me like he meant it, before begging me to go home with him.

Obviously, I said no. Even if I was ready to let a man into

my life, which I'm not, there's no point in starting a relationship.

The second I graduate, I'm on the first plane out of here. The urge to see the world eats at me, and now thanks to my job at the Luxor Lounge, I'll be able to afford it.

Shane didn't try to kiss me again after that, and somewhere along the line we sort of became study buddies. It helps having someone to bounce things off, even if his eyes sometimes linger on my lips a little longer than study buddies should.

I shake my head at Shane and offer a tight smile.

Eventually, class ends.

When Professor Buckley finally draws the lecture to a close, Shane rises from his desk and perches on the side of mine. His neatly clipped fingertips graze over the scratched pine as I stuff my notes into my satchel.

'Want to go for a drink? It's Friday, after all.' He cocks his head and flashes that famous grin, showcasing years' worth of expensive orthodontics. His bright blue eyes glitter with hope.

'I can't tonight.' I push my chair back with the backs of my thighs and stand. 'But I'll see you next week.' I scurry out of the door with the weight of Shane's gaze on my back.

Reaching into the front pocket of my satchel, I fumble around for my mobile, an iPhone as old as the hills, with the scratches to prove it. Even now I have the money to upgrade, I won't. I don't need a fancy camera or access to a hundred stupid social media sites. Apart from Avery, there are only two people who ever call me.

Eleanor Thorne, my former teacher and saviour in my hour of need.

And Nathan Sterling, the detective in charge of my mother's case. The man who convinced me to testify against my stepfather. Not that I needed much convincing. Jack

O'Connor claimed he was unaware my mother was in his whiskey distillery when he burnt it to the ground, but I don't believe that for one second.

The man is unhinged. Why my mother married him in the first place is beyond me. Clearly she had a thing for bad boys, given my birth father was a professional fighter back in his day.

Nathan checks in on me periodically. He'd have preferred it if I'd left Dublin after the trial because of the threats I received from Jack's sons. The parting words of my stepbrother, Declan, ring through my ears as fresh as the day he spat them in my face. '*If I ever see you again, I'll kill you.*'

But given my scholarship offer from Trinity Business School, and my lack of other options, Nathan and I agreed I'd change my name and start a new life.

I scroll a thumb over the scratched screen of my phone and call Eleanor's number. She answers on the fourth ring.

'Scarlett.' There's a maternal warmth to her tone. My heart aches in my chest, remembering my own mother. They say time heals pain, but it doesn't. Not really. You just learn to live with it.

'Hi Eleanor. I'm just checking in.' I stride through the bustling streets of Dublin, pressing the phone tightly against my ear. It's not even five o'clock but the sky is a shade of midnight and there's a fierce wind whipping against my face.

'You don't need a reason to call.' After my mother's death, Eleanor fostered me until I turned eighteen. It couldn't have been easy for her but I'll always be grateful for what she did for me.

'I was thinking about you earlier.' She pauses, 'You know, with your mother's anniversary coming up.'

I flinch. I never visit my mother's grave. Not because every fibre of being doesn't want to, but because the danger of being seen, of giving away my new identity, is too great.

The O'Connors are a formidable family. I wouldn't put it past them to be watching, waiting for me to show up.

'I miss her,' I say. They're the only words I can muster.

'I know, sweetheart. I'll lay some flowers on her grave for you.' Eleanor's kindness knows no bounds. 'Are you okay? Do you need anything? Have you got enough money?'

'I'm fine, thank you.' I blink back the tears forming in my eyes. 'I got a job in a bar.'

'Is it safe?' Concern taints her tone.

'Yes, it's low key. The uniform is...' Can you call designer lingerie a uniform? 'It makes me unrecognisable, even to myself.'

'You're on the home run. Last semester, then the world is your oyster,' Eleanor reminds me with a hint of pride.

'I know. I can't believe it.' I've spent the last five, almost six years, in survival mode. I can't imagine what it'll be like to truly live.

'You're amazing Scarlett. Your mam would be so proud of you.'

My chest tightens. My fingers instinctively reach for the cross around my neck. 'That means a lot.'

'I wish you'd come over. I'd love to see you.' Eleanor sighs.

'I don't want to put you at risk.'

'So much time has passed. Surely by now...' she trails off.

'Maybe you could come to my graduation?' Eleanor is the closest thing I have to family, although we barely manage to see each other twice a year, at most.

Her smile is evident in her voice. 'Honey, I wouldn't miss it for the world.'

'Great. I'll check in again soon.'

'Do.' Eleanor says. 'And please, visit. Anytime.'

I hang up before she can pin me to a date and time. My solitude is her safety. After everything she's done for me, I'm unwilling to jeopardise that.

I slip the phone back into my bag and weave through a throng of commuters. My studio apartment is only a ten minute walk from college. Despite the college's prestigious reputation, it borders some less salubrious areas, but at least the accommodation is affordable. Well, it was, until my dickhead landlord raised the rent.

Thank God for the Luxor Lounge. Cole wires my wages weekly. And don't get me started on the tips. Someone anonymously left me five grand on my first night. The cash is tucked away in my lingerie drawer, which is now overflowing with decadent silk, chiffon and lace, thanks to my open credit limit at Belle de Nuit.

As the weeks are progressing, so is my confidence. Dancing feels as natural as breathing. And if I'm honest, being admired and desired so carnally does things to me. Things that ignite a fire in my stomach and lower.

I love commanding the attention of every eye in the room.

Even if none of those eyes feel a fraction as intoxicating as James's.

The memory of our conversation, of how it felt to be in his proximity, is seared into my soul as if it had taken place minutes before, not weeks. I'd do well to remember the man is a notorious player.

He's a client of the club.

And he has no real interest in me.

Chapter Nine
SCARLETT

The sun is dipping low behind the building when I reach the paint-peeled front door of my apartment building. I jam my key in and twist, glancing over my shoulder as I step into the cold concrete hallway. The stairs are a winding, creaky affair that spiral up five floors. They're a death trap. I always cling on to the wobbly handrail, even if it's grubby and questionably sticky.

I jog up the steps and let myself into my apartment, if you can even call it that. There's a tiny sitting/kitchen area and a bedroom/ensuite. I've seen bigger shoe boxes. It's single-glazed sash windows render it absolutely freezing. The décor can only be described as shabby at best, but I keep it spotless.

It's a far cry from the manor house where I was raised, but it's all mine, as long as I keep paying the rent. Which won't be a problem now.

Eleanor is right. I'm on the home run.

I heat up some leftover stir-fry and spend two hours with my nose buried in my textbooks. At nine o'clock, a sleek black SUV pulls up outside my apartment building to transport me to the club. It's an unbelievable service. I wouldn't get it working in McDonalds.

My contract stipulates I work four nights a week, but on my second night, Christopher asked if I'd consider doing five.

My answer?

Hell, yes.

I've got five months until graduation to make as much money as I can. I'll work seven nights a week if he wants. If there's a chance I can pay off some of my credit card debt this decade, I'll take it. The scholarship only covers tuition fees and living in Dublin is expensive.

I grab the coat Avery gifted me for my audition, a knee-length fitted black cashmere, which covers the simple black dress I'm wearing underneath. I need to buy more 'work dresses'. Not that I wear them for long, but I can't travel to and from the club in my lingerie.

Thankfully, the driver doesn't want to make small talk. At the club, I head straight to the changing rooms and greet several of the other dancers with a smile before heading to my allocated vanity station to get ready.

I spot the flowers as soon as I round the corner. It would be impossible to miss them. What looks like three hundred scarlet, velvety roses wrapped with a red velvet bow dominate my make-up station.

'Someone has an admirer,' Layla, one of the friendlier dancers comments, firing me a knowing wink as she passes.

It's not uncommon. Avery is regularly showered with gifts, but this is the first time I've received any. Unless you count the copious amounts of cash thrown my way each night.

My fingers search the stems until I locate a small white envelope; meanwhile my heart beats double time in my chest. The stupid, foolish, hopeful romantic in me is silently squealing, praying they're from James, but why would they be?

I tear the paper open and gasp.

> *Not many things shock me. You, Scarlett, are shocking in the best possible way.*
> *James*

He's not the only one who's shocked.

I bite back the grin tugging my lips and try to restrain the millions of butterflies soaring through my stomach.

It's just flowers. He probably got his secretary's secretary to send them.

They don't mean anything.

Tell that to those pesky butterflies though.

I stuff the card in my coat pocket for safekeeping and begin to get ready. Tonight's wig is a pastel pink affair that flows down my back in soft bouncing curls. It's the same shade as the silk scrap between my legs and over my nipples. I'm lashing mascara on to synthetic eyelashes when Avery bounces in. 'Oh, gorgeous flowers. Who are they from?' She fumbles through the roses for the card.

'I'll tell you later,' I whisper, not wanting to draw the attention of the other dancers. Why, I don't know.

Avery looks at me quizzically, then her eyes fall to my ensemble. 'Nice outfit,' she exhales a low whistle. 'I must see if Belle de Nuit stocks that in my size.'

Where I'm tall and lean, Avery has curves to kill for.

'Thanks. Shopping for lingerie has become my new favourite lunchtime pastime.' I swivel on the stool, crossing one long thigh over the other.

'I hear you.' Avery motions over her own lingerie, an electric blue lace corset and a tiny lace thong. 'There's a big crowd out there tonight.' She nods towards the double doors leading to the main lounge.

It's on the tip of my tongue to ask if *he's* there. But I don't.

Owen and Tristan, the two security guards from my first night, appear in the doorway. 'Next set please.'

I stand, along with six other women, and stride across to the door.

'I'll have a glass waiting for you,' Avery promises, sliding into the vanity station next to mine, reaching for her face powder.

'Thanks.' I don't need it. Not like I did the first night. But I've developed a taste for it, along with my new found love of luxurious lingerie.

The familiar scent of orchids fills my senses as I enter the main lounge. Avery wasn't joking. The place is packed. I scan the room, hating myself but unable to stop.

There's no sign of James, but I spot his brothers. Disappointment seeps into my soul.

Christopher Cole is perched by the long ebony bar sipping something small and potent. He's immersed in conversation with several other regulars. My boss is a millionaire. He doesn't need to be here. Which means he *wants* to be here.

His head twists in my direction, gleaming eyes settle on the silk between my legs. and he offers one swift nod of what looks like approval. It would appear my new boss and I share similar taste in lingerie.

A cold shiver of apprehension steals over my spine.

Chapter Ten
SCARLETT

I strut across the main stage in six-inch platinum peep-toe stilettos that cross and tie at my ankles. Grabbing the pole, I lift a thigh and hook the back of my knee around the cool chrome, arching backwards until I'm upside down.

Thank God the candy-floss-coloured wig is pinned firmly in place. The low hum of conversation dips as men gravitate towards the stage.

I spin and twist and hoist myself upwards again, my biceps flexing as I climb higher and higher until I'm almost at the top.

My eyes fall back to the Beckett brothers. The youngest one is staring at me like he hasn't eaten in years. The stern-faced one remains, well, stern-faced. The smiley one is staring at the screen of his phone and typing. The last one motions a passing server to fetch another round of drinks.

Where is James?

With someone who's too classy to be mistaken for a woman who would accept money for sex?

So why send me flowers?

And why now?

When the music changes, I slide from the pole and strut across the stage to the steps in search of Avery. I could do with a glass of champagne right about now.

As my heel connects with the floor again, a warm hand grips my elbow. I flinch as my head whips round. No one is supposed to touch me. Not without my permission.

Christopher releases his grip and flashes a creepy smile. Tiny hairs prick on the back of my neck. I glance around for Avery but she's preoccupied with the rock band.

I swallow thickly. Was it naïve to think I could come here and just dance?

Christopher's hand lifts to graze my cheek. 'How would you like to make twenty grand right now?'

Twenty grand is half of my credit card debt.

But at what cost to me?

'I, err...' Worry slithers into my stomach.

'Dance for me.' His eyes darken and fall to my lips. 'In one of the private rooms.'

We both know what he's asking for, and it isn't a dance.

My chest tightens. This man pays my wages. If I refuse him, will I still have a job?

'Okay.' he says brushing a stray stand of hair from my face. I flinch. . 'You drive a hard bargain. I'll make it twenty-five grand.' He says it like it's a done deal.

I battle to regulate my breathing and buy myself time to find the words to refuse him without risking everything.

'I can't,' I blurt after what feels like minutes, not seconds.

'Can't or won't?' Christopher scowls.

'Can't,' a deep, rich voice decrees from behind us. A huge, hot hand lands on the base of my spine. The shivers that skim my skin aren't out of fear. They're an entirely primal response to the owner of that booming baritone.

The scent of citrus and raw masculinity surrounds me.

James.

Christopher's gaze snaps to the man behind me, his hand falling from my face.

I take a step back, leaning against smooth silk and solid muscle.

'She already agreed to dance for me tonight.' James's tone is eerily neutral but still weighted with a warning.

'Is that right?' A tight smile lifts Christopher's lips. 'Well, well, well, there's a first for everything.' His eyes jump curiously between James and me. 'Scarlett doesn't normally do private dances and you never normally avail of them.'

'There's never been anyone worth availing of before.' James maintains an air of boredom despite the tension swirling in the air.

'I offered her twenty-five grand. What are you prepared to pay for a... dance.' Christopher pronounces the word 'dance' like it's a drug.

'Fifty.' James's tone is final.

I clear my throat, unsure if I should be horrified or flattered that they're bartering over me. The club takes twenty percent of every private dance but I'm pretty sure Christopher doesn't give a shit about the money. This negotiation is a power struggle. And there is one clear winner.

'She's due on the main stage again in an hour.' Christopher's biceps flex beneath his suit as he folds his arms across his chest.

'And she'll come back to me again after that.' James's voice is calm but there's a cold, dangerous edge to it.

'Do I get a say in this?' I glance between the two men displaying a confidence I don't feel.

Christopher's jaw tenses. 'Of course you do. Private dances are at your discretion.' Funny how he's doing a one-eighty now James is here.

'In that case...' I swivel towards James, 'I'll dance for you.'

It's not about the money. I'd dance for him for free.

It's about the man.

I've been obsessing about him since the first night. I'm not going to let the opportunity to spend some time with him alone slip through my fingers, even if I wasn't being paid a ridiculous amount of money for the privilege.

'How about seventy grand?' Christopher arches an eyebrow in question. 'I don't mind sharing.'

A thunderous expression flickers across James's features. 'I don't share.' His hand remains protectively on my lower back as he ushers me towards a mirrored doorway. 'Send in a bottle of Dom Perignon, will you?' he calls to Christopher over his shoulder, like he's no more than a glorified waiter.

Christopher pauses for a beat, a thunderous expression flicking across his face as he turns on his heel.

My stomach flips.

And who the hell pays fifty grand for time with me?

It's beyond flattering.

It's exhilarating and terrifying in equal measure.

He nudges me through the mirrored door and it closes behind us with a definitive click.

Chapter Eleven
SCARLETT

The room is twenty feet wide in each direction. In the centre is a small circular podium made of shiny black marble, complete with a centrally positioned chrome pole. Lilac uplighters line the circumference. A huge ivory leather couch lies against the far wall. Candles dot the perimeter. A sensual beat plays through carefully positioned speakers, but at a lower volume than in the main lounge.

'Thank you,' I say to James.

'For saving you from Cole? Don't mistake me for your saviour. I'm the most unapologetic sinner I know,' his lips curve upwards and my stomach flips.

He loosens his crimson silk tie and undoes his top button. My eyes fall to the smattering of dark hair contrasting his crisp, white shirt.

I blow out a breath and step up onto the podium. It's what I'm being paid to do after all.

'Wait.' James sinks into the couch and raises his hand to halt me. 'Have a drink with me.' He motions to the space next to him. 'I enjoyed our chat the other night, before you ran out on me, that is.' He smooths a hand over his broad chest. 'I'd like to continue the conversation, if that's alright with you?'

I pause for a beat and suck in a breath before nodding. For fifty grand, I can't exactly refuse, can I? I step off the edge of the podium towards the sofa.

'Tell me, Scarlett,' he beckons me closer with a single index finger, 'why are you still a virgin? Is it a religious thing?' he persists, manspreading across the leather.

I stand in front of him. If I were to take a step closer I'd be between his open thighs. 'No.'

'Are you saving yourself for marriage?' Big black eyes bore through me, like he's searching for my soul beneath my skin.

'No.' I shake my head. 'I'm not sure I even believe in marriage,' I admit.

He arches an eyebrow. 'We have that in common. Tying myself to someone forever isn't a prospect I'm comfortable with.'

'Yeah, until death do us part doesn't do a lot for me either.' It certainly didn't do a lot for my mother.

His chuckle rumbles through the air. 'I knew I liked you.'

'Thank you, I guess.' His compliment stirs something in my stomach. I smooth a hand across it and watch as his eyes follow the movement.

His eyes dart up again, a startled expression hijacking his features. 'You *are* into men?'

I swallow down another laugh. 'Yes, but I've been avoiding them, mostly,' I admit.

'Why?' Thick eyebrows knit together.

My eyelids flutter closed as I force away the memories. 'It's a long story. One I'd rather not go into.' And one he'd probably rather not hear about, given the rivalry between the O'Connors and Becketts is notorious.

His knuckles graze over his stubble contemplatively.

'I know it's weird that I've never...' I raise my hands.

'It's not weird. It's fucking wonderful.' His espresso-coloured eyes glint. 'I'm just surprised none of those college boys...'

An image of Shane Stenson flashes into my mind. Like he can sense it, James's lips purse together in a tight line. 'Ah, so there is a college boy. Tell me, Scarlett, who is he?'

I swallow hard feeling ridiculously guilty all of a sudden. 'No one. There was a guy once. We kissed in the campus nightclub. That was all.'

James's jaw clenches.

Why did I even admit that?

'I don't have billions in the bank,' I say, lifting my palm. 'I don't have a business. I don't have a family, not anymore anyway.'

A curious look crosses his face but he doesn't interrupt my flow.

'But what I do have is that part of myself. And when I give it away, it'll be because I want to, not because society thinks I should, not because a college boy thinks I should, and certainly not for money.' My tone is unwavering.

'I respect that more than you'll ever know.' His eyes bore into mine.

He's so hot. So intense. So *male*. At thirty-three, he's ten years older than me, (I *might* have done a little googling), but he has a twinkle in his eyes which is practically adolescent. His confidence is sexy beyond measure.

'Scarlett,' he drags my name across his tongue like he's savouring it, 'I think you may be the most attractive woman I've met in my life.'

'Thank you.' My nipples pebble beneath the flimsy silk. 'And thank you for the flowers.'

'The red velvet petals reminded me of you.' His throat flexes as he swallows. 'When you dropped the V-bomb on me, it was like striking a match in a petrol station. I haven't been able to get you out of my mind.'

My face heats. 'I didn't mean to blurt it out like that, but I wanted you to know I'm not easy.'

A low rumble of laughter tumbles from his chest. 'Believe me, I know you're not easy. Which only adds to the appeal.'

My fingers nervously reach for my necklace.

He thrums his fingers against the leather again. 'You exude an innocence that every man in this club would give their right arm to corrupt.'

'Every man but you.' I twist my torso and lower my backside on to the couch, the leather cool beneath my ass cheeks. 'Attraction or no attraction. Because you don't indulge in *extra* activities with dancers.' I mimic his words from our first encounter.

'And you neither require any extra tuition, or offer any *extra* activities– of any description.' His pupils gleam.

Touché.

'In that case, what are we doing here?' I gesticulate around this lavish private chamber.

He straightens in his seat and edges closer to me, his expression almost as dark as his onyx-like eyes. 'The thing is, Scarlett.' He glances at his hands. 'I have a different proposition for you.'

Chapter Twelve
JAMES

I might be the one paying for this private room, but there is no doubt she's in control. She holds all the cards, she just doesn't know it yet.

I tried to stay away. Tried to follow my father's instructions. Tried and failed.

Every day for the past two weeks, I've endured a different date, chosen by my parents. Every night for the past two weeks, I've rushed home to beat off in the shower imagining my fist was Scarlett's tight, hot, slippery channel.

My father warned me from a young age that temptation is a fool's game. Yet, inch after inch of smooth olive-coloured skin tempts me more than I've ever been tempted by anything in my life. Which makes me a huge fucking fool for Scarlett.

But I've come up with a plan. One that will keep my father off my back and allow me to scratch this itch with Scarlett.

A pole dancer is unequivocally not Alexander Beckett's idea of marriage material, and I'm pretty sure the Board would agree.

But that doesn't mean she can't *pretend* to be, for a few months at least.

Scarlett speaks with the same eloquent accent as the other girls at the Luxor. I'd bet my life she was educated privately, probably in some fancy girls-only school, and she's clearly intelligent, given she won a scholarship to the Trinity Business School.

If she's willing to play along until I secure the Imperial Winery acquisition, I could overturn my playboy reputation, and show the Board and my father that I'm capable of commitment, and have some fun in the process.

My hand falls to Scarlett's bare thigh. Her quad flexes beneath my fingers as she sucks in a sharp breath. As I trace languid circles across her silky skin, a ripple of satisfaction slides over my spine at the goosebumps trailing in my wake.

What is it about her that makes me feel like a fucking schoolboy?

Just like the first night, the attraction between us crackles and fizzes like a live wire. There's an intensity to it that's borderline painful. It's like nothing I've ever experienced before. It's no wonder I haven't been able to get her out of my head.

Christopher chooses this exact moment to burst in with the champagne. No danger of him sending one of the girls, or even knocking.

He might not have had his way tonight, but that won't stop him trying tomorrow. The thought pierces my chest like an arrow. I've known him a long time. He won't give up. Not while he's employing her. If anything, my intervention will only make him more determined to have her.

Cole pauses, taking in my hand on Scarlett's leg, before sliding an ice bucket complete with champagne bottle across the podium, along with two flutes. He hovers for a second, as if he's contemplating opening his mouth.

'That will be all.' Cole's eyes flicker with a burning rage at my abrupt dismissal.

I stand and follow him to the door. When it closes, I turn the lock.

I pour two glasses and hand one to Scarlett before dropping back onto the couch. 'I'm curious. What's this proposition?' Scarlett takes two large mouthfuls of champagne.

I raise my glass to my lips and drink deeply.

'I want to pay you to pretend to be my girlfriend.' I rock back against the leather, deliberately giving her space. 'My father and the board of directors are putting pressure on me to...' I search for the right words. 'Settle down.' I let my words sink in for a second, willing the stupid nerves in my stomach to quell. I've made many propositions in my lifetime, yet for some reason, this feels like one of the more significant ones. Probably because I want this—her—more than I've wanted anything in a long time. Maybe even ever.

Champagne splutters from her mouth. 'You're kidding? Why?' she asks, incredulous. 'Don't tell me. Because you were photographed on that yacht with those women?' Her grey irises twinkle.

I roll my eyes and choose to ignore her quip. 'You know I'm attracted to you. I think you're attracted to me. We could put on a convincing show.'

A wry smile twists her lips. 'I suppose you're not too bad to look at. But why me? Half the women in the country are attracted to you.'

'They're attracted to my bank balance. They're not really interested in me.' An image of yesterday's date pops into my mind. Jessica De Burgh, in a high-necked designer dress, blonde hair twisted into an immaculate chignon. Make-up applied so subtly I'm supposed to believe her beauty is natural. Perfectly manicured nails. A pearl necklace – not the type I've been fantasising about giving Scarlett, either.

Her family owns a global chain of Michelin-starred restaurants. On paper, we might be a good match, but in reality, there was no spark. No connection. Nothing. I made my excuses and left as soon as I finished dessert.

It was a total waste of time.

As were the dates I had with Aisling Kavanagh, Saoirse O'Sullivan, and Lady Fiona Harrington. I exhale heavily. Lunch with Lady Harrington was particularly painful. There was nothing ladylike about her. She chewed with her mouth open, talked about herself incessantly, and her high-pitched voice would grate on the nerves of a nun.

'Are you sure it's your money they're after?' A small smirk lifts Scarlett's lips as her eyes dart to my crotch the way they did the first night I saw her dance.

'You know, for a virgin,' I lean forwards and offer her a wink, 'you're pretty forward. If you keep looking at me like that I'm going to rip that pretty little scrap of silk from your pussy and bury my tongue in it.'

Scarlett's pupils dilate to huge lava-like pools. All traces of teasing evaporate from her face. Vulnerability and desire duel in her silver eyes and something sharp twists in my chest.

I want to corrupt her so badly, but she also provokes a mad urge to protect her, take care of her, lavish her beautiful body with affection and attention.

She leans in closer and my eyes are drawn to her spectacular tits.

'But why me?' She shimmies towards the edge of the leather and crosses her long tanned legs.

She has absolutely no idea how insane with lust she drives me. 'Because you're a million times more interesting than any of the society wannabes. Because you're gorgeous. Intelligent. Well spoken. Well educated. And you're about to graduate in finance. We're practically soul-mates.' I take a sip of my drink.

'What school did you go to?' I nip the inside of my cheek, praying my assumptions are right.

'St. Jude's Girls' School.'

I expected as much. St. Jude's is the most exclusive girls' school in the country.

'There you go then.' I raise my hands to emphasise my point. She might be a pole dancer, but she is equally qualified to be a private equity manager– or she will be in a matter of months at least.

How was Scarlett able to afford to attend the country's most prestigious girls' school and yet now she's here at the Luxor Lounge dancing for tips to pay back forty grand of student debt?

Where are her parents?

If they could afford to put her through private school, why aren't they helping her through college?

'I don't have a family, not anymore.'

I swallow back my curiosity. I don't need to know. What I need is an answer to my proposition. Every single atom in my body vibrates with the need for her to agree to fake date me. Because there's nothing fake about the attraction between us but while she continues to work at the Luxor as a pole dancer, there's no way we can explore it further.

I want her away from Cole and the other predators. Predators like me.

I want her to myself.

In any capacity.

'You know you can't carry on working here. Nice girls like you don't belong here.'

Scarlett's fingers strum over the stem of her glass. 'What makes you so sure I'm nice?'

'I'm never wrong about people. And you're one of the good ones.' I rub a thumb over the stubble dusting my chin. 'But Cole is like a hound chasing the scent of blood. He didn't like what happened tonight. He didn't like losing you to me. He's not going to forget. He's going to keep coming after you.'

I watch as my words sink in. Her expression falls.

'Help me, Scarlett, please. Pretend for a while. I have a big deal I'm working on and it would really help to get the Board and my father off my back, at least until the deal's done. It might take a few months, but I'd pay you well for it. How does three hundred thousand sound? And, unlike your current boss, I won't pressure you into sex. If you come to me looking for it though...' My lips quirk at the serious expression pinching her face.

It's impossible to miss the way she presses her thighs together. The slight roll of her slim hips. The way her tongue dips over her lips.

'What would I have to do?' She sucks on the inside of her cheek contemplatively.

'Resign from this place for a start. Attend my boring as fuck societal obligations. Publicly date me. Don't worry, Scarlett, this isn't a trap. I won't corrupt your virtue. Unless you want me to, that is.'

She stares into space for a long beat, seeing something that isn't there. I'd love to know what she's thinking.

Eventually, she stands, downs the remaining champagne in her glass and places it on the floor beside the couch. Every muscle in my body tightens, bracing itself for disappointment, waiting for her to walk out of the door.

But she doesn't.

Instead, she struts purposely towards the podium and steps up. 'I'll think about it. Let me dance for you. It's what you paid for, after all. And if I accept your offer, I might not get to do it again.' She grips the pole and pushes herself against it, swaying those hips in a hypnotic rhythm that's animalistic, agonising and utterly enthralling.

My cock is rock solid in seconds.

If I get my way, she will dance for me again, but it will be naked in my bedroom.

Because as much as I need to get my father and the Board off my back, what I desire more than anything, is time alone with her.

The need to know more about this woman is consuming me.

Chapter Thirteen
SCARLETT

Avery allowed me to leave the club on Friday night without a full debrief, but on the promise I meet her for Sunday brunch and a badly needed shopping spree. And apart from the fact I'm dying to discuss James, I'm also in desperate need of some new clothes.

Who knows? If I accept James Beckett's proposition, I might just need them.

But what if he finds out I'm the step daughter of his family's biggest rival? I'm all too aware of the legal battles, the public showdowns. I know how James's father, Alexander, got that scar on his face. And it's not a pretty story.

No. There's no way James can ever find out. I've changed my name. Cut my ties. There's nothing that can link me to the O'Connors. In fact, they're as much my enemies now as they are the Becketts'.

If I accept James's proposition, it could potentially set me up for life.

Plus, I'm insanely attracted to him. More attracted than I've ever been to any man.

'If you keep looking at me like that I'm going to rip that pretty little scrap of silk from your pussy and bury my tongue in it.'

I got myself off twice when I went home that night, just imagining it. Of course, if I were to agree to his proposition, we couldn't complicate our arrangement with sex.

There's a reason he wants a fake girlfriend, not a real one.

By the time I stride into the restaurant to meet Avery, I've made my decision.

Chez Blanc is a Michelin-starred restaurant offering French-inspired dishes in an elegant and intimate setting. Two weeks ago, it would have been so far out of my price range it's not even funny. After a couple of weeks dancing in the Luxor Lounge, it's irrelevant.

Large windows line one side of the restaurant, allowing the natural light to flood in and offering a spectacular view of the bustling city streets below. The Southside of Dublin has a completely different vibe to the North side, where I grew up.

'Can I help you?' A waitress approaches before I have time to stumble too far down memory lane.

'Table for two.' I force my lips into a wide smile.

She takes me to a table in the window. The weak wintery sun spills across the spotless tablecloth. I slip into the high backed seat and stash my handbag beneath the table.

'I need details.' Avery squeals as she parades into the restaurant two minutes later in a cloud of Jo Malone perfume and knee-high Jimmy Choo crocodile boots.

Her shoulder-length blonde hair falls freely over her camel-coloured cashmere coat and she looks every bit the privately educated college graduate she almost is.

Mind you, in a Ralph Lauren shirt dress, and a pair of last season's Claudie Pierlot ankle boots, (Avery's cast-offs, of course), I do, too. No one in their right mind would ever suspect we're a couple of high-end pole dancers.

Avery slides into the plush velvet seat opposite me, excitement dancing in her eyes. 'Details. Tell. Me. Everything.'

'Can we at least order a drink first?' It's midday somewhere and I'm not working later.

'Fine, but make mine a champagne.' Avery slips her coat off and slings it on the back of her chair. 'This life is for living. There will be days where we get away with bubbly breakfasts, and there will be days where we're bogged down with menial duties like dropping kids to school and holding down real jobs. I say, let loose while we can.'

Kids.

A family of my own.

A pang of longing hits me like a train. One day, maybe. One day.

Let loose is all very well coming from a woman who's biggest worry is if she'll be able to snag one of the ten limited edition Givenchy handbags coming to Brown Thomas next week.

The waitress drops two menus to the table. I scan mine mindlessly.

'What are you thinking?' Avery asks without looking up.

I'm thinking about James Beckett.

About his big molten eyes.

Eyes that I could drown in.

'Earth to Scarlett.' Avery waves a hand in front of my face. 'What are you thinking?' she repeats slowly.

'Sorry.' I blink. 'Avocado toast with poached egg and microgreens. Are you working tonight?' I place the menu onto the crisp, white linen table cloth.

'No.' She shakes her head. 'Stop deflecting.'

The waitress chooses that precise moment to return to take our order. Only when the bottle of champagne is open and poured do I start talking.

'Christopher offered me twenty-five grand to dance for him.' I run my finger up the stem of the champagne flute.

Avery hunches closer across the table. 'The going rate is five. He must have really wanted that dance.' She emphasises the word *dance*. 'Cole can be a bit... intense.' She frowns.

'James overheard and offered me fifty. Christopher's proposal sent him all alpha.' More alpha, I should say. The man radiates sex hormones like a silent mating call. 'Next thing I know, I'm drinking champagne with him in a private room.' I lift the glass and bring it to my lips, watching over the rim as Avery's chin practically hits the table.

'No fucking way!' she shrieks, attracting the attention of several neighbouring diners.

I shoot them an apologetic wince. 'Shh. Keep it down,' I plead. It's one thing being looked at on the stage, in a wig and enough make-up to conceal Beyonce's identity, but here in the city, even on the Southside, you never know who's around.

Which is why, *if* I agree to fake date James, he'll have to promise me I won't be photographed in those high society magazines that he so regularly features in.

'Fifty grand?' Avery hisses, wide-eyed. 'Holy fuck. You know he never paid any woman for anything before, right? Please tell me you finally parted with that invisible chastity belt?'

I swear if Avery's eyes get any fuller they're going to pop out of her head.

'No! Jesus, Avery what do you take me for?'

'A mug, Scarlett, clearly. I take you for a mug.' Her blonde hair swishes across her face as she shakes her head in disbelief. 'I would let that man do anything he wanted to me for fifty grand. Hell, I'd let him do it to me for free! He's the most perfect example of the male species to grace this earth!'

'That at least we can agree on.' I purse my lips to halt a grin from splitting them open.

'And did you do *anything*?'

'I danced for him.' I shrug, like it's not completely crazy that a billionaire paid me fifty grand to dance for him.

'You didn't...' She gestures with a perfectly manicured hand and nods towards my body. 'He didn't...'

'Nothing.' I confirm. 'And the money was wired into my bank before I even got home, minus Christopher's twenty percent of course.' I take a sip of my drink then nod. 'That's not all.'

'Go on.' If Avery arches any further forwards her generous-sized chest will be crushed on the table. 'You're killing me, Scarlett. Spill the fucking beans.'

Where do I even start?

'The flowers were from him. He wants me to fake date him,' I whisper, glancing sidewards to check no one can hear us.

'No. Fucking. Way.' Her head snaps up so quickly she should probably be treated for whiplash.

'After that New Year's Eve yacht scandal,' my cheeks flush, 'he's coming under pressure to at least *appear* like he's behaving.'

Avery's eyes look like they might actually pop out of their sockets. 'Please, please, please tell me you said yes.' She reaches for my hand over the table and squeezes it.

'I didn't say no.' I shrug.

'James might be a lot of things, but he'll be good to you. Accept his offer. Hang off his arm like you're the next Harry and Meghan. Lose that damn V-card if you get the chance! Fuck's sake, girl, you've been hanging on to it way too long...' She licks her lips lasciviously, her blue eyes twinkling with mischief.

'I can't sleep with him, Avery. No way.'

'Whether you sleep with him or not, you have to accept his offer. You'll graduate college debt free. And you'll have access to your own personal tutor through your finals.' She winks. 'I'm sure he could teach you a few good lessons. Take whatever pleasure you can get and milk it for all it's worth.'

'I told you no sex!' I hiss.

'Why not?'

I stick out my index finger. 'Because it would be like he's paying me for it, which feels wrong on so many levels.'

'He's paying you to pretend to be his girlfriend!' Avery snorts. 'You could at least throw in the sex for free!'

I shake my head in disbelief, though her blasé attitude doesn't surprise me.

'It reminds me of Julia Roberts in *Pretty Woman*.' Avery sighs dreamily.

'Huh.' I offer her a swift, sharp dig to her shin beneath the table and she squeals.

'What was that for?'

'I'm a virgin, and you're comparing me to a hooker?'

'Oh honey, if James Beckett gets his way, you won't be a virgin for much longer.' She waggles her eyebrows. 'He might be paying you to go out in public with him, but I'm pretty sure if you chose to "pretend" in the bedroom, he wouldn't say no either.'

'Have you forgotten he's never been pictured with the same woman more than once? At least not since Cynthia Van Darwin.'

I pored over the pictures of them together in the papers. They split unexpectedly and the world never found out why. 'Imagine if I gave him the goods then he didn't want anything to do with me. It would make our arrangement pretty fucking awkward.'

'Pah,' my friend gestures over my body. 'As if.' Her loyalty knows no bounds.

I do want to lose that pesky V-card. I'm not saving myself for marriage. I'm saving myself for a man that will make it memorable.

And James Beckett would certainly make it utterly memorable. He's so hot, he's on fire.

But I, of all people, know what happens when you play with fire.

You get burnt.

'What if I get hurt?'

'Don't overthink this. Take it for what it is and enjoy the ride.' Avery says encouragingly.

Avery lives for the moment.

Maybe just this once, I should too.

Chapter Fourteen
JAMES

'Any progress with the Imperial Winery Group acquisition?' My father perches on my desk like he owns it.

'I'm working on the full proposal but I've made my intentions very clear. Unfortunately, O'Connor's appear to have the same idea.'

My father's face darkens four shades at the mere mention of our rivals. Our families have been locked in a bitter feud for generations. My grandfather, Benjamin Beckett, co-founded the original whiskey distillery with Seamus O'Connor. But while Benjamin was the epitome of perseverance and integrity, Seamus was driven by greed, seeking to exploit the distillery as a facade for more illicit ventures.

They parted ways and the O'Connors fell into bed with Ireland's biggest crime syndicate. Rumour is, they use their legitimate businesses as a front for drug trafficking and God only knows what else.

Needless to say, we avoid them wherever possible, but Dublin isn't a big city.

'It's far from ideal, but I'll deal with it.'

'Why would they be interested in the Imperial Winery

Group? They're a bunch of glorified thugs.' My father's hand smooths over the distinctive scar on his left cheek, a reminder of the brutality of the family, and Seamus O'Connor's son, Jack, in particular. Its deep purple shade has faded over time but the memory of the attack remains with me as vividly as if it were yesterday.

'Perhaps for the same reason as us. It could help their reputation. Plus, it could be a great front for whatever illegal shit they've got going on across Europe.' I clear my throat.

'Be careful of those mad bastards, son. They're liable to stoop to anything,' my father warns in a grave tone.

Don't I know it. Jack O'Connor is currently serving time for manslaughter. He's so deranged he set fire to his own distillery – with his second wife in it. Now his sons run his empire for him. Declan O'Connor, his eldest, is rumoured to be more vicious than his father.

'I'm dealing with it, Dad.' And so is Killian. Only he's dealing with it in his own unique way.

My father's shoulders relax a fraction. 'And any progress on the other *proposal*? I heard you had lunch with Jessica De Burgh. How did that go?'

'As expected, of course. It was boring as fuck.' I battle an eye roll.

My father sighs. 'You'll find your match yet. I have every faith in you. At least while you're dating these high society women, you aren't being photographed with half-naked employees.'

Heat ignites my blood. I hesitate for a split second, before saying, 'There is one woman with potential.'

'Oh, who is the lucky lady?' His voice hitches with interest.

'You don't know her. She's not on the usual social circuit.'

'Is she from a suitable family?'

'I believe so.' I clear my throat, realising I know nothing

about Scarlett's family. 'She's exceptionally intelligent, well-educated, and she's beautiful.'

'Well, well, well...' He runs a finger over the desk like he's inspecting it for dust.

'But she's,' I pause before admitting, 'younger.'

'How young?' His head whips up and a line deepens between my father's eyebrows.

'Twenty-three. She's months away from obtaining her masters in finance.'

'From which college?' Dad asks.

'Trinity Business School.'

'Impressive.' He clears his throat. 'Ten years isn't too much of an age gap. I mean it's not like you're corrupting some innocent young virgin.' He chuckles again.

Guilt stokes my gut. My arrangement with Scarlett, if she chooses to accept, isn't for sex, it's for show. But given half the chance, I'll drag her to my bedroom and show her exactly what her body was made for.

'What are your plans for tonight?' My father glances at his Rolex. It's getting late.

'I still have a couple more hours to do here.' I motion to the computer. And then, I plan on going straight to the Luxor Lounge to see if Scarlett has come to a decision. Fuck. Excitement and nerves battle for dominance in my stomach. I'm like a teenager with an all-consuming crush.

'I know you want to put things right, make up for your indiscretions, but don't work yourself into the ground. Your mother would love to see you. Come by this week.' My dad stands, smooths a hand across his suit and claps my back before he leaves.

Three hours later, I stride into the Luxor Lounge with a

casualness that completely contrasts with the thrumming in my veins.

What if she turns me down?

Keep it together, fuck's sake. It's no different to any other business deal.

Except it is, because I've never been as attracted to anyone I've made a deal with before, and I'm only lying to myself by pretending otherwise.

Even on a Monday, the place is packed. Rian and Killian are sitting on tall stools beside the bar. Caelon and Sean are nowhere to be seen.

Avery is on the main stage. Eight other dancers dot the smaller podiums. I scour the room with narrowed eyes. There's no sign of Scarlett.

There's also no sign of Christopher Cole.

My fingers curl to a clench. Has he got her holed up in one of those private rooms with him? Is he laying his dirty hands on her right now?

Blood roars in my ears. I should have got here earlier. Should have been here for opening. I didn't want to come on too strong but fuck it, I should have had Killian watch out for her.

Though, that would mean telling him I care. Because I do care, strangely enough. I care about her more than is healthy.

Then again, if she agrees to act as my girlfriend for the next few months, Killian will expect me to care. He'll insist on a background check, of course. It's a matter of protocol.

I greet my brothers with one question. 'Where's Cole?'

Rian's fingers whiten around his whiskey tumbler and his smile freezes on his face when he cops my thunderous expression.

'What's he done now?' Killian lurches from the bar stool, ready for whatever the night brings.

'I'm not sure yet, but I need to find him. Like, right now.' I scan the crowd until I locate his manager, Giselle.

She must feel the heat of my stare because her head snaps up and she's by my side in a matter of seconds. 'Mr Beckett, good evening. Can I assist you with something?'

'Where's Cole?' My voice is cold and low.

Giselle flinches and glances towards one of the narrow corridors branching off the main area. 'In his office, dealing.'

I take off with Killian and Rian at my heels. The soles of my shoes thud against the marble flooring. There are four doors to the left and three on the right. Light spills from beneath the last door on the left.

I push it open with the silent calmness of a man in complete control, even though my pulse is pounding.

Scarlett is standing to the right of a huge cherrywood desk, wide-eyed like a startled deer staring at the barrel of a rifle. In her hand is a small white envelope.

Her resignation?

Probably, given the incensed expression on Cole's face.

She's so much better than this place. It's irrelevant how much the membership costs. Or how much Cole pays for that fancy fucking orchid scent. Or that the clientele is mostly made up of Dublin's millionaires and billionaires.

Scarlett is above all of it.

I know it, Cole knows it, and every man in the place knows it, which is why they all want a piece of her.

Cole's towering over her, his thin lips curled into a snarl. 'You can't quit,' he spits. 'You made a commitment to dance at my club. Dance for me now. I fucking own you.'

His hand reaches for her wrist and my final cord of restraint unravels.

I clear my throat loudly.

Cole's head whips round, sadly not fast enough to snap his

neck. I've never committed murder. But I might, if he's so much as harmed a hair on her head.

'She'll never dance for you.' My voice is eerily calm, borderline bored, in complete contrast to the storm swirling inside my body. I close the distance between us. 'And you don't own her.'

'This is a private conversation, in a private area of my club.' Cole's hand drops to his side as fast as a flash of lightning. His false confidence isn't convincing any of us. He glances to the panic button on top of his desk, which is laughable really. Killian's men will burst in. Cole might hire them, but their loyalty is not to him.

My eyes roam over Scarlett, searching for any sign of injury, but she looks unscathed, on the outside at least. In an ivory silk balconette bra, and matching thong, she is the epitome of every virgin fantasy I've ever had. A pearl embroidered suspender belt drapes from her waist complete with sheer ivory stockings.

Tonight's honey-highlighted wig extends all the way to her almost bare ass. It's no wonder she's driving normally sensible men to stupidity. She's driving me to it too, but the difference is, I would never place a hand on her if she didn't want me to.

'This conversation is over.' I step in front of Scarlett and a relieved sigh escapes her lips.

Killian paces the front of the office at an unnervingly slow pace, eyeing every detail in the room like he's looking for evidence of something untoward and committing it to memory.

Rian leans against the doorframe casually, but there's nothing casual about the grimace on his face. He might be the baby of our family, but all of my brothers are a force to be reckoned with. We were raised to treat women with respect, regardless of what walk of life they're from.

'She signed a contract.' Cole's voice wavers. He knows it's

over, but still he can't shut his mouth. 'She needs to work out her notice.' His beady eyes rove over her flesh. 'Why are you taking so much interest anyway? She's no more than a high-class whor—'

Rage rises in my torso like a riptide. My fist smashes into his face with a satisfying crunch before he can even contemplate finishing his sentence.

The metallic scent of blood saturates the air as it spills over his chin and onto his shirt. His hands fly to his face.

'You broke my nose!' His tone is incredulous.

'Think yourself lucky that's all I broke, my friend.' My voice remains cool as I take a step back and slide off my jacket before slipping it around Scarlett's shoulders.

I usher her towards the door, shooting Cole a murderous look. 'If you lay so much as a finger on any of the women here without their permission, I'll break every bone in your spineless body.'

Cole's jaw locks tight but he doesn't dare open his mouth again.

'Are you okay?' I slip an arm over Scarlett's shoulders protectively as I guide her through the corridor with Killian and Rian close on our heels.

She's visibly shaking. 'I don't like violence. I've seen enough of it to last me a lifetime.'

Curiosity piques, but now is not the time for questions. 'It's okay, sweetheart. You're okay. It's over now. He won't touch you again.' I nudge her through the crowd. It feels like every eye in the place is focussed on us. 'Let's get you out of here.'

'My stuff.' Scarlett glances towards the changing rooms.

'Killian will get it for you.' I turn to my stony faced brother and speak directly into his ear. He nods before slipping away.

A security guard looks at us questioningly, but I raise a hand to convey I've got this.

'I'm sorry.' Scarlett says shakily as we leave the club. Her breath fogs in front of her face and she pulls my jacket tighter around her torso. Thankfully, on her, it's long enough to cover the sexy suspenders because I'd hate to have to kill every man who looked at her out here.

Scarlett shivers under the starlight.

'Don't be sorry. He employed you to dance, not be his plaything. Men like Cole can't help themselves.'

'And you?' The whites of her eyes are luminous beneath the moonlight. Her skin so flawless. So fresh – a reminder of exactly how young she is. But despite her sexual naivety, she exudes a knowing. Like someone who has seen too much but experienced too little.

'You're safe with me, I promise.' I pluck my phone from my pocket and text my driver, Tim.

'Do you think he'll come after us?'

'Who? Cole?' I scoff. 'He wouldn't fucking dare.'

Her shoulder's relax visibly. 'Thank you. For coming in like that.'

'You're welcome.'

Killian appears with a tan leather bag and oversized coat. He holds the coat out to Scarlett and the bag to me. 'Rian and I are going to stay for another drink.' He holds my stare pointedly. Translation *'Rian and I are going to stay and remind Cole not to try anything stupid.'*

'Good idea. I'll see Scarlett home. And I'll see you in the morning.'

Chapter Fifteen
SCARLETT

James's driver, Tim, arrives in a sleek black Mercedes. He opens the door and James motions for me to climb in.

'Are you hungry?' James slides along the cream leather beside me. His eyes are brimming with concern.

I shrug. 'I haven't eaten since lunch.'

'That's no good.' James says something I don't quite catch to Tim, then presses a button to raise the partition, giving us some much needed privacy.

For the second time in my life, I'm alone with Ireland's most eligible billionaire.

'Are you sure you're okay?' He checks again, flexing his fingers and examining his knuckles.

'I'm fine. I've come up against a lot worse than Cole and lived to tell the tale.' *Just*.

'He's scum in a suit.' He says, as the city lights whizz by. 'So, I guess you're officially unemployed.' There's a hint of amusement in his tone. 'Unless...' His eyes linger on my lips and his throat bobs as he swallows.

'I'll do it.' I eye him steadily. 'On two conditions.'

'Just two?' He swipes a thumb over his strong jawline. 'I assumed you'd have a list.'

'What can I say?' I sigh. 'I'm low maintenance.'

'One of the things I lo– like about you.' His head dips closer to mine and I get a brief whiff of his expensive cologne. 'What are your conditions?'

I wet my lips. 'Firstly, I won't have sex with you.'

His mouth opens, then rapidly closes. 'Okay.'

I exhale a heavy breath. That was easier than I thought. Given the way he flirts with me, I assumed he'd at least try to put up an argument.

'And the second condition?' He smooths his hands across the front of his suit.

'I can't be photographed with you,' I blurt. I've managed to keep my head down and my nose clean for the past few years. I can't risk everything now. 'I'd rather not be in the spotlight.'

Low laughter rumbles from his chest and echoes around the vehicle. 'Like you said, you're low maintenance.'

'And that's funny?' I arch an eyebrow.

'It's actually utterly endearing.' He turns to me through the moonlight and cups my face in his hands, angling it to his. Our breath mingles and a hot shiver of desire courses over my spine. 'You have a beautiful face, Scarlett. It's a face any red-blooded male would want to photograph. I can't guarantee we won't get papped, but trust me, I'll make sure the papers don't show your face. I have a few connections. I can pull a few strings."

Huh. An image of James's debauched behaviour on that yacht in Dubai that made the headlines a few weeks ago flashes through my mind. He didn't manage to pull a few strings to stop that one appearing with the faces, and a lot else besides, most definitely on show. A flicker of envy flares in my chest.

Just because I said we *can't* have sex, it doesn't necessarily mean I don't *want* to.

'Any other requests?' His hand drops to my knee and a jolt of energy strikes me right between my thighs.

'No.' I pause for a second, my mind wandering back to last week's lectures where I'd been so distracted with thoughts of him that I barely caught a third of the information I needed. 'Well, I might cash in on the tuition you offered.' The man has a master's in the subject I'm hoping to graduate in. Plus, he has the business acumen and experience I'm lacking, and I have a dissertation to hand in.

I get a flash of straight white teeth through the darkness. 'I'll give you all the tuition you need. All you have to do is ask.'

A hot flush inches over my skin and my stomach somersaults.

He removes his hand from my knee as the car pulls to a stop outside Juliana's, the most exclusive Italian in town. I assume we're getting take out, given we don't have a reservation.

He glances out of the window, watching as Tim steps away from the car and enters the restaurant. 'You like Italian?'

'It's my favourite.' My fingers reach for my scalp where a hundred bobby pins are securing tonight's wig in place. I tentatively loosen a few and slip them into my coat pocket.

'Need a hand?' His gaze trails over my face like a caress.

'Just loosening these pins. Please tell me a wig isn't necessary in my new job.' Though it might not be a bad idea, especially if we are papped. I can't take the risk of being identified. Not after all the trouble I've gone through to keep a low profile all this time since the court case.

'It's not necessary. The lingerie is optional.' He winks and my stomach flips again. 'Let me help you with those.'

Thick fingers sweep over my temple with a tenderness he

doesn't look capable of. Following my hairline with the pads of his fingers, James skims my skin until he touches a sliver of metal, then wiggles the pin out.

For a man of his size, he's surprisingly gentle.

I wonder if he'd be gentle with me in bed, too?

"Don't worry, Scarlett. This isn't a trap. I won't corrupt your virtue. Unless you want me to, that is."

No. No. No. No. Don't go there, Scarlett.

James drops pin after pin into my lap. I work from the back of my neck and he works from my temples. Every time our fingers graze a hot bolt of electricity charges up my arm like a live wire. When all the pins are out, he moves his hand to the nape of my neck. 'Do you mind if I take your wig off?'

'Sure.'

He tugs gently, the wig falls to my lap and he hisses out a low breath. 'Stunning, Scarlett.' Uncoiling my French twist, he drags his fingers through it in a slow, sensual motion that sets goosebumps rippling across my skin. A quiet moan of appreciation escapes my mouth.

'I've been wondering if your hair was as dark as your eyebrows.' He grabs a handful and pulls it to his nose, inhaling deeply. 'It's absolutely stunning. Like dark liquid chocolate.'

My chin juts out, my face angles upwards, until we're sharing the same breath. Every cell in my body hums with a longing like never before.

'James.' There's a warning in my tone. We're three minutes into our agreement and I'm already fighting to remember why I'm not supposed to throw myself at him.

From my periphery, I spot Tim leaving the restaurant. I jerk backwards before he opens the car door. 'The table is ready when you are, sir.' He closes the door quietly again.

I glance at James, who is motioning me to get out.

'Where are we going?'

'On our first date.' He flashes a devastating grin.

'You can't be serious?' My eyes fall to my coat, specifically, what little I've got on under it.

'As much as I'd love to sit across the table from you in that decadent lingerie, don't you have other clothes in that bag?' He motions to my handbag that Killian collected from the changing rooms.

'Oh, right.' I put my hand in and search around for the little black Reformation dress I found in the Brown Thomas sale with Avery yesterday. Thank God for that little shopping spree.

I pull it out and wait for him to turn away or something.

He doesn't.

'Don't pretend you're shy now, Scarlett,' he teases. 'Not when you've danced for me. Not when you've admitted how intoxicating it is to be watched on stage. You like being seen.'

He's uncannily accurate.

I slip the coat from over my shoulders. The heat of his stare blazes a trail across my body as I tug the dress over my head.

He lets out a whistle that sets my insides fluttering again. 'Yep. Nobody in their right mind will struggle to believe we're a real couple.'

His fingers dart over his lips and my eyes follow. His hands are so huge. What would they feel like on my body? In my body?

'Scarlett. Sex isn't part of the job description, but,' his voice is low and guttural, 'I warned you the other night if you keep looking at me like that I'm going to bury my tongue in you.'

Fuck, if *he* keeps looking at *me* like that, it'll be impossible to remember why I'm not supposed to let him.

Chapter Sixteen
SCARLETT

The restaurant is long and narrow with high ceilings and elaborate coving. With ambient lighting and soft classical music, it radiates a rustic charm. The delicious scent of garlic, herbs and freshly baked bread wafting through the air makes my mouth water.

Or that could just be the sight of James's marble-sculpted ass in those tailored trousers.

Most of the customers are finishing the last dregs of their wine, the last few morsels of dessert. It's close to midnight, but the restaurant is showing no sign of shutting.

We're led to a table elegantly set with crisp white linen and gleaming silverware. The waitress pulls a cushioned chair out for me and I sit, smoothing down the front of my dress.

'We'll have a bottle of Barolo, please.' James slides into the seat opposite and flashes the waitress a quick smile before returning his attention to me.

I take the leather-bound menu the waitress offers and flip it open.

'What do you fancy?' He glances up from the menu with a crooked smile.

'I'm not sure.'

'Want me to order for you? I think I know what you'd like.' A hint of devilment dances in his dark irises.

'Are you always such a shameless flirt?'

'Just practising a little role play, you know.'

Heat inches up my neck but before he can flirt anymore, the waitress returns with the bottle of red and pours a small amount into my glass. James encourages me to taste it, his expression almost daring me not to like it.

I raise the glass to my mouth, watching him over the rim as the wine passes my lips. It's heavenly. My expression must give me away because James's chuckle rumbles across the table.

'I think it's safe for you to pour,' he instructs the waitress.

'Are you ready to order?' The waitress takes a pen and a small notebook from the pocket of her black embroidered pinafore.

'We'll have the wagyu beef tagliolini, and the foie gras ravioli, please.' He closes his menu with a small thud and hands it back to her.

'Certainly, sir.' She nods at him, then at me. 'Madam.'

'Do you come here often?' I lift the glass and swirl the liquid, watching as it streaks the inside of the glass.

'Only when I'm really trying to impress.' His lips quirk as he shrugs off his suit jacket and slips it over the back of the chair. Deft fingers swiftly roll his sleeves up to reveal taut, tanned forearms rippled with enough veins to form a road map. 'Is it working?'

'You don't need to impress me, remember?' I lower my voice and arch my torso. 'It's not a condition of our arrangement.'

'Yes but, I'm hoping those conditions are up for negotiation. And by the way, I have a few conditions of my own.' His eyes pin me in a powerful stare.

A ripple of nervous apprehension rises in my gut. 'Go on.'

'Firstly, I'm giving you a credit card. Buy whatever you want. Text books. Clothes. Make-up.' His focus falls to my dress as if he can see beneath it. 'Lingerie. Whatever you need or want.'

'I–' He cuts me off before I can protest. He's already paying me a fortune.

'Scarlett, you just resigned from your job to work for me. I want to make sure you're better off for it.' He pulls his phone from his pocket and hands it to me. 'Put your phone number in here, please.'

I tap in the digits and hand it back.

'Secondly, I need at least three public dates a week if I'm going to convince the Board we're serious.'

I nod. Three dates a week with this gorgeous creature isn't exactly work. Unless you count the effort of not throwing myself at him and begging him to make good on his promise to bury his tongue in me.

'Thirdly, though, I'm pretty sure I don't need to even voice this one, I need your assurance you won't see anyone else. You mustn't be caught even speaking to another man.' His jaw ticks, like he's seeing it in his head in multi-coloured flashing images. 'And God help anyone you might kiss in a nightclub.'

Clearly, I'm never going to live that down.

'As if I would.' It's a battle not to roll my eyes. 'But tell me, I'm still curious to know why a man like you, who could have any woman he desires, needs a pretend girlfriend?'

His mouth curves in a slight smile. 'Because real ones get big ideas about marriage and babies.'

I take another large mouthful of wine. 'You don't want babies?' He's already told me he's not interested in marriage but surely a man like him would want an heir.

'No.' His tone is final. 'And especially not with some society wannabe.'

'What do you want then?' The words are out of my mouth before I can stop them.

'Right now, I want to get to know my pretend girlfriend.' He reaches across the table and takes my hand, drawing small circles on the back of it. Every fleeting flick of his fingers has my insides melting.

'I hope this is okay.' His eyes fall to the table. 'It's important we put on a convincing performance.' His eyes dart around the room, but no one is looking our way.

'Next you'll be kissing me in public, too.'

'You can bet your life on it, sweetheart.' He wets his lips. 'And I'm going to enjoy every second of it.'

'James,' I scold. 'You can't say that.'

'Why not?'

'Because I told you, I'm not going to... we can't...' The mere thought of his naked body on top of mine makes me unable to form coherent sentences.

'I want you, Scarlett,' he says in a low, velvety voice that sets my pulse fluttering. 'I've made no secret of that. And I intend to do everything in my power to convince you to let me have you.'

My mouth is suddenly drier than the bottom of a bird's cage.

'Why have you been avoiding men?' His thumb strokes over mine in what is both a soothing and sensual motion.

I pause for a second, wondering how to explain without revealing too much of my less than pleasant past. 'Let's just say, I've had some bad experiences.' I fiddle with the stem of my wine glass.

'What happened?' Sympathy crossed with something like anger pinches his features.

'It's a long story. I'd rather not discuss it tonight.'

James brings my hand to his mouth and presses his lips against my skin. His eyes exude a heat that scorches my soul. 'While you are mine, no harm will ever come to you. I'll make sure of it. This arrangement between us might be business,' his throat bobs as he swallows, 'but if there's anything I can do for you, just say. I want you to be happy.'

'Thank you.' His kindness is unexpected. I blink back the hot well of tears forming behind my eyeballs.

Thankfully, the waitress returns and places two steaming plates of food between us. James raises his wine glass and clinks it against mine. 'To fake first dates.'

'To fake first dates.'

He stabs the beef with his fork and I watch with envy as it passes his luscious lips. His moan is borderline sexual. Or maybe it's just on me. From the second I laid eyes on James Beckett, I've barely thought of anything else but sex. The allure of the unknown has never been more, well, alluring.

'So good,' he murmurs, stabbing another piece of succulent beef. This time, instead of raising his fork to his own lips, he raises it to mine. It feels even more intimate than the hand holding. My mouth opens of its own accord. The cool metal of the fork contrasts with the heat of the dish. A burst of flavour hits my tongue before the beef melts in my mouth.

My own moan is positively orgasmic. 'So good.'

'Right?' James grins at me. 'I love a woman who loves food. It's the second greatest pleasure on this earth.' He shoots me a lascivious wink.

'Tell me, why did you choose to study finance?' James asks, between mouthfuls of ravioli.

'What's this? An interview?' I tease. 'I thought I already got the job?'

'You did, but when I introduce my "girlfriend" to my family, I'd like to know a little about her.'

'Numbers are the only constant thing in a world that's ever changing. Opinions change. Theories change. People change. But numbers never let me down.'

He nods with approval.

'How about you?'

'Duty,' he admits. 'I'm the oldest Beckett. It was always going to fall to me to run the company. My brothers got to choose their subsidiaries, but I didn't have that luxury. Which is why I refuse to permit my father to pick a wife for me, too.'

'Do you get along with your family?' I ask before popping another piece of beef into my mouth. All I ever wished for in life was a normal family. When my mother married Jack O'Connor, I was young enough to think I might have found it. How wrong I was.

James's throat bobs as he swallows. 'They're everything to me.'

'Even your dad? Even when he's pressuring you to get married?'

'*Especially* my dad. He taught me everything I know. He's hard on me for my own benefit, but he's also my biggest champion.' James puts his fork down and rocks back in his chair. 'He's actually a ridiculous romantic. He and my mother still go all doe-eyed when they see each other. I think he wants that for me.'

'Sounds lovely.' I'd imagined Alexander Beckett to be sterner.

'What about you?' James's head tilts to the side.

I shrug. 'There's not much to know. My father died when I was two. My mother died when I was seventeen.' I stare at the wine in the bottom of my glass. 'That's it.' My throat tightens at the memory, but I don't want to dwell on it. I don't want to cry. Not in front of James.

He winces, genuine horror crossing his face. 'Jesus, Scarlett, I'm so sorry.' His fingers dart over the back of my hand again. 'Any brothers or sisters?'

I blow out a breath. 'No.' *Not anymore.*

'Sounds lonely.' He studies me with sympathy.

'I've learnt to take care of myself.' I don't need or want his, or anyone else's sympathy.

'So, what's the end game?' he asks. 'What are your plans after you graduate?'

'Get out of the city. See the world.' I tuck a strand of hair behind my ear.

'Where do you want to go?' James asks.

'I've never been to Paris.' I shrug. 'I might start there.'

'Why Paris?'

'Emily.' I smile.

'Who's Emily?' His brows furrow.

'It's a show, *Emily in Paris*. I'm obsessed with it. The fashion is gorgeous but the male lead is pretty easy on the eye too.'

James harrumphs. 'Easy on the eye? Really?'

'You should see him, ' I swoon. 'Model worthy bone structure to die for.' My gaze lingers on James's sharp cheekbones. In truth, James's bone structure is more striking than any model I've ever seen.

'Anything else?' He's staring at me with an intensity that heats my skin.

I pause for a second to think. 'He has this twinkle in his eyes that just screams "come to bed".'

His eyes flash. 'What do my eyes scream, Scarlett?'

'They don't scream.' I swallow, gazing into his dilating pupils. 'They smoulder.' My cheeks heat as I tear my gaze away.

The waitress reappears with the menus. 'Would you like anything to finish?'

'I was just about to ask the same thing.' He smirks. His innuendo isn't lost on me.

'Not for me.' I address the waitress and ignore the chemistry crackling across the table. 'I'm trying to be good.'

James's chuckle rings through the air like a deep, hypnotic melody. 'Come on then, let's get you home. You've got school tomorrow.'

'School is for children. I have lectures.'

'Semantics.' James shrugs with another smirk. He pays the bill, leaves a hefty tip and escorts me out into the chilly night where his driver, Tim, is waiting for us.

'Where do you live, sweetheart?'

I hesitate for a second before giving him my less than desirable address. Crinkles form around the corner of James's eyes, but he doesn't comment.

The car ride is quiet. James taps away at his phone, while I gaze up at the stars and wonder which one of them is my lucky one, which one I have to thank for my unusual proposition.

'I transferred two hundred grand into your Revolut account.' He says two hundred grand like it's twenty euro. His eyes don't even veer from his screen. 'I'll transfer the other hundred afterwards.'

Afterwards.

I can't even think about afterwards, when we're only just commencing our 'arrangement.'

'I'll have a credit card delivered to you before lunch tomorrow,' he continues.

I grew up in an affluent family, before I fled for my life, but the Becketts are on another level.

James tucks his phone into his pocket as the car pulls to a stop outside my apartment building.

I squint through the darkness towards the front door.

Several students ramble by, leaving a trail of raucous laughter in their wake.

'This it?' James's head snaps up. Frown lines crease his forehead.

'This is it. Home sweet home.' I shrug, taking in the shabby, broken front door and the litter discarded either side of it.

James pinches the bridge of his nose and exhales heavily. 'Not anymore it isn't. You're coming home with me.'

Chapter Seventeen
JAMES

Scarlett opens her mouth like she's about to protest, then closes it again.

Even through the moonlight, it's clear the front door is hanging from its rusty hinges. The wood is so splintered, the slightest puff of air could blow it down.

It's about as secure as a matchbox.

I sigh. Moving my fake girlfriend into my house wasn't part of my plan. I never take women home. Ever. But Scarlett isn't just any woman, she's the one woman I haven't been able to erase from my mind from the moment I laid eyes on her. Having her under my roof will prove to be a special type of torture, given her 'conditions'.

But I can't leave her here. Actually, I don't *want* to leave her here.

I thought I was obsessed with her before, but after tonight's dinner, that obsession has only intensified. And this shit show of an excuse for an apartment block is the perfect excuse to take her home with me.

'I know it's far from pretty but it's fine for me.' Scarlett's teeth tug at her lower lip.

'It's not a matter of aesthetics, it's a matter of safety.' I shove my phone in my suit trousers and slide across the leather. 'Let's get your things.'

'Really, there's no need,' she insists as Tim opens the door.

'Scarlett, I have fourteen guest bedrooms. You can take your pick but you're not staying here.' A needle I spot discarded in the gutter reinforces my point.

Her eyes dart between my face and the building she calls home. 'Honestly, go home. I'm fine.'

'Over my dead body.' She flinches. 'I'll help you get your belongings, but this isn't up for negotiation. In fact, I'm officially making it a condition of our arrangement.'

Her shoulders sink, like she finally realises I'm not going to take no for an answer. 'How about I stay for a night or two, until we can get the door fixed?'

I inhale slowly. 'We'll explore the logistics later.' Right now, I just need to get her the hell away from here. 'Do you have the keys?' I motion to her handbag.

'This is crazy,' she says. 'We barely know each other.'

'Perhaps it's the perfect opportunity to get to know each other, given we're going to have to convince my family we're in love.' I pause.

'But –' she opens her mouth but I cut her off.

'No woman of mine is staying somewhere like this.'

'I'm not your woman. I'm pretending to be your woman. It's different.' She flicks her hair back from her face defiantly.

I take a step towards her, until we're toe-to-toe, hip-to-hip. Energy thrums and vibrates between us. Tim shifts on his feet and looks the other way.

I cup her chin and tilt her face up until our eyes lock. 'You agreed to be mine, on paper at least. And I take care of what's mine.' Prising the keys from her hand, I take them in my own, stride towards the front door and unlock it.

I glance through the dim dingy hall. 'No lift?' I hiss and she scoffs, striding in behind me.

'Welcome to the real world, Mr Beckett.' Amusement tinges her tone.

The place is eerily silent, bar the noise from the passers-by on the street outside. I take the stairs, two at a time. They're a fucking death trap. One misplaced foot and it's game over.

Scarlett points to a door at the far end of the corridor. I slide the key into the lock. Before my foot is even fully inside the door, I vow she'll never spend another night here.

Scarlett flicks the light switch on. I blink, adjusting to the brightness. The apartment is tiny. The kitchen is older than my granny. Candles are dotted around the room. A cream fleece throw is draped over the back of a worn faux leather couch. A tiny TV sits on a small dresser. The room is colder than an industrial-sized freezer, but Scarlett has the place clean and smelling surprisingly inviting.

My heart breaks for the woman beside me.

How did she go from an education at St. Jude's to living here, in one of the roughest parts of the city? I can only imagine that when her mother died she was left with nothing.

But how?

I nod towards a pile of textbooks sitting on a small, semi-circular table next to an ancient-looking laptop. 'Grab those, Tim.'

There's no way she's staying here. Not when I have so much space. So much of everything.

I turn to Scarlett. 'Pack a bag. Get whatever you need.'

'Seriously?' She stands, dusting invisible lint from her dress. 'My front door locks. I know it's far from fancy, but it's fine, for me.'

'Can you stop saying fine "for you"? Like you deserve less? You're moving in with me until after graduation.' My tone is final. 'Even if the front door and stairs weren't dangerous, the temperature in here is lethal.'

Her huge grey eyes dart to the floor.

'There's no shame in this. You should be fucking proud, sweetheart. You've survived God knows what, alone. You're months away from graduating from Trinity Business School. I don't know what you've been through but whatever it is, you're not alone anymore.' I clear my throat. 'Besides, we have an arrangement, and if I want you to hold up your end of the deal, I need you safe, warm and protected. When I get the acquisition over the line, and you graduate, you'll go your own way. See the world. Whatever it is you want to do. Until then, let me take care of you.'

Scarlett folds her arms over her chest. I've got a feeling she could be stubborn. Proud even.

'You'd be doing me a favour. When my family and the Board hear I've moved my 'new girlfriend' in so quickly, they'll have no choice but to take me, us, seriously.'

Her throat flexes as she swallows. 'I don't need your pity,' she murmurs.

'I know you don't.' I lower my mouth to her ear, my breath brushing over her sensitive lobe. 'Don't mistake me for a good man, Scarlett. My intentions for you are purely selfish.'

She shivers. I'd like to think it's anticipation, but equally it could be the Baltic temperature.

'Fine.' She stalks towards a narrow door which I can only assume is her bedroom.

Tim grabs her books and the laptop. 'Shall I put these in the boot?'

'Do.'

Twenty minutes later, we're back in the car. The scent of Scarlett's exotic shampoo invades my lungs.

What have I done?

Chapter Eighteen
SCARLETT

James is silent for the duration of the journey, but intermittently I feel the heat from his stare.

It's just a job. It's just a job. It's just a job, I repeat in my head like a mantra.

Okay, it's not your typical nine-to-five, but then neither was dancing at the Luxor Lounge.

We're half an hour outside of the city, with the mountains to the left and the Irish Sea to the right, when the car slows to a stop. I peer through the darkness. Huge black electric gates mounted on ivory limestone pillars swing open.

Even through the darkness the mansion beyond is... majestic. I spent the last half an hour trying to imagine what James's home might look like. In my wildest dreams, I couldn't have come up with anything as grand.

The imposing façade is comprised of warm, toned, aged stone. Rising above the main structure, multiple spires and turrets pierce the sky. The largest tower is centrally positioned, its dome gleaming under the moonlight. Huge stone pillars bearing the Beckett family crest flank the doors.

James turns to me. 'Welcome home, Scarlett. Tim will bring your belongings in. Let me give you a tour.'

His fingers skim over my lower back as he ushers me into a huge hallway. Ignoring the crackling surges of electricity coursing over my skin, I soak in my temporary new home.

Where the outside of the building is archaic, inside it's bright and modern. The floor is laid with polished marble, not entirely dissimilar to the one in the Luxor Lounge, but where that is a sleek black, this is a brilliant gleaming ivory. A huge solid wood staircase sweeps to the upper levels. Fancy artwork hangs from the wood panelled walls.

'Wow.' My breath whooshes from my lungs.

'Not what you expected?' Amusement tinges James's tone.

'I expected a penthouse somewhere. Something sleek and shiny and cold,' I admit, absorbing my surroundings.

'That's more Killian's style.' James leads me through the hallway, the echoes of our shoes on the marble ringing through the otherwise silent house.

'This is the main living area.' He pushes open a heavy oak door. An immense fireplace dominates the far wall, its mantle carved from marble.

I can't bear open fires. Can't stand the sounds of the cracking and popping as the flames consume the wood. The red hot heat that radiates from it. The burning scent that steals the breath from my chest.

Any type of fire reminds me of what Jack O'Connor did to my mother. Forces me to imagine what she must have gone through at the end. Even the thought of it chills my bones and makes me want to run a mile in the other direction.

Thankfully, it's not lit.

I close my eyes for a second, instinctively gripping my necklace.

'Are you okay?' James asks, placing a steadying hand on my forearm.

I blink back the images cascading through my brain. 'Do you ever light that fire?'

'Not usually.' His black shiny shoe taps the floor. 'I had underfloor heating installed a few years ago. But I can ask the servants to light it, if you'd like?'

'No.' The word comes out sharper than I intended. 'Thank you.'

As my pulse comes back under control, I ask, 'Servants?'

James shrugs. 'You don't think I have the time or inclination to do the dusting?'

'I could help out,' I offer.

'Absolutely not.' His head whips towards mine. 'You have a different job.'

As James continues the tour, he takes me into a formal dining room that boasts a long oak table capable of seating twenty guests. An ornate drawing room. A games room with a full-sized snooker table. A library lined with wall-to-wall shelving overflowing with thousands of old leather-bound books.

There's a cinema room. A gym with more equipment than a professional sports centre.

And most incredible of all, a full-sized heated outdoor swimming pool.

'You can't see much now, but the view is pretty spectacular in the daylight,' James says, with a casual shrug. 'This is your home, now. Make yourself comfortable. Use it how you want. Unfortunately, the businesses take me away a lot, so you'll usually have the run of the place. I want you to be happy here.'

It's phenomenal.

'I'll show you your room.' His dark eyes twinkle.

'My room?' I repeat like a moron.

'Yes, Scarlett, *your* room.' He flicks off the lights and closes the door to the pool. His hand settles on my lower back again. 'I know I said you could have your pick, but trust me, you'll love this one.'

James leads me through the wide corridors back to the staircase. Suddenly I'm bone tired, the weight of the events of the day catching up with me. 'What about my stuff?'

'Tim brought it up already.'

'Does he live here?' My feet sink into the plush carpet upstairs as we walk side-by-side to the sleeping quarters.

'He has his own house at the rear of the property. You'll see it tomorrow.' James stops outside a door and his hand falls from my back. 'Rosa, my housekeeper lives there, too.'

'How many people do you have working here?' I ask.

'Five more, in addition to Tim and Rosa. Ask them for anything you like. Rosa will be ecstatic to meet you.'

'Really? Why do you say that?'

'Because this is the first time I've ever brought a woman home.' His Adam's apple bobs as he swallows. Our eyes lock and something unspoken passes between us.

'I'd better leave you here, Scarlett.' His gaze falls to my lips and something undecipherable flashes over his features.

I'm drowning in his expensive cologne and heady stare. My hand reaches for the brass door knob but I don't turn it. 'What about tomorrow?'

He glances at the chunky silver watch on his wrist. 'It's already tomorrow.'

'I have class in the afternoon.'

'Tim will take you. I'll drive myself to the office. If you need anything, I'm only a text or a phone call away.'

I swallow the emotions forming in my throat. 'Thank you.'

'Thank *you*.' He flashes me a devastating smile, revealing a perfect set of white teeth. 'For agreeing to be my fake girlfriend.'

'I think I might be getting more out of this agreement than you are,' I say, gesturing to the grandeur of the house.

He inches closer to my ear until his hot breath is searing my sensitive lobe. 'I think you'll find we could both get a lot more out of it, if you're prepared to renegotiate the conditions.'

His fingertips graze over my waist for a fleeting moment before he disappears down the corridor.

Chapter Nineteen
SCARLETT

I blink hard, my bleary eyes struggling to adjust to the weak winter sunlight sneaking through the cracks between the heavy velvet drapes and the huge sash windows.

My bedroom is every bit as opulent as all the other rooms in James' mansion. The walls are painted a deep dusky pink. Thick ivory cornicing lines the room. A chandelier hangs from the double-height ceiling. The pristine Egyptian cotton sheets are like silk against my skin.

What I really notice though, is the warmth and the silence.

There's no nip in the air. My nose doesn't feel as if it's about to drop off. And I can't hear any traffic. No neighbours. No passing students strolling raucously by.

For the first time in a long time I feel... safe.

I reach for the bedside locker to find my phone.

The screen shows six texts I missed from Avery asking where I went last night, each one more panicked than the last.

There's also one from Shane asking if I want to study

together tonight. I regret the day I ever gave him my phone number.

And there's a text from a contact I didn't add into my phone. *Boyfriend.* I snort. James must have put it himself at dinner last night. I open it with a grin.

> I got called away on an unexpected business trip. Help yourself to anything. Rosa will make you breakfast. There's a present in the dining room for you.

I try to tamp down my disappointment as I fire off a quick text to Avery assuring her that I'm fine, and that I'll meet her in the campus canteen at lunchtime.

I don't reply to either James or Shane.

Flinging back the covers, I dart out of bed. Nerves and excitement mingle in my stomach as I pad across the plush carpet to the ensuite. Twin ivory sinks are set into a marble counter top. A mood shower like something out of a luxury spa occupies the far corner of the room while a claw-foot bathtub dominates the centre of the room. Complete with the entire miniature Molten Brown range, this place is more luxurious than a five-star hotel.

I brush my teeth, shower, and pull on a casual jumper dress, tights and the Claudie Pierlot ankle boots I wore to brunch. That feels like a lifetime ago.

Stepping out of the bedroom, I glance down the corridor. Silence rings through my ears as I retrace my steps from last night, down the wide wooden staircase and into the dining room. It's even more spectacular in the daylight with the sun streaming through the windows, illuminating all the gilded paintings and a dizzying array of ornate objects.

At the far end of the table is a new laptop. A new phone. And a shiny black credit card with my name on it.

It's too much.

'Miss Fitzgerald,' a musical voice calls and I jump, spinning on my heels. 'I'm Rosa.' A beautiful blonde woman stands in the dining room door wearing navy dress pants and a white chiffon shirt. 'Sorry if I startled you.'

Rosa is stunning. If I had to guess, I'd put her at lates thirties. She's the epitome of sophistication. She's not what I was expecting from James's housekeeper. I expected someone older, more maternal. Not someone who looks like they've stepped off the catwalk. I like her already.

'Please, call me Scarlett.'

Rosa beams at me and takes a step closer, scrutinising my face with an excited curiosity. 'Tim said you were pretty.'

'He did?'

'Yep. I'm still in shock.' Rosa takes another step forwards. 'It's been a long time since there was a guest to take care of. And never a woman. Well, not since...' Rosa trails off.

'Oh.' My heart flutters in my chest.

'Anyway, here I am, shooting my mouth off. Mr Beckett will be cross.' She pulls out a high-backed dining room chair and gestures for me to sit. 'Would you like some coffee?'

'I'd love some, thank you.' I sit because I have no idea what else to do. Have I died and gone to heaven? Been slipped a ruffie and I'm hallucinating? How else would you explain the two hundred grand sitting in my bank account and my opulent new home?

'I'll be right back.' Rosa shoots me a parting smile and strides out of the room, her kitten heels clicking across the marble floor.

I pull out my phone, open the message from *Boyfriend,* and begin typing.

> It's too much. I don't need all this.

A reply pings back before I put the phone down.

> James Beckett's girlfriend has to have the best of everything. No one will believe you're mine otherwise. Tim will take you shopping after school ;) We'll be going on lots of dates. Buy some dresses.

It's not real. It's not real. It's not real. It's a job.

An agreement.

An arrangement.

But tell that to my twirling tummy.

Rosa returns with the coffee as I'm powering up my new phone.

'How about some eggs?' she offers, slipping a tray of coffee and toast onto the table in front of me.

'No, I'm fine, thank you.'

'Mr Beckett left strict instructions that I was to cook something hot for you.' Rosa hovers by the table.

'I never normally eat breakfast,' I admit.

'Do you normally wake up in a billionaire's mansion?' Rosa wiggles her eyebrows and I have to laugh.

'I guess not.'

'So, scrambled or poached?' Her hand rests on her hip.

'Poached, please.'

As promised, Tim drops me at college. He's also waiting for me when class is over.

As I stride over to the gleaming black car, he opens the door for me. 'How was your day, Miss Fitzgerarld?'

'Please, call me Scarlett.' I duck into the back seat, the scent of James's cologne lingers in the air along with upholstery cleaner and the tang of leather. It's just a shame he had to go away. How is it possible to miss a man I barely know? But I do.

'It was grand, thank you.' Clutching my handbag and laptop against my chest, I stare out of the window as my fellow classmates traipse by, eternally grateful for the tinted windows. James may not be paying me for sex but I'm sure that's what it would look like to anyone looking in.

'Mr Beckett asked me to take you shopping,' Tim says before closing the door.

I assumed shopping meant Grafton Street. Brown Thomas, specifically. Dublin's most decadent department store. I assumed wrongly.

Tim parks outside a three-storey building down a side street I never even knew existed.

Curiosity twists in my stomach. My phone vibrates.

> Martha will take care of you. Buy whatever you like. But don't forget to get lingerie. I'm going to burn every single piece paid for by Cole and his club.

Is James tracking my movements? Or is his timing just uncannily accurate?

Tim opens the car door and offers me a leather gloved hand out. I pause in front of the gleaming glass door. James's credit card burns in my pocket.

He's already given me a safe place to stay, a new phone and laptop, not to mention the two hundred thousand euros in my account which I still can't quite believe is real.

My phone vibrates again.

> Go burn some of your "boyfriend's" cash.
> New condition– I want to see you model the clothes you pick.
>
> Especially the lingerie.

James's flirtation is powerful enough to ruin my panties from however many miles away he is.

I type out a reply.

> Remember the conditions of our arrangement?

His reply is instantaneous.

> There was no condition on looking. As I recall, you like being looked at. In fact, I'd even go as far as to say you're an exhibitionist. And I'm going to devour you with my eyes until you're ready for me to devour you with my tongue.

Oh. My. God. I've never been more turned on in my life. Before I can think up a reply another text pings in.

> Be ready for an inspection when I get back.

James Beckett fights dirty.

> And when exactly will that be?

> A couple of weeks, unfortunately. Missing me already?

> You're trouble.

> You have no idea ;)

. . .

I inhale a deep cold blast of air and ring the doorbell. Within seconds, I'm greeted by a flawlessly made-up assistant in a long-sleeved tailored pencil dress, thick-rimmed Chanel glasses, and a pair of patent pumps.

'Scarlett.' Her pink painted lips lift into a genuinely welcoming smile. 'Come in. I'm Martha. We've been expecting you.' I step into the hallway and she takes my coat, her eyes sharply assessing my frame, sizing me up.

'He wasn't wrong.' She tsks, seemingly more to herself than me. 'I'm guessing you're a size eight or ten?'

I follow her into an enormous room with big bay windows overlooking the street below. Racks of dresses, suits, shirts, skirts and blouses line the room. I'm no fashion expert but even I can see the labels in here are on par with the most high-end department stores across the world.

This place makes Brown Thomas look like Zara.

A younger woman enters the room with a polite smile. She's carrying a glass of champagne. I accept it along with my fate. James Beckett wants to ruin me.

Who am I to stand in his way?

Martha clicks her pink painted fingers. 'Let's begin,' she says.

Chapter Twenty
JAMES

Knowing Scarlett is in my house while I'm working stirs some sort of primal instinct in me. I had hoped having her under my roof would at least mean she's no longer living rent free in my head.

I was badly mistaken.

If anything, my obsession is only escalating.

Did she eat?

Does she have everything she needs?

Is she currently wearing anything?

The list goes on.

I'm finally back in Dublin, but now I'm snowed under with an avalanche of shit. The Imperial Winery Group acquisition is far from straightforward. These things take months of work, but time is of the essence given the competition.

HR is breathing down my neck about some scandal in our New York division. And I've had weeks of meetings with none too happy investors.

On the plus side, I haven't had to endure any further mundane dates.

Unfortunately, I haven't had any electrifying ones either.

My relationship with Scarlett, our fake relationship, has so far mostly been comprised of regular text messages, most of which include me asking if she's okay, and her responding that she's fine. Despite demanding three public dates a week, I've managed to take her out for dinner precisely twice since she moved into my house.

Which is why I'm looking forward to taking her out tonight. It's the opening night of Rian's new nightclub. And it's time to introduce the world to my new "girlfriend."

And what better night than Valentine's to do it?

The sooner the Board, our investors and my family know about my new relationship, the more credibility it will give it.

I haven't been photographed with the same woman twice since Cynthia Van Darwin. Being photographed with Scarlett will certainly get them talking, even if I have to have them pixel out her face. Of all the conditions she could have come up with, not being photographed with me was an odd one.

Killian found nothing unusual on her background check. Her digital footprint is practically non-existent. It's as if Scarlett Fitzgerald has been hiding under a rock. Which only fuels my curiosity about her past.

Chantel pops her head round my door. 'Heads up. Your mother is in the building. Fifty euros says you're the first son she'll call on.'

A long, low groan rumbles from my throat. It's not unusual for her to stop by, but today I'm itching to get home to Scarlett. It's bad enough that I'm going to have to share her at the nightclub opening tonight, let alone miss the rare chance of having dinner with her.

Six minutes later, Vivienne Beckett, my effusive mother, strides into my office in a cloud of Coco Chanel Mademoiselle. Like Dad, she doesn't look her age, though that's mostly down to her talented plastic surgeon rather than healthy living. My parents enjoy the good life. Cocktail parties. Charity galas for random obscure animals no one has ever heard of. Dad always says if Mother got invited to the opening of an envelope she'd go. Which is why I'm so sure she'll be at Rian's opening night later, even though she's thirty years older than his target market.

'James.' She leans over the desk and air kisses both of my cheeks.

'Mother, what a wonderful surprise.' If she notices my dry tone, she doesn't acknowledge it.

'I was in the city getting a blow out for tonight and I thought I'd call in. Dad says you're working too hard. You've been halfway around the world over the past few weeks.' She slides into the seat opposite my desk and crosses her legs.

'Well, a few weeks before that I was partying too hard, according to the tabloids. So, I can't win.' I relax back into my chair.

'Oh, darling.' She swats the air in front of her face. 'Let's put that distasteful business behind us. Dad says you've been dating.' Her chocolate-coloured eyes twinkle. 'Tell me, what did you think of Lady Harrington?'

I clasp my fingers together and rest my hands on my desk. 'I thought she was as boring and bad mannered as the others.' My nose wrinkles in distaste. She's a million miles from the woman I've moved into my home, but now might not be the best time to drop that bombshell.

'Her mother is exactly the same. It's impossible to get a word in edgeways. Talks incessantly.' My mother chuckles.

'The apple doesn't fall too far from the tree.' I wonder if Dad ever borrowed the company yacht back in his day.

Chantel knocks and enters with a pot of tea and two china cups. I glance at my watch wondering if it's late enough for a whiskey, and how much longer I have to sit here before I can get home to Scarlett.

I had three hundred velvety, scarlet roses delivered to her college today, because it's Valentine's Day, and because I wanted to make her smile. Okay, I also wanted to remind those college boys that she's spoken for.

'So, Dad said there was a girl with potential?' My mother resumes the conversation as if Chantel isn't in the room.

'Woman,' I correct her. 'She's young, but she's all woman.' My lips lift in a smirk as my mother's nose crinkles.

'I don't need those type of details. If you could try to keep your penis out of the press with this one, your father and I would really appreciate it.'

'Don't worry, Scarlet's not *that* type of woman.' Pride tinges my tone. We might only be faking this relationship, but I can't help but admire her integrity. Her pride. The way she knows her own worth and how she's not prepared to sell herself out.

There's something about her that's so intriguing. The way the platinum pools of her eyes flit between a knowing depth, and a naivety that I'm dying to fuck out of her.

I'm a bad man. I can't help it. Even when I'm pretending to be good, all I want to be is bad.

My mother's mouth drops open as she lifts her teacup. 'Is that genuine warmth I detect in your tone?'

'You know, I think it is.' My phone vibrates on the desk. I snatch it up.

Scarlett.

> There was no need for the embarrassingly large bouquet, but thank you. It is gorgeous.

My thumbs dart across the screen.

> You're gorgeous. Happy Valentine's Day.

> You are a shameless flirt.

My mother's brow creases as I type.

> Role play–remember? :)

> You should come with a health warning.

> Why? Are your panties on fire?

> My cheeks are.

> We're going out tonight. There's somewhere I need to take you–other than heaven, that is ;)

I bite back a smile, but not before my mother catches it. She clears her throat pointedly.

'Sorry. Just a second.' I tear my eyes from the screen and fire her an apologetic look.

'Is that her?' My mother is not a woman who's easily shocked, but right now, she looks positively stunned.

Before I can answer, my phone vibrates on the desk again.

> *Inserts eye roll* I never had you pegged as cheesy! And I'm not sure I believe in heaven.

> Remind me again what that billionaire does to Anastasia Steele when she rolls her eyes at him... And heaven is real. If only you'd let me show you.

I laugh out loud as I hit send.

> You read Fifty Shades? *inserts wide eyes*

> I was curious.

> I have no words.

. . .

Laters, baby. *inserts winky face*

I'm still grinning like an idiot when I drop my phone back on the desk.

My mother is positively preening. 'So, this looks like it could be serious.'

'Stranger things have happened.' I knew Scarlett and I were capable of putting on a convincing show. We're nailing it and she's thirty miles away.

'You have a huge heart . Don't think your father and I don't see it.' Mother waggles her pointer finger over my sternum.

She's not wrong, but the last time I showed it to someone, it didn't end so well. Which is why I've never tried since, why I need a fake girlfriend, and why it's a good thing there's an end date on our agreement.

God forbid I'd be the one to get attached. Scarlett is so young. She has no family depending on her to carry on the family business and name. She has her whole life ahead of her. A life full of travel and new experiences, free of responsibility.

My life is here. With my family. Running our businesses. It will always be.

Which is why I'm determined to make the most of the next few months of fun.

'Don't let your past ruin your future.' My mother clicks her tongue against the roof of her mouth. 'So, Scarlett... what's her surname? Who are her parents? Your father said she's studying finance at Trinity.'

'Does it matter who her family are?' Irritation flares in my chest. 'Look at the Van Darwins. They had a great name, great reputation and look how that turned out.'

My mother has the grace to look at the floor.

Cynthia was employed as one of our accountants. She came from a respectable family. Old money. But that didn't stop her embezzling Beckett money. I don't know what was worse, that she tried to steal millions, or that she actually stole my heart in the process.

To this day, I still don't know if any of what we had was real, or if it was all just a distraction ploy. The stupid thing is, if she'd have just come to me, I would have given her the money.

I force away the memories, clenching my knuckles. 'Scarlett's parents have passed, Mother. Please, for the love of God, do not bring them up tonight.'

'Were you fighting?' My mother's hawk like eyes zone in on the grazes on my knuckles.

'Tim and I were sparring in the gym.' Tim is the only person mad enough to get in the ring with me, so I avail of his foolishness several times a week.

Mother shakes her head. 'I wish you boys would take up golf or something. It's far more dignified than taking chunks out of each other.'

'But nowhere near as satisfying.' I grin.

'So, back to Scarlett.' She's like a dog with a bone.

'Stop with all the questions. You'll meet her tonight.' I rake my fingers through my hair. 'Try not to terrify her with the Spanish Inquisition.'

My mother lurches forward in her seat. 'For real?'

'Yes.'

'I'm not sure what's more exciting, that you're going on a date on Valentine's night or that you're finally bringing a girl to meet us. How exciting!' My mother puts her cup down in its saucer and stands. 'Now, I must go, darling. I have a nail appointment in ten minutes.'

'I can see how busy you are.' I shake my head but my heart squeezes. If I thought I could find a love as strong as my parents share, or like Caelon and Isabella, I wouldn't shun the idea of marriage.

But the problem with letting someone in, rather than pretending to let someone in, is that you open yourself up to get hurt.

Which is why I vowed never to put myself in that situation again.

Chapter Twenty-One
JAMES

An urgent phone call from Julian Jones, the Chairman of the Board, holds me up for another forty-five minutes. Then he demands an update on the acquisition, and my love life. Both of which I'm able to report are progressing nicely.

When I eventually hang up, Chantel appears to clear away the tea. 'Someone's sent you a Valentine's present,' she singsongs, twisting her ponytail around her fingers.

'Put it in the bin.' It's not the first time. Once, some opportunistic stranger sent lingerie.

'I think you'll want to see this one.' Chantel eyes me smugly.

'Doubtful.'

'A courier arrived with it fifteen minutes ago. It's from Scarlett.' Chantel is up to speed with our arrangement. I can't keep secrets from her.

I yank my eyes from my computer screen. 'You opened it?'

'No. She wrote her return details on the packaging. I'll fetch it for you now. I thought this thing between you was for the benefit of the Board?' Chantel teases, shimmying her hips.

'It is.' Mostly. 'Where is it?'

'Give me a second.' She takes the tray and returns thirty seconds later clutching a small box, wrapped in brown paper and tied with a scarlet bow. I pull the string, but then think better of it with Chantel peering over my shoulder like a pirate's parrot. 'A little privacy please.'

'Don't leave me hanging!' Chantel begs as I shoo her out the room and close the door. 'Go home,' I shout before it slams shut.

The box burns beneath my fingers, curiosity curling in my core. I tear the paper clean off, and laugh as it falls to the office floor. A neat crimson box with a clear plastic lid reveals a designer tie in a familiar shade of grey. I open it and pull out the tiny card attached.

Thought you could wear this laters, baby.
Scarlett x

I pluck my phone from my pocket and message Tim. I can't wait another second to see her. We might be pretending to be in a relationship, but I've never pretended I don't want her physically.

Tim drives frustratingly slowly, religiously sticking to the speed limits. Clearly, he's not as eager as I am to get home.

The smell of roast chicken and thyme permeates the air as I step into the hallway of my home. A thrum of anticipation ripples down my spine.

Rosa strides into the hallway and takes my coat. I scan the room. 'Where is Scarlett?'

'In the dining room, sir.' Rosa points to the door, even though I'm well aware of where my own dining room is. I grab a bottle of Beckett's whiskey from the bar in the sitting room before making my way into the dining room.

Scarlett is perched at the top end of the table, with her nose buried in her new laptop. A pile of textbooks sits beside her. She glances up as I enter, a small smile playing on her crimson-painted lips.

In a figure-sculpting black cocktail dress that dips into a low V at the front, she looks elegant, endearing and utterly enticing. The elaborate bouquet I bought her sits in the centre of the table.

'You're home!' Is that pleasure in her tone? There's a hint of mischief in her kohl-lined eyes.

'I am, thank goodness. It's been a long day. Scratch that, it's been a long few weeks,' I drag in a breath and blow it out slowly. 'Especially knowing you were here.' I cross the room to stand beside her.

The scent of her perfume lingers in the air between us.

I want to inhale it.

I want to inhale her.

'Did you miss me?' I pull out the chair beside her and lower myself into it.

'Was it a condition of our agreement?' she teases.

'It was a question.' I drop the bottle of whiskey on the table and pour two large measures but I don't drink it. Not yet. The only thing I want to drink in is the woman beside me. The way her lips turn up at my words. The way her platinum eyes blaze with a need she has no idea how capable I am of satisfying.

'Maybe. This is a big old place to ramble around in alone.' She glances up at the high ceilings.

'Tell me about it. I've been doing it for years.' A small tinkling laugh permeates the air. God she's so beautiful. Of all the times I've summoned her face to my mind over the past few weeks, I realise my memory never once did her justice.

'Bloody hell, Scarlett, you look incredible.' Gone is the girl-next-door look, replaced with expertly tailored dresses and a newfound air of sophistication. She always had it, but now it radiates from her. And I'm happy to see she's put on a little weight. She was too skinny before. Rosa must be taking good care of her.

'I hate that we have to go out tonight. We could have so much more fun at home.'

'Not part of our arrangement.' She smirks as she closes her laptop. 'Might be safer if we go out.'

'That's a killer dress.' As good as it looks on her, it would look better on my floor.

'Thank you.' Her eyes rake over my suit, before returning to my eyes. 'You spoil me.' She sweeps a hand across her outfit and glances at her phone.

'And you spoil me.' I pull out the tie from the inside pocket of my suit and place it on the table.

Heat flushes her cheeks. 'It was sort of a joke.'

'Sort of?' I zero in on her lips, the way she licks them with a nervousness, or perhaps hunger. 'Do you sort of want me to tie you to my bed post with this?'

Her eyes glaze like she's imagining it and her throat flexes as she swallows. 'What I want, and what I can have, are two very different things.'

'Actually, Scarlett, they are one and the same. All you have to do is say the word.' Why is she holding back on me? Nerves? Fear of the first time? Energy swirls between us in a thick haze of sex hormones. 'Did I buy you this dress?' I appraise her like a lion sizing up its prey.

'You did.' She crosses one long leg over the other.

I run a finger over the silky fabric of the dress, cruising from her waist, over her hip, and sliding off her thigh. A tiny gasp permeates the air. 'Give me a twirl.' I make a circular motion with my finger.

She rises from the chair and slowly spins on her heels. The back of the dress is entirely absent, showcasing the elegant curve of her spine and a swathe of silky skin. Her head angles as she spins. Those enormous eyes seek something from me. Admiration? Approval? Either way, she has both, by the truckload.

I devour every inch of her with my eyes until she stops where she started, her breasts rising and falling mere inches in front of me. 'You're killing me, Scarlett.' My voice rasps with need.

Mischief gleams in her eyes. 'You weren't wrong in your text, you know.'

'I'm never wrong.' My Adam's apple bobs. 'But specifically?'

'I like your eyes on my body. On my skin. I feel like I've been in hiding for years, but now finally someone sees me.'

'I see you, sweetheart.' I swallow hard. 'Every damn time I close my eyes and even when I dream. I see you.' My hand reaches up to stroke her face, but Scarlett's mobile buzzes on the table, piercing the heavy air surrounding us.

She glances at the screen, then snatches it up so fast her fingers fumble and she drops it on the floor between us.

I crouch and swipe it up. A name glares back at me from the screen. *Nathan.*

'Who's Nathan?' The question comes out more suspiciously than I intended thanks to the green-eyed monster sitting on my sternum.

'No one.' Her quick response oozes guilt. 'Well, I mean, he's an old friend.' Her eyes travel the entire room twice, before returning to mine. 'Of my mother's.' She swallows hard. 'Sort of.'

Curiosity supersedes my jealousy, but before I can ask any further questions, Rosa arrives with entrees. 'Happy Valentine's Day, lovebirds,' she coos.

I have no choice but to swallow down my questions and wait.

Chapter Twenty-Two

SCARLETT

Silence stretches between us as we tuck into the dinner Rosa prepared for us. Nathan's call was a nudging reminder of exactly why I shouldn't want James. History has proven how dangerous getting involved with men can be. But judging from the dull ache in my lingerie, my vagina still didn't get the memo.

James studies me curiously, his eyes lingering on my lips. 'I'll wear you down eventually, you know,' James murmurs seductively, his foot hooking around the back of my calf. 'I always get what I want, Scarlett. And what I want is you.'

'It's not that I don't want you...' I blurt, lifting my wine glass.

James's eyes whip to mine at my sudden burst of honesty. 'So, what's holding you back? We're both consenting adults.'

I place my fork down on the table, unable to swallow another mouthful. 'I'm worried that if we have sex, it will... complicate things.'

'It won't. This is already the least complicated relationship I've ever had. We both know where we stand. I won't hold you back in your plans for after graduation.' He presses his shoulder against mine, leaning into me. 'We have an arrangement, with an end date. That's all.'

'And that's why we can't compromise it,' I sigh, as his eyes bore into mine. 'Being with you has transformed my life in a matter of weeks. I sleep peacefully behind the high-gated walls of this mansion. I've come to rely on Rosa's cheery 'good mornings.' I look forward to Tim's company on the way to college. I haven't been fussed over in years, and I know you pay them to do precisely that, but they already feel like friends. It's nice not being alone.'

He opens his mouth to speak, but I raise my hand to halt him. 'I've managed to write twenty thousand words of my college dissertation in three weeks. My grades are up. My stress levels are down, and for the first February since I can remember, I'm not freezing.'

'I'm happy to hear it, but I still don't see the issue.' His hand falls to my thigh. I cross my legs. Not because I don't trust him, but because I don't trust myself. There's a perpetual throbbing in my underwear whenever he's near, and it's getting stronger by the day.

'Sex will change everything and I can't risk ruining this.'

What I can't risk is giving him that part of myself, in case he discards me afterwards, like he's done with all the other women before me. And truthfully, it's not just because of the arrangement; it's because I'm terrified of catching feelings for him. More feelings, I should say. Because I've had feelings for him since the first night I laid eyes on him, and with every shared smile, every dinner, every witty text, those feelings have intensified.

A knock at the door stops James from arguing with me. Tim appears. 'The car's out front whenever you're ready.'

Those espresso-coloured irises twinkle as James brings my hand to his lips and kisses the back of it. 'I'm pretty sure Scarlett's almost ready. I mean, she's dragging her heels, but I'll coax her along...' James smoulders, his innuendo clear.

He's alarmingly close to the truth.

Rian's new nightclub is five storeys high with a different DJ on each floor. There's a queue a mile long outside, but James leads me straight to the front where we're ushered into a VIP area and handed champagne.

The entire décor is comprised of glass walls, mirrors, and chrome furnishings. Hundreds of helium heart balloons hang from the ceiling to celebrate Valentine's Day. An eclectic beat bumps through carefully positioned speakers, vibrating through the floor beneath my stilettos.

The place is wedged with designer-clad bodies. I glance around at the clientele. Half the Irish rugby team is here, a young TV presenter who's dating a high-profile fashion blogger, a former Olympic swimmer. Hell, there's even a movie star and his wife drinking wine at the long granite bar. But no one is paying any attention to them, because everyone is staring at us.

A tremor of unease sweeps down my spine. What if someone snaps a picture of us? James might have influence over some of the papers, but even he can't stop ordinary people taking shots on their phones. 'Remember the clause about the pictures being pixelated?' I remind him.

'Relax.' James's palm skims over my back, sending goosebumps scattering over my skin. 'This is a no-camera club. If anyone attempts to take pictures, they'll be banned for life.'

Relief trickles through my veins like sweet soothing honey.

Several businessmen advance towards us. Some extend a hand to James. Others nod their silent greetings and gaze in awe at Ireland's most eligible billionaire. A number of stunning women, all hair and teeth and fluttering eyelashes, flock towards us, but my date brushes them off with a short, sharp dismissal.

'Are you okay?' He leans to speak into my ear, his breath sending shivers over my skin.

'I'm fine.' I raise a champagne glass to my lips and take a large mouthful.

'Fine's not good enough.' James shakes his head. 'I want you to feel amazing.' Those dark eyes burn with an unspoken promise. 'I could make you feel amazing, Scarlett, if you'd renegotiate our terms.'

My eyes fall to his lips. It would be so easy to give into him. The bubbles must have gone straight to my head because instead of deflecting, I blurt out what I couldn't bring myself to say earlier at the table. 'The entire world knows you never have sex with the same girl twice. If we sleep together, it'll be game over. You'll have had your fill. Which will complicate things, given I'm living with you until after graduation.'

His huge frame towers over me, pinning my body against a chrome pillar. He's so close I can feel the heat as it radiates from his body. His hips rest against mine and something hard presses against my stomach.

Oh. My. God.

The sheer size of it.

Hot lust builds in my core.

'Perhaps I haven't made my feelings for you clear enough. If you ever think I'll get my fill of your pussy, you are delusional.' His velvety voice sends shivers skimming over my skin. 'I spend every second of every damn day thinking about it. Imagining what it looks like. How sweet it would taste. What it would feel like to slide my cock into your tight walls and unleash myself on you.' The subtle grind of his hips has me simultaneously swooning and sweating.

'So, one thing you don't have to worry about is me "having my fill." I could spend every minute from now until your graduation with my head, hands, and cock between your legs and it still wouldn't be anywhere near long enough. The first night I saw you on stage at the Luxor Lounge, I fucked my fist twice in the shower thinking about you.'

It's suddenly stifling in here. 'You don't mean that.'

Desire consumes me. If I tilted my chin up even an inch, our lips would be touching. My skin pricks with a need I didn't know I was capable of.

'Well, well, well, what do we have here?' Rian, James's youngest brother, strides over, surprise written into every line of his face.

James turns his head to look at his brother, tearing his hips from mine and his hands from the pillar. 'Ah, the man of the minute.' He slaps his brother on the back in an affectionate gesture.

'You mean the man of the hour, at least. Give me some credit, brother.' Rian grins, his eyes darting between us with open curiosity.

It's obvious from his face he recognises me, even without the elaborate wigs and make-up.

'Rian, you remember Scarlett.' It's not a question.

'Of course. A... face like hers is impossible to forget.' Rian's eyes roam over my outfit and it's obvious it's not just my face he's recalling.

James's nostrils flare as he jabs Rian's bicep hard enough to make him cry out. 'Careful, brother. If you look at my woman like that again, she might be the last thing you'll ever see.'

'Your woman?' Rian's eyebrows skyrocket as he rubs his arm.

'Yes,' James hisses.

My core clenches. It might be an act, but it's hot as fuck.

'Since when?' Rian seems genuinely intrigued.

'Since I punched the last guy who touched her.' James's hand settles on the base of my spine. Tingles radiate in every direction.

Rian's palms raise in surrender. 'Well, in that case, I'm delighted for you both.'

James's thumb strokes over the bare skin on my back, his fingers continuing a blazing trail towards my shoulder blades and back again.

'Congratulations on the club. It's amazing.' I flash a small smile Rian's way.

'Thanks.' Rian soaks up the décor with pride. 'Mother is looking for you,' he says to James.

'I bet she is.' James's lips purse.

'Your mother is here?' I squeak.

'Yes. And she's dying to meet you.' James's eyes flash with devilment.

The prospect shouldn't make me nervous. It doesn't matter what she thinks of me, because our entire relationship is for show, but for some reason, I'm desperate to make a good impression.

Through the throng of bodies, I spot the other three Beckett brothers approaching. James gave me a rundown of his siblings in the car on the way here. Names, ages, occupations. From what James said, they're a tight-knit family.

I suck in a breath as I'm surrounded by tall, dark, handsome men. What a gene pool. They're all exquisitely attractive in their own way, but none of them radiate the same powerful presence as James.

'Here's the cavalry.' James flashes a genuine smile before extending his hand to greet them. 'I was just introducing Rian to my girlfriend.'

Caelon almost spits out his drink. Sean eyes me with a

quiet curiosity. Killian simply nods in an unspoken greeting. He appears to be a man of few words.

'You're a fucking dark horse.' Caelon's bright eyes blaze appraisingly. 'Isabella will be so thrilled to have another female in the family.'

The family.

The words make my heart clench with longing.

'Where's Isabella?' James asks, scanning the room.

'With Zara, on the first floor.' Caelon shrugs.

'Zara is here?' James's voice is thunderous.

'Relax, Isabella is taking care of her. She's not going to let her out of her sight.' Caelon grips James's forearm.

'Make sure she doesn't. Especially with all that other business unresolved.'

Curiosity kindles like a flame, but I don't ask any questions. He's paying me to be his fake girlfriend, not to nag him like a real one.

'Speaking of which, I need a word.' Killian's features form into a deep frown.

'Sure.' James scans the room again.

'In private.' Killian's head jerks in the direction of the door.

'I'll keep an eye on Scarlett for you.' Rian smirks. Clearly, he enjoys poking an angry bear.

'And I'll keep an eye on Rian.' Caelon's elbow connects with Rian's ribs in a playful gesture.

'Ow, why does everyone keep hitting me?'

I stretch up onto my toes and lift my lips to James's ear. 'I might just go to the ladies' restroom to freshen up.'

James pauses for a long beat. 'Meet me back here in five minutes.'

'I will.' He inches down until his full lips meet mine in a fleeting kiss, marking his territory for everyone to see.

It might only have lasted two seconds, and it might have been for show, but it still sends a hot thrill thrumming through my blood.

Chapter Twenty-Three
SCARLETT

I stare at myself in the huge, gilded mirror over the basin. My dark hair is loose in bouncing waves across my back, and my skin is flushed from the permanent state of arousal caused by James's close proximity.

It's easier to deny him when he's God knows where on business. Resisting him in the flesh is testing every ounce of my willpower.

Being on his arm is intoxicating.

Being in his company is intoxicating.

I can only imagine what being in his bed would be like.

Two stunning women fall through the restroom door giggling like schoolgirls. Their laughter is infectious. The blonde is wearing a silver sequinned midi dress that's so beautifully cut it must have cost at least four figures. She looks to be older than me, maybe twenty-seven or twenty-eight. The brunette is wearing a simple but elegant black dress. She barely looks old enough to be in a club. Her huge dark eyes twinkle with fun. There's something familiar about them.

'If James sees you getting chatted up, there will be murders, Zara,' the blonde warns.

Zara?

This has to be James's sister.

'By all accounts, he's too busy with his new woman.' Zara waggles her eyebrows at the other woman. My lips stretch even further. 'Mother said he was grinning when he was texting her earlier. Grinning. I mean, when have you ever seen James grin?'

The two women proffer a smile as they fall into the same toilet cubicle, the way women do.

It's a battle not to follow them in and beg for more details.

It's not real, Scarlett.

Of course, he's going to put on a good show for his mother. It's all part of the act.

And James Beckett is a very convincing actor. Case in point, the filth that fell from his tongue minutes earlier was exceptionally convincing. I don't doubt he wants to have sex with me, but lines like 'I could spend every minute from now until graduation with my head, hands, and cock between your legs and it still wouldn't be anywhere near long enough,' has to be a lie.

The giggling continues from inside the cubicle as I reapply my crimson lipstick. With a final glance at myself in the mirror, I stride back out into the bar area to wait for James. The song booming over the speakers is one of my absolute favourites.

My hips instinctively sway to the beat.

Dancing has always been my outlet, my way of releasing the pent-up energy buzzing through my veins. And thanks to James, his filthy mouth and fuck-me-sideways stares, I have copious amounts of pent-up energy.

How am I going to survive months of this?

I'll be tripping around like a pheasant in mating season, dizzy with desire.

With the bass thrumming through my blood, I gravitate to the middle of the dance floor instead of the VIP area.

My limbs sway as I shake and shimmy in time to the beat. Smiling strangers surround me. My shoulders slacken as my eyes close. Every single cell in my body surrenders to the beat.

'Scarlett,' a familiar voice yells, but it's not the voice I was expecting.

My eyes snap open. Shane Stenson, my study buddy and previous kiss, is beaming at me like he hasn't seen me in years instead of hours. 'I had no idea you'd be here.' His words are slightly slurred, but his eyes are sharp and keen as they rake over my dress.

The man is the human version of a golden retriever. Sunshine in a shirt and suit pants. He's the polar opposite of James.

'Come on, let me buy you a drink.' He takes my wrist and tugs me towards the bar, wiggling through the crowd until he reaches a free space on the marble counter.

'I shouldn't.' I scan the room looking for James. I barely know him, but I do know he won't like this. In fact, not being seen with another man was one of his conditions.

But Shane is my friend. It's different.

'One drink. Please, indulge me. It's been ages since I saw you out of class.' His big blue eyes widen like a goddamn puppy's.

'I'm here with—'

Before I can finish, Shane pulls me to his chest. 'Scarlett.' His gaze falls to my lips. 'I'm crazy about you. Every time I see you swinging around that pole in the college gym it does things to me.'

A hot hard expanse of muscle slams against my back and the scent of citrus and pure masculinity steals my senses. 'Remove your hands from my girlfriend or you will lose them.' James's cold, calm voice cuts deep, even over the music.

Strong arms wrap around my torso, wrenching me from Shane's grip. James's hands roam languidly over my body like he's marking every inch of skin as his. Shane's eyes follow the movement and his mouth drops open as James's palms pause just below my breasts.

'I...' His huge blue eyes dart between James's hands and my face. 'I didn't realise,' Shane stutters.

'Well, now you do.' James's voice is as hard as steel as his smooth hands slide up a few inches, grazing over my breasts in a possessive claim.

Shane raises his hands and backs away.

James spins me around. 'What the fuck was that, Scarlett? Do you know how many eyes are on us tonight? How many people are whispering about us, wondering who you are, what you are to me? It's not every day I introduce my family to my girlfriend.' He hisses out a breath, sliding his hands lower until they settle on my hips. 'I leave you alone for two fucking minutes and you let some guy put his hands on you.' His pupils flash with anger.

'I'm sorry. It's only Shane. He's in my class. We study together sometimes. We're friends. Sort of.' The sentences stream out like one.

James's expression darkens. 'Friends?' His hands reach around to grip my ass, yanking my pelvis against him hard. The sensation is a delicious slap to the sensitive spot between my legs. 'Friends don't tell friends they're crazy about them, Scarlett.' His voice is dangerously low as he leans into my ear to be heard over the music. 'And what did he mean about the college gym?' His eyes are so dark they're almost black as they burn through me.

'There are poles for fitness in the gym. It's where I learnt to dance.' I should back away, but I don't want to. I like his hips pressing against mine. Like the way our thighs are lined up and our chests are pressed tight enough for me to feel the thudding of his heart beneath the hard muscles of his torso.

His jaw ticks. 'You dance at college?'

'Only for fitness.'

His eyes narrow to slits. 'For fitness?' he repeats. Something flashes across his face. 'You're killing me, Scarlett. You know I could show you a million other ways to keep fit, if only you'd let me.'

'Might not be appropriate here in the nightclub...'

'Wait a minute,' realisation flashes over James's features. 'Was he your nightclub kiss?' James growls.

Why the fuck did I ever mention I kissed someone in a nightclub? James has a habit of dragging the truth from me. 'It was months ago.'

A vein pulses in his temple. 'He knows what your mouth tastes like.' His arousal digs into my pelvis and flames lick every inch of my skin. 'I want to taste you. I want to touch you. And I want to fuck you.' Fire blazes in his eyes. 'And I think you want it, too.'

'I told you, we can't,' I say, but my throbbing clit and needy nipples scream the exact opposite and I can't for the life of me remember any of my earlier compelling arguments why we shouldn't. I can barely remember my own name.

'Are you still attracted to him?' James inches his face closer until we're sharing the same breath.

'No.' I shake my head.

'Prove it.' James's tongue wets his lower lip, his eyes blazing like an inferno. 'I need him and everyone else in this club to know you're mine.' His fingers trail up from my ass to my waist, then up under my breasts again. It's agonisingly arousing. If he wants proof of who I'm attracted to, he'd only have to check my panties. Because a jealous James is even hotter than a calm James.

'Kiss me,' he demands. 'Show him, and every other man in here, who you belong to.'

Desire shimmers around us. I'm wound so tightly, I'm close to snapping.

My chin juts out of its own accord. It's millimetres, but it's like I flung the gates open wide as an invitation. James's full hot lips crash onto mine with a carnality I couldn't have dreamt up.

His tongue invades my mouth, plundering and conquering and claiming, devouring me like a man who has been starved.

Molten desire sizzles through my blood, searing every single inch of me from the inside out. His right hand grips the nape of my neck, angling my head higher, demanding deeper access. His left hand makes small circular motions on my hip that set shivers across my spine.

I've been kissed before but never like this.

Never with so much need.

So much passion.

It's too much.

It's not enough.

I want it all.

I want him.

Lust laps over my entire body as my fingers slide over the hard planes beneath his crisp shirt.

All too soon, he tears his mouth away. My lips feel bruised and bereft.

Huge dark eyes gleam through the dim nightclub. 'That was one hell of a first kiss. If you fuck like you kiss, you might just be the death of me.'

The feeling is mutual.

Chapter Twenty-Four

JAMES

Scarlett presses her fingers against her lips, a look of shock in her silver sparkling eyes. I graze my knuckles across her prominent cheekbone, committing every second of this moment to memory. She wears an expression as if she's lived a hundred lives but still not quite found what she's looking for, and it stirs something deep in my soul. Something that makes me want to plug that void for her. Be the very thing she's looking for.

But why?

What is it about this woman that has me in knots? I've never wanted anyone the way I want her. Is it simply because I can't have her? Or is it something more?

'Will you dance with me?' she says, with a pleading expression.

'Here? Now?' I gaze around the nightclub. She can't be fucking serious. I don't dance. Ever.

She nods, her teeth digging into her lower lip, and there's something so endearing about it.

Fuck, I've known her all of a few weeks and already I can't

say no to her. Who is this mysterious white witch? And what is she doing to me?

I buy myself time. 'Why?'

Her throat bobs as she swallows. 'Dancing is my outlet. My way of letting off steam.' Her admission is like an invitation she has no idea she's issuing.

Steam?

My little virgin needs a release. There's no way I'm letting her walk around this nightclub with all that pent-up lust sizzling beneath her skin. I'm the only man allowed to touch her. It's time she let me do exactly that.

'Oh sweetheart, there are so many other ways to blow off steam.' My lips dip and I trail my tongue across her jawline to the sensitive spot behind her ear. 'Let me help you.'

She pauses, staring up from under elongated eyelashes. 'James...'

Even the way my name sounds falling from her lips is sexy as fuck. I want to hear her scream it while she comes on my face, on my hands, and on my cock.

I reach up to tuck a stray strand of hair from her face, then let my finger trail down her neck and across her collarbone. My eyes fall to her dress where twin peaks rise on her breasts. She's horny as hell, and she can deny it as much as she wants, but she needs this.

It's time to show her what she's been missing.

I tell myself I'm doing it for her, but deep down, it's all for me. I need to make her come. I need to watch her face as she breaks and shatters. I need her to cry my name as she explodes with ecstasy. And I need it now.

I murmur, pressing a kiss to her temple. 'Didn't I say I'd take care of you until graduation?'

The faint trace of a smile ghosts her lips. Her eyes fill with a trust I don't know if I deserve. She could be the undoing of me.

'Let me take care of you the best way I know how. Let me make you come. Just once. Please. It's the least I can do when our agreement prevents you from getting it elsewhere. It doesn't have to mean anything.' I scan the club, searching for the quickest exit.

Lies, lies, and more lies. I'm going to make her come so hard she'll be banging down my bedroom door begging for more. I slide my hand into hers and tug her through the throng of people in search of somewhere more private. I can't risk taking her home. Even if I could sneak out of this nightclub and past my family, the fresh air and thirty-minute car journey will give her too much time to overthink this. To change her mind.

Instead, I lead her up the stairs, taking them two at a time.

'Just this one time,' she repeats more to herself than me.

'Call it a public service,' I call over my shoulder. 'I can't have you walking around this nightclub like a gasket ready to blow.'

'Where are we going?' she asks breathily, glancing around.

I swivel into her, planting another dizzying kiss on her lips. 'There's a viewing lounge on the top floor. We should find a little privacy there. Okay?'

She gazes up from hooded eyes as her hips buck almost involuntarily against mine, and I have my answer.

I thank my lucky stars I got a tour of this place in the daylight, or else we could be locked in a toilet cubicle right now instead of opening the door to a viewing point overlooking the city spiralling below. The moonlight spills in through floor-to-ceiling windows. Hundreds of stars punctuate the navy sky outside. It's the perfect backdrop for the first time I get to touch the woman who's been haunting my every waking thought.

A small circular bar occupies the centre of the room,

flanked with ten high-backed bar stools. 'This is for more intimate meetings.' My innuendo is lost as Scarlett strides across the floor to admire the view. The only view I'm interested in is her.

I follow her, slipping my arms around her waist. I rest my chin on her shoulder as we gaze out at the city together, and my hands slide upwards to palm her tits, so full, so round, so perfect.

She twists in my arms until she's facing me. I keep one hand firmly on her lower back for support and skim the other hand over her thigh and under her dress.

Our eyes collide as I inch slowly upwards over smooth satiny skin until my fingers seek out the scrap they're searching for. 'Did I buy this lingerie?'

'You did.' Her head lolls back, exposing her long, elegant neck.

'I believe I warned you I'd want to inspect it,' I hiss as my fingers slide over the saturated silk. She gasps as I stroke over the material from her clit to her slit. 'You are soaking, sweetheart.'

'You tend to have that effect on me. Even when you're in another country.' Her admission stirs something deep in my stomach and it takes a minute to pinpoint the feeling.

Satisfaction.

Her skin is flawless beneath the moonlight. Flawless and youthful. She's so fucking young, probably too young for me, but now I've got her here, now I know she's soaking for me, there's no way my conscience is going to impede me.

'You don't mind that I'm older?' My finger inches to the side of the silk, searching for the seam to slip beneath.

'Your experience terrifies me and turns me on in equal measure,' she pants.

'Never be scared of me, sweetheart.' I gently suck on the skin sheathing her rapid pulse. 'I'll never hurt you.'

Someone did though, given what she's told me. God help that person if I ever find out who.

'I only want to give you pleasure.' I pull my hand away from her pussy and disappointment flashes over her face. 'Now take off that lingerie so I can do exactly that.'

Chapter Twenty-Five

SCARLETT

The throbbing between my legs is overriding all rationale. I reach beneath my dress, hook my fingers inside the waistband of my thong, and slide it down my legs. I'm about to bend down and pick it up when James beats me to it.

He crouches at my feet, snatches up the silk, and raises it to his face. His head angles up and his torrid eyes burn into mine as he inhales. It's primal. Rising slowly, he tucks the lingerie into his trouser pocket and dips a hand beneath the hem of my dress again without breaking our stare. Teasing fingers skim my inner thigh, inching higher. The anticipation of his touch is almost enough to get me off alone.

'Has anyone else touched this pretty pussy?' His pupils gleam as his fingers glide through the slickness down there.

'Only me.' There's that uncanny ability he possesses to extract the truth from me. My gaze falls to the floor.

'Do you know how much that turns me on, Scarlett?' He uses his free hand to tilt my chin up so I have no choice but to meet his eyes. Twin flames burn with a desire on par with my own. 'Knowing that I'm the first man to touch you?'

Apparently, it's a rhetorical question.

'But tonight's not about me. It's all about you.' His fingers slide either side of my clit, driving up and down with the perfect amount of pressure.

'Open your legs wider, sweetheart.' His dominance serves to soak me further.

I obey, willingly.

He pushes a fingertip at my entrance while his thumb works maddening circles around the most sensitive parts of me. Heat pools in my core as my limbs tighten. Fireworks dance across my skin. I fall forwards onto his chest, my fingers gripping the lapels of his suit jacket.

'How does that feel?' His breath caresses my ear.

'Unbelievable,' I moan. 'You're going to wreck my dress.' My protest is feeble. It might be a Rebecca Vallance, limited edition and the most stunning dress I own, but I'd sacrifice it for this pleasure.

'You're going to wreck me, Scarlett. I've known it since the second you walked onto that stage.' His face inches forwards until we're sharing the same air. His lips brush over mine then he runs his tongue over my bottom lip.

'I need to get a closer look.' His fingers slow to a stop but before I can even protest, he kneels in front of me.

James Beckett, billionaire bachelor, is on his fucking knees inspecting me, and it's the hottest thing I've ever seen.

'Pull your dress up around your waist. I want to watch you come on my fingers.' I do as I'm told, too wanton with lust to even contemplate being shy. His face presses against my sex, and he inhales deeply again. For a second, I wonder if he'll put his tongue there, but he doesn't.

One strong hand cups my ass cheek as he buries his fingers between my legs, applying the perfect amount of pressure to my needy clit. It's the single most intoxicating experience of my short life.

'You're so fucking sexy, sweetheart.' His voice is so breathy, I almost believe him.

My legs tremble as I try to hang on, nowhere near ready for this to be over, but it's impossible. The pressure builds below until I'm blind with the need to come. Hot white stars burst behind my eyelids and my entire body ignites into flames. The pleasure is paralysing.

James pumps my entrance with his fingers relentlessly, like he's savouring every second. His hand doesn't stop until he's wrung every ounce of pleasure from my body and my limbs are limp with exhaustion.

Eventually, he slides his fingers out, brings them to his mouth, and sucks them. 'How's that pent-up pressure? Still need to hit the dancefloor?' He rises from the floor and presses his mouth to mine.

I'm still dazed when he pulls back. 'Fuck. That was... the hottest experience of my life.'

'Shame it was just one time then, hey?' He winks, and I slap his chest. 'Happy Valentine's, Scarlett.'

'Happy Valentine's,' I murmur, wondering if I should give him another type of present.

He pats the pocket containing my lingerie. 'By the way, these are mine now.'

'And what will I wear?'

'Nothing, sweetheart. And when we're out there with my family, I'll have the pleasure of knowing the last thing that touched that pretty pussy was me.'

'You're a bad man, James Beckett.' I stand still as he wiggles my dress down over my hips, smoothing the material over my still shaking quads.

He flashes me a wolfish grin. 'Next time you need to let off some pent-up energy, you know where to come.'

I'm officially ruined.

. . .

An hour later, I'm still reeling. Like a drug addict floored by her first hit, I'm already wondering how I can get my next one. So much for just one time.

Getting intimate with James goes against everything I said, but that was before I knew what pleasure he could bestow.

I need more.

It's all I can think about.

He's created a monster.

His hand rests on my bare leg as we sit on the low velvet couches with his brothers. Every now and again, his thumb swipes in a circular motion over my skin. From his subtle smirks and sideways glances, he makes it clear it's a deliberate reminder.

As if sitting here panty-less isn't a reminder enough.

I sip on a glass of champagne while James talks shop with his brothers. From their pinched expressions and hushed whispers, it's obvious there's some sort of problem.

It can't be too serious, given James was happy to abandon the discussion to get on his knees for me.

'You have got to be fucking joking me.' James's voice is calm but it's tinged with a hard edge. Every hair on my neck stands to attention.

I follow his gaze and my blood runs cold when I spot Declan O'Connor, my former step-brother, flanked by four of his henchmen.

I could pick out those cold, callous eyes in a sold-out stadium. They haunt my dreams and fuel my night terrors. The pleasure of the present is eradicated by the pain of the past.

Declan's eyes narrow as he zeros in on us. I twist my torso so my back is to him. My heart pumps furiously in my chest. *'If I ever see you again, I'll kill you myself.'*

If it weren't for my other stepbrothers, I'm pretty sure he would have already made good on that promise. After all, their father is rotting in a prison cell because of me. Mind you, he's not dead, which is more than I can say for my mother.

My fingers gravitate towards the cross nestled in the hollow of my throat. My chest constricts. My legs tremble. This time, not with pleasure but with panic.

I need to get out of here.

The walls are closing in.

There's no air.

Dread crushes my chest.

James's thumb slows to a stop on my leg, and he inclines his body in front of mine protectively, almost as if he knows. But he can't. How could he?

'Scarlett, I need you to go home with Tim now.' It's not a request. He stands in front of me, sheltering me, blocking me from sight.

I don't need to be told twice.

Keeping my back to Declan, I nod.

Tim appears out of nowhere.

James presses a kiss to my temple and there's nothing fake about it. 'I'll see you at home, okay?'

Home.

His mansion.

It might be his home, but it'll never be mine.

Seeing Declan again reminds me why I can't let James, or any other man, get close to me. It's not safe to form attachments.

I need to stay away from James Beckett, and every other man in this city, focus on graduation, then get the hell out of Dublin. Get the hell out of here, out of this life.

Before I suffer the same fate as my mother.

Chapter Twenty-Six
JAMES

'Where are Zara and Isabella?' I growl at Caelon.

'Gone.' Caelon straightens himself in the seat next to me. 'They had too much to drink. Mother stumbled across them coming out of the toilet and made them get a ride home with her and Pete.'

Pete is one of Killian's top security guys, which is why he's assigned as our mother's driver. My shoulders relax slightly. If the shit hits the fan with the O'Connors tonight, I don't want any of my women anywhere near it.

'Can you believe the fucking cheek of it?' Caelon shakes his head in disgust. 'Not only to threaten us earlier, but to gatecrash Rian's big night.'

'I think we're supposed to be intimidated.' Rage ripples beneath my skin.

'Where are the rest of them?' Killian glances around the room looking for Declan's brothers.

'That's the million-dollar question.' They'd be foolish to instigate trouble publicly, but the O'Connors aren't the smartest of families.

Killian fires off a quick text, no doubt alerting the club's new security team, all vetted and hired by his firm. Within seconds, the doors are flanked by a team of his men, literally dressed to kill with concealed weapons hidden beneath their black tuxedos.

The music continues to blare and the dancefloor remains packed, partygoers utterly oblivious to the chaos that's seconds from breaking out, depending on how the O'Connors decide to play this. I pin Declan with an icy stare as I take a sip of whiskey. Beckett's Gold, of course.

Killian flanks my right. Sean to the left, while Caelon and Rian pull their stools in closer to form a tight circle. Even without the extra security, we could probably handle the O'Connors, but I'd prefer to avoid another public scandal with the Board breathing down my neck.

Eventually, after what seems like hours but is only a couple of minutes, Declan's cold, blue eyes find us. A slow, cruel grin reveals a flash of teeth. Of all the O'Connor brothers, Declan is notoriously the most dangerous. Quick to act. Slow to think. He operates with the brutality of a nineteen-fifties gangster but with the IQ of a gnat.

I offer him a languid smile, like his presence here was expected, welcome even.

He strides across the room to the VIP area, lifts the red rope and ducks into our space like we're old friends, not rivals.

'Not a bad establishment, I suppose.' His narrow eyes dart around at the décor appraisingly.

'If that's your way of saying congratulations, then thanks,' I drawl, taking another sip from my glass.

Declan pulls up a stool between me and my brothers. He's either very brave or very stupid.

'I bought the warehouse across the road,' he drops in casually. 'Think I might turn that into a nightclub too.'

Rian's jaw locks and Caelon puts a subtle hand on his thigh to restrain him.

'What do you want, Declan?' I adopt a bored tone, shoving my free hand casually in my trouser pocket.

I'm not a patient man. I can't even pretend to be. Thanks to this arsehole's arrival, I've had to send my girl home, and I'd have much preferred to be looking into her stunning face than this neanderthal's.

His lips purse into a grimace. 'Back off the Imperial Winery acquisition. It's not your kind of deal.'

'Really. And why is that?'

Declan shrugs. 'Trust me. You don't want the trouble.'

'It's a good fit with our business.'

'Actually, it's really not. Find something else.'

'We had it in the bag until you intervened.' I approached Lucien Moreau, the owner, long before the O'Connors showed any interest.

'Semantics.' Declan shrugs again. 'The winery is mine. And I don't like people touching things that belong to me.'

'That's just it though, it doesn't belong to you. Nor will it ever.' The O'Connors might be ruthless, but so are we.

Acquiring the Imperial Winery is important to secure my position as CEO of my own family's company and to prove my worth to the Board, but more than that, I *want* those vineyards.

And Declan O'Connor has the fucking gall to come here and threaten me? I'll never let him get his hands on the business. Over my dead body.

I'll work myself into the ground to get this deal done, even if it means playing dirty.

Besides, no one threatens the Becketts and gets away with it.

Declan O'Connor will have to learn the hard way. We

might like to wear designer suits and drive fancy cars, but my brothers and I are not afraid to get blood on our hands.

'We'll see about that.' Declan flashes a cold, crooked smile, scanning the nightclub like he's searching for something. Or someone. 'But if you fuck this deal up for me, I will come after you and everyone who means anything to you. Everyone you care about. I will bring so much heat to your door, you'll suffocate on the smoke before the flames even get near you.'

A cold, icy tendril curls in my core.

The O'Connors' speciality is playing with fire. Or at least, that's what they like people to believe. But one isolated fire doesn't make a conflagration.

Their father might be doing time for arson and manslaughter, but it could have been sheer bad luck that his wife was in the building at the time.

If it wasn't, they're all more deranged than even I can comprehend.

'Don't threaten me, Declan.' I eye the security guards flanking the room and glance at my four brothers. The air is seething with anger.

'You're in no position to tell me what to do,' he hisses with a callous grin. 'Especially when you've just sent your pretty little woman home to a big empty house. And where's your sister and your sister-in-law? Where's Mammy?'

'You wouldn't fucking dare.' My fists clench, white with rage. My house is better armed than an army barracks, but the thought of the O'Connors anywhere near Scarlett sends a shred of panic skating down my spine.

'Easy.' Declan raises his hands playfully. 'I'm here talking to you, aren't I? This is just a friendly conversation between two businessmen.' He shrugs. 'My brothers though, I'm not sure where they are tonight. Keith has a vested interest in those vineyards. He has a real thing for French pussy, you know?' Keith is the second oldest, and the brother responsible for breaking three of my ribs in a nightclub four years ago. If I ever see him again, I'll take his head clean off his neck.

Declan picks up my whiskey glass from the table and downs the contents. His weathered face creases with distaste. 'Tastes like shit.' He bangs the glass back down. 'I'll have some O'Connors' sent over to you. Can't have you scaring all the punters away, can we? The first ten crates are on the house.'

He stands, making prolonged eye contact with each of us in turn before striding away.

Killian's men block the door preventing his exit. Killian gives them the nod. As much as I'd like to physically remove Declan's cruel grin along with his too-white teeth, too many people have seen us together tonight.

Declan turns back to face us and lifts his hands in a patronising wiggle of his fingers that says *toodle-oo* and *fuck you* in the same arrogant gesture.

Chapter Twenty-Seven
SCARLETT

The memory of James's hands trailing over my body is seared into my soul. Unfortunately, so is the memory of seeing my former stepbrother, which is why I've been burying my head in my books all week.

The timing was freakish. It was like a badly needed reminder of why James and I shouldn't get involved, even if we had the time. James works ridiculously long hours, even when he's in the country. He's gone in the morning before I even drag myself downstairs and doesn't arrive home until after I go to bed.

He hasn't sought me out and I haven't gone looking for him. Though, I'm not entirely sure our reasoning is the same.

I've passed him briefly in the corridors several times, but he always appears to be distracted. Part of me wants to ask him about the other night, about Declan and whatever threat he and his brothers were discussing, but the other part of me thinks I'm better off not knowing.

Footsteps approach across the marble flooring. I lift my gaze from the dining room table in anticipation.

It's probably Tim coming to see if I'm ready for college. He's a stickler for punctuality.

But it's not. It's James in a tight white vest that clings to his sculpted torso. His bare arms are ripped with muscles. A smattering of dark hair peeps from the top of his vest. Grey sweatpants hang from his hips low enough to flash a hint of the V leading straight to heaven.

Oh, sweet Jesus. The man looks mouth-watering in a suit – but this... it's a unique type of torture. I drag my eyes from his crotch to his face.

Sweat clings to his skin, glistens on his forehead, and dots his upper lip, which is stretching into a mile-wide smile. How many times has he caught me staring at his crotch now? Two? Three? I'm dying to find out what he's packing down there.

Crimson heat colours my cheeks. 'Oh.' I fluff my hair and smooth my clammy palms across the slim-fitting dress I selected this morning. The soft cotton material is casual but the lacy hold-ups I'm wearing beneath it are anything but. Since James expressed such an interest in my lingerie, I've been upping my game—just in case. 'I didn't realise you were still here.'

Amusement crinkles the corners of his eyes as he slides into the seat next to me, despite the fact there are nineteen other free chairs around the table. He's already testing my willpower and he's only just walked in.

'I work from home on Fridays when I can.' He motions to his sweat-drenched vest. 'Tim likes to batter me with boxing gloves in the gym. It's a great way to let off steam.' He shoots me a wink.

I squeeze my thighs together and suck in a breath, picking up my coffee mug just for something to do.

Those long dark eyelashes should be illegal on a man. 'I hope you're well settled in at this stage.'

'Yes, thank you. You have a beautiful home.' I place the

mug down again. This is a far safer topic than how to let off steam.

'It's your home now too, for the next few months at least. Enjoy it. Use the pool or gym or anything else you like. Sorry I haven't been here.' His pupils dart over my lips. 'There've been a few...' he pauses while he searches for the right word, 'complications this week.'

'Everything okay?' My fingers automatically reach for the cross around my neck.

James blows out a breath. 'This acquisition isn't going to be as straightforward as I'd hoped, but I'll make it work. The O'Connors, our biggest rivals, and frankly the spawn of Satan, have been sniffing around. Killian is monitoring things on the ground while I've been crunching the numbers.' His lips lift in a wry smile.

Rosa stalks into the dining room carrying a tray with a fresh pot of steaming coffee, fresh buttery toast, and today's papers. She places the tray in front of James and he grabs a piece of toast.

I watch as his lips close around his food and a hot jolt of lust strikes my core. I never realised it was possible to be jealous of a carbohydrate until now.

'You two made it into Friday's Fashion Fix.' Rosa opens the paper and pulls out the glossy magazine tucked inside.

A sense of dread sinks into my stomach as she flicks through the pages until she finds a selection of pictures from Rian's opening night. I spot the Rebecca Vallance dress right away, its intricate cut so stunning, it's easy to pick out even in a crowd of opulent outfits. While you can clearly see my dark hair and James's arms draped possessively over my shoulder, my face has thankfully been pixelated out.

A heavy sigh of relief slips from my lips.

'What does it say?' I lean closer to James to peer at the

glossy pages and I'm immediately enveloped by the raw scent of his sweat.

Oh my fucking God.

I thought his expensive aftershave was intoxicating but it has nothing on this. Every single cell of my body remembers what he's capable of. The pleasure he's capable of giving with his touch.

It's far easier to remind myself why we can't complicate things when he's away on business. Or even thirty minutes away in his office.

Here, in his house, over the breakfast table, I'm thirty seconds away from throwing myself at him. I'm not even averse to begging.

'"James Beckett photographed with mystery brunette. Could she finally be the one to tame him?"' He snorts. 'You'd swear I was a wild animal or something.'

'You two look fantastic together.' Rosa beams, glancing between us as she backs out of the door, presumably back to the kitchen. Pride flickers in my chest.

'It's a nice start to convincing the Board.' James takes another bite of his toast and I force myself to look out of the window over the immaculate grounds.

'Speaking of which, there's a charity function next weekend at Dublin Castle. I'm expected to attend, with a date, of course.'

'I'll go with you. That's what you pay me for.' I raise my eyes to meet his.

'It is, isn't it?' Devilment twinkles in his eyes. 'So, be ready for seven o'clock tomorrow night.'

I'm acutely aware I didn't get to meet his mother amongst all the drama of the other night, and if we're to convince his father this thing between us is legitimate, then that will have to happen soon.

'There's somewhere I'd like to take you.' He grabs another piece of toast.

Somewhere he'd like to take me. Not somewhere we ought to be seen together. I try not to read into it. 'What shall I wear?' I mentally scan my new wardrobe for something appropriate.

'Something loose-fitting.' He smirks, trailing his index finger over my jean-clad thigh. 'It's not really a place you can dance, so on the off chance you need to let off some steam again, I'll need access to that sweet little pussy.' Filth rolls from his tongue like a lullaby.

The heat of his stare sparks an inferno in my panties. 'We agreed just one time.'

'But we didn't shake on it.' James's accompanying grin isn't even remotely apologetic.

Tim enters the dining room before I can form any sort of response. Dressed in a fitted black suit as usual, he looks like he's going to a black-tie event, not driving me to college. Does he know this thing between James and me is a business arrangement? Or does he think it's real?

'Are you ready, Miss Fitzgerald?'

'Please, call me Scarlett,' I say for the hundredth time, rising from the table.

I still have half a cup of coffee left and I'm reluctant to leave it behind. Seeming to sense it, James prises the cup from my hand. Gold-flecked eyes glint with amusement as he raises it to his face and presses his lips against the exact spot mine just touched.

'Until later, angel.' If he only knew. I might be a virgin, but I'm no angel. I'm the former stepsister of his biggest rival.

Yep, definitely best if I don't mention it.

Chapter Twenty-Eight
SCARLETT

I grab my gym bag before heading out the front door to where Tim is waiting for me. James might have been joking about letting off some steam, but the struggle is real. Pole dancing is perfect for fitness but there's also something cathartic about it, too.

Swinging around the college gym pole might not be as thrilling as dancing nearly naked for James in the Luxor Lounge, but it should hopefully burn off some of the wayward desire pumping through my body.

Shane's given me a wide berth this week, opting to sit with some of his football teammates in class rather than in his usual spot beside me. It's probably better that way, but I do miss having someone to share notes with.

I sit through a two-hour lecture on fintech and digital finance. Professor Buckley is in his usual twitchy form. I don't dare sneeze for fear of drawing attention to myself.

When we are finally free to escape, I make my way across campus to the brand-new purpose-built gym, coincidentally funded by Shane's father.

The scent of chlorine and cleaning solution hits my

nostrils as I stride through the tiled corridors towards the gymnasium and the adjacent female changing rooms.

I pass by several workmen in hard hats. They're carrying scaffolding poles under their arms. Is there work going on? A new wing of the gym? A new upstairs workout area?

But why would they be carrying scaffolding poles out of the building instead of into it?

It doesn't make sense.

I nudge open the door to the pole dancing fitness class and my jaw hits the floor.

It wasn't scaffolding they were carrying.

It was our poles.

'What's going on?' I ask a guy wearing a luminous yellow jacket and a frown.

'Health and safety. Poles have to be removed,' he says in a monotone voice.

'What do you mean health and safety?' I fold my arms across my chest. 'They've been fine for the last four years. Why now?' Even as the words leave my lips, I know the answer.

'Someone made a complaint. Not only are the poles a health hazard, but they're an inappropriate form of fitness for an establishment of this calibre.' The man drawls out the word calibre like he actually means bullshit.

James Beckett.

A memory of our conversation at the club replays in my head.

'You dance at college?'

He wouldn't.

Would he?

I glance around as the last pole is carried out of the building.

He just did.

I pull out my phone and type a text before I can overthink it.

> How could you?

Three dots appear immediately.

> Working off steam elsewhere is cheating.

> Taking away my only other outlet is cheating. You're incorrigible.

> No, I'm insatiable. It's different.

> Maybe I'll take up running.

> You can run… but you can't hide, sweetheart ;)

I find Tim outside the gym. His lips twitch like he's holding back a laugh. The bastard is in on it. And I thought we'd sort of become friends.

Hysteria rises in my chest, but truly there's nothing funny about it.

It's frustrating that I can't dance, but there's also a part of me deep down that's oddly flattered that a man like James would go to such lengths to prevent me releasing my tension elsewhere.

No man ever cared for me before. Let alone a man who could have any woman in the world.

'You ready to go home, Miss Fitzgerald?' Tim opens the back door for me.

'I guess so, seeing as there's not a lot else I can do,' I huff as I slide into the backseat.

'I know it seems extreme,' he says, holding onto the door. 'But it's actually a compliment.'

'It's the most fucked up compliment I've ever seen.' I hold my bag to my chest like a shield.

'James has some unusual methods, but there are two things you should know about him.' Ah ha, so Tim is aware our arrangement is strictly business. Does that mean Rosa is too? 'One—James always gets what James wants. Two—he's crazy about you, whether you believe it or not.'

He closes the car door before I can reply.

Half an hour later, I march through the grand entrance to James's mansion, my heels clicking furiously against the marble. 'Where is he?' I demand as poor Rosa appears from the kitchen carrying a vase of fresh peonies to put on display on the table in the hall.

'In his office, I believe.' She rolls her lips and presses them together.

Is everyone in on this?

I drop my bag on the gleaming floor and charge down the corridor in search of James. When I reach his office, I fling open the heavy door and strut in. James is spread out on the huge leather armchair behind his enormous desk in those damn sweatpants.

I drag my eyes away, heat tearing up my throat.

His eyes glint with a hint of mischief.

'Scarlett, come in. I don't bite. Unless you want me to, that is.' His voice oozes amusement. 'It's lovely to see you in the flesh.'

In the flesh? What's that supposed to mean?

His bare feet rest languidly on the top of the dark oak desk next to his computer. He makes no move to cover what is definitely an erection beneath his sweats. The man is shameless.

Even though I'm supposed to be mad, it's not anger that's

causing an ache between my legs. The room is filled with the scent of him. That distinct male scent that drives me insane with lust.

'You had the poles taken out of the college gym.' It doesn't come out nearly as angrily as I intended.

'And?' He folds his arms defiantly across his burly chest.

'Why?'

He rocks forwards in the chair and beckons me with a single finger. 'Come here and I'll show you.'

I take a small step closer, unable to shake the feeling I'm stepping into the lion's lair. 'You'll get a better view if you come round to this side of the desk.'

I take three steps closer with more conviction than I truly feel. He points at his computer screen and my pulse spikes. A twenty-eight inch image of me fills his screen, there in all my semi-naked glory. I'm on the stage at the Luxor Lounge wearing nothing but three tiny crimson silk triangles. My legs are split wide open against the pole, my fingers gripping the cool metal, supporting my weight as I spin. My eyes are closed tight, seemingly oblivious to the world around me.

'Where did you get that?' I whisper, utterly transfixed.

James Beckett is turned on looking at a picture of me.

'Killian's company provides the security for the club, including their CCTV.' He shrugs as if it's no big deal that he's sourced semi-naked images of me.

'Look at you, Scarlett.' He motions to the screen. 'You're every man's fantasy. But you're my girlfriend, on paper at least. And I don't share.'

'But–' My protest dies in my throat as heat stokes my core. I want to be annoyed with him, I really do. But I'm vibrating so hard with that damn pent-up energy again, the only thing I really want is to see what he's got beneath those grey sweats.

'The agreement is you're mine. And while you're mine,

I'm the only man who gets to watch you dance.' The bulge beneath the grey is growing by the second, straining against his pants, pulling the material so deliciously taut across his crotch.

'Like what you see?' He motions to his crotch. I wet my lips and swallow hard. 'Because while you are mine, I am yours. You're the only woman who gets to see me.' His eyes darken to almost black. 'You do want to see me, don't you, sweetheart?'

Chapter Twenty-Nine

SCARLETT

I do want to see him. More than anything I want to see him. I shouldn't, but I do. It's supposed to be a fake relationship, but deep down it's always been real, for me at least. I love the lengths he's going to for me. I'm so turned on it's not even funny. I barely hesitate before panting out my answer. 'Show me.'

'First, show me today's lingerie and then I'll show you what you do to me.' No wonder he's so damn successful. He's the king of negotiating.

I reach around the back of the dress I'm wearing and grip the zip, tugging it until the air hits the base of my spine. Sliding the cotton over my body, I let it fall to the floor. The front fastening balconette bra is so sheer it's almost entirely see-through and the ebony lace thong does nothing to hide what's beneath.

James's pupils dart to my lace-topped hold-ups. An appreciative hiss slides from his lips. His hot and greedy gaze on my skin is addictive. 'Look what you do to me.' His hand slides beneath the band of his sweats and grips his cock.

'Let me see you,' I demand breathily.

'Take your bra off,' he bites out, eyes blazing.

I glance at the door. 'What if someone walks in?'

'I guess that's a risk we'll just have to take.' He shrugs casually, but there's nothing casual about the set of his jaw, the throbbing in his throat, or the way his breath comes in ragged bursts. 'Unhook that bra, baby, please. I've been dying to see your perfect tits from the second you walked onto that stage at the Luxor Lounge.' He drags his feet from the desk, plants them on the floor and straightens himself in the chair.

His uninhibited desire sets my core clenching. I want to show him. I want to give him everything he wants, I'm just not sure I'm ready to give him *everything* right now.

But I can give him this.

My fingers fiddle with the clasp until it pops open and my breasts burst free. My nipples immediately stand to attention. Silently begging for his touch.

He licks his lips. 'My god, you're so fucking beautiful. On the desk.' He nods for me to perch on the edge of it. 'Spread those legs. Let me see you.'

This is so fucking hot.

He's so fucking hot.

The fact that any of the staff could walk in is so fucking hot.

'You can look,' I tell him with more confidence than I feel. 'But you can't touch, okay?' I back up to the desk until the solid wood hits the backs of my thighs. I'm going to draw this out. Drive him demented with desire, the way he does to me.

'Fine. I won't touch you, if that's what you want. But I'm telling you now, Scarlett, before you leave this office, you'll be begging me to touch you, lick you, or fuck you.'

My skin simmers with heat as his huge hands grip my waist, hoisting me up onto the desk. Our eyes lock and he tears his hands away and raises his upturned palms in the air in surrender. I sit back and part my thighs slightly.

'Wider,' he commands. 'Show me how wet that pretty pussy is for me.' My thighs part and his head dips closer until his face is inches from my sex. His breath brushes over me and every single hair on my body pricks to attention. Every single cell begs to be touched. 'Move the lingerie to the side, or I will. But if my fingers get anywhere near your pussy again, it will take the entire fucking army to drag me away.'

I reach for the lace and pull it to the side, exposing myself to him. He hisses again. 'Fuck, Scarlett, even the sight of you turns my world upside down.' A pained look pinches his face.

'Your turn. I want to see what's mine.' *Mine.* That word feels so good rolling from my tongue.

Something like approval flits across his features. His hand jerks his cock free and oh my fucking god, it's enormous. My jaw falls open as I take in the length, the sheer thickness, the slick, shiny tip, glinting with precum. Every furious vein commands my attention.

I watch entranced as he grips himself and pumps. My eyes roll upwards, imagining what it would feel like to touch him, to take him.

I want him so badly.

My eyes flutter closed as lust rages against logic in my head.

'Want to play a game?' he whispers.

'What sort of a game?'

'One where we both get to come so hard we see stars.' Those huge pupils pin me in a promising stare. I squirm on the desk, searching for friction.

'How do we play?' My voice is thick with want.

'You can either play with yourself, if you really don't want me to touch you again. Or we can play with each other.' He shifts closer, dragging the chair with him beneath his backside, his sweats sitting beneath his cock.

I drink him in. 'I don't know how to play with you,' I admit, sinking my teeth into my lower lip.

'Oh, sweetheart, I'll teach you everything you'll ever need to know.' His fingers whiten as they tighten around his length. 'How about some of that tuition we discussed?'

I shouldn't.

We shouldn't.

But fighting this attraction between us is like fighting a bushfire with a watering can.

Like a disease, James Beckett has crawled beneath my skin and conquered every cell in my body. Every waking minute is consumed with thoughts of him. Of this.

'Teach me.' Those two words will either kill me or cure me.

'With pleasure. But first, you need to know the rules of the game.' His eyes blaze as his hand pumps again.

'Go on...'

'There's really only one rule.' His expression is solemn. 'Ladies first. Always.'

James yanks his hand out of his sweats and presses his palms against my inner thighs, spreading them, until I'm practically doing the splits again. He manoeuvres the chair so he's sitting between them with a first row seat to what I'm certain is about to be the utter undoing of me.

'We're going to take this slowly.' His fingers inch higher. 'I'm not going to teach you to fuck until you're ready. But I will teach you what your body was made for.'

Oh my god, this is so hot I could actually spontaneously burst into flames. 'Shall I call you "sir"?'

'You can call me anything you like, sweetheart, as long as I get to worship you.

Today's lesson is what I call "hands on". As much as I

want to bury my tongue in you, that will have to wait until our next lesson. It's important to ascertain a firm grip of the basics.'

'Didn't we cover the basics in the nightclub?'

'Greedy girl. So impatient.' He bends forwards and nips my inner thigh with his teeth. 'That was rushed. I want to savour it this time.'

With one swift tug, he tears the lace panties from me, leaving me bare for him. 'So pretty,' he murmurs, eyes darting from between my legs to my breasts.

'And that's taking it slowly?' My nipples are like bullets begging to be touched. As if he can read my mind, his lips graze over my stomach and inch higher. His tongue darts out to swirl around my nipple before capturing it in his mouth and sucking hard enough to make me scream.

His laugh reverberates around my breast. 'Shh, or Tim will come rushing in here to save you.'

Save me?

'Would you like that?' James angles his face up, teasing my nipples with his tongue. 'Naughty girl. I bet you would. You'd like him to see you up here, with me between your legs, sucking your tits and playing with your tight little cunt.'

A moan slips from my lips and my fingers dig into the desk. It's not about Tim, and James knows that. It's about being seen. Yep, I'm officially an exhibitionist.

'So wet for me, sweetheart.' His knuckles glide across either side of my clit and a million volts of electricity shoot through me. 'I've been thinking about your wet pussy all damn week.'

His fingers slide lower, playing with my entrance as his thumb takes over a relentless assault on my clit. I reach for his shoulders, fingers digging into his flesh through his vest.

'Good girl,' he purrs. 'You're already acing this class. You're a natural.'

The sight of his hand between my legs is the most erotic thing I've ever seen. I can't wait to see what his head looks like down there, because we both know it's inevitable.

My legs shake, my thighs tighten. I'm physically trembling with every touch.

His left hand skates up my body, pinching and rolling my nipples, whilst his right hand continues to devastate the sensitive spot between my legs. He watches on with fascination as he drives me closer to the edge.

'Come for me, angel.' He slides two fingers deep into my core and pumps. White hot lust lances every single cell in my body as wave after wave of pleasure destroys me in the most decadent way.

This might only be my first official lesson, but I've already learnt that however many times James does this to me, it will never be enough.

Chapter Thirty
JAMES

Watching Scarlett come undone at my hands is the most hedonistic experience of my life. Her core tightens and pulses around my fingers and those shockingly silver eyes glaze with lust as her fingernails dig into my shoulders hard enough to draw blood.

'Such a good girl,' I repeat, sliding my fingers from her and bringing them to my mouth. Her eyes flare as I wrap my lips around them and suck. She tastes like heaven. My sweet girl is definitely an angel, even in those sheer fuck-me stockings and six-inch court shoes. 'You taste so fucking good, Scarlett. If I thought you were ready, I'd clean you up with my tongue until you make a mess again, but for now, let me get you something.'

She sits, legs spread as I reluctantly scoot back in the chair in search of a wad of soft tissues. 'You look incredible.' My throbbing cock is a testament to it. 'I'd keep you on my desk permanently but I'd never get any work done.'

I grab the tissues and glide back over to her, gently cleaning between her legs. 'The right job would be a bath.' I glance at the clock on the wall by the door. It's almost five o'clock, the end of the working day for most people, especially on a Friday. Not for me. I was supposed to be on a call with the company's director of finance fifteen minutes ago, but I don't regret missing that meeting. I'll call Chantel and ask her to tell him something came up.

Literally.

'Give me two minutes, and I'll go up and run the jacuzzi.'

Scarlett's gaze falls to my crotch again. 'Are you coming in with me?' There's a hint of mischief in her tone. 'Because this lesson is far from over. Teach me how to touch you.'

The earnest expression etched on her face twists something in my chest. Not to mention my cock is weeping for her and my balls are blue, but I don't want to put too much on her in one day.

'As much as I'd love to feel your hands around my cock, it's not necessary. I told you, Scarlett, while you're mine, I'll take care of you.'

'And while you're mine, I want to take care of you, too.' There's a defiance in her eyes. 'I'll run the bath. Come up when you finish in here.' She slides off my desk and wiggles her hips back into her dress. The door clicks closed and I'm alone again.

I fire off a quick email to Chantel, asking her to put off the meeting until Monday. It's easier than calling her and having to answer five thousand questions she would undoubtedly throw at me. I never cancel meetings. Ever.

Scarlett's ripped lingerie lies at my feet. I snatch it up, fingering the flimsy material. What is it about this woman that has me driven so fucking demented with lust? Is it because she's a virgin?

No, it's her. The way she's so cautious, yet so trusting.

Vulnerable in some ways, yet so certain in others. Agreeable but defiant. There's a depth beneath those platinum eyes that I've barely scratched the surface of, yet when her pupils morphed with her irises and she came hard on my hand, I swear I glimpsed into her soul.

And it was fucking beautiful.

Two minutes later, I dart out into the corridor. All the decadent things I want to do to Scarlett have me propelling towards the staircase faster than Usain Bolt.

Tim is carrying Scarlett's schoolbag upstairs. She must have left it in the hall. Schoolbag. Fuck. How awful does that sound? College bag doesn't have quite the same ring to it.

For a split second, guilt flickers in my chest. A ten-year age gap isn't a lot. Especially if I ignore the fact she's closer in age to my baby sister than she is to me. She's also someone's daughter. Someone's friend.

'But she's yours now,' my inner devil whispers.

I'll take care of her.

I'll be good to her.

And when this arrangement between us is over, I'll make sure she's set up for life. She deserves that. And not because I want to fuck her, but because she's one of the most decent women I've known, which has been abundantly obvious from the first time we met.

Tim glances around at the sound of my footsteps. His eyes flicker with knowing. 'Did you manage to appease Miss Fitzgerald?'

It's a battle to fight the upwards pull of my lips. 'I believe I did.' And I hope to again.

'Good.' At the top of the stairs, he heads towards the bedrooms while I veer towards the main bathroom, following the sound of cascading water.

I nudge open the door. Huge sash windows overlook a sprawling emerald expanse outside stretching all the way to the Irish Sea, while the sun is setting over the water, casting hues of pink and gold across the twilight sky.

Scarlett bends over the clawfoot jacuzzi tub, swirling her

hand in the water, checking the temperature. Her slim frame inclines over the side, causing her dress to hitch up, giving me a glimpse of flesh between the top of the lace hold-ups and the hem of her dress. The sight alone could bring me to my knees.

'How long is this arrangement for again?' I ask, tracing a finger across the top of her stocking.

'Until you get your deal done and I graduate.' She turns slowly, her teeth digging into her bottom lip.

'You know, I might need you to hang around for the next acquisition as well, just in case.' My lips brush over hers and electricity short circuits between us.

Where the fuck did that come from?

'Sorry, James. There's an entire world out there and I'm determined to see it.'

Ouch. We both know there's an expiry date on this thing, but when she says it like that, it's like a kick to the crotch.

But that's the arrangement—until graduation. What did I expect?

Her hands reach for the hem of her dress. She tugs it up and over her head, exposing inch after inch of taut olive skin. It's only been minutes since I last laid eyes on it, but it feels like a lifetime ago.

'I could look at you all day long.' I cup her pussy and she moans. 'As much as I love the stockings, I want to see you naked.'

'What about what I want?' she whispers breathily. Wild eyes roam over my torso and lower.

'What do you want?' I growl.

'I want to see you. I want to touch you. And I want to drive you over the edge.'

I don't say that she already has. That I'm cancelling meetings to prioritise making her come.

I tear off my top, kick off my sweatpants, and slide my

underwear down my thighs while she watches on, transfixed. 'Get in the tub.'

She sheds her shoes and stockings and climbs in, giving me a decadent view in the process. I step in beside her, sinking to the ledge seat beneath the bubbles. The tub is big enough for eight, but even eight inches between us is too much.

I turn off the taps and reach for her, my palms settling on either hip. She's weightless beneath the water as I pull her onto my thighs, facing me. Her knees rest on either side of my waist. She's far enough back from my cock that it doesn't touch her. But fuck, does it want to.

Her chestnut brown hair cascades over her shoulders, the ends grazing the top of her perfect tits. She's like a goddamn goddess on my lap.

She grinds herself against my thighs as the steam swirls between us.

'You're a natural, Scarlett. Sensuality oozes from you.' I rest my head against one of the bath's cushioned headrests and skim my hands over her hips, and upwards, until I'm cupping her breasts and rolling those twin peaks between my fingers.

She tuts and swats my hand away. 'This is supposed to be about you, remember?' Her hands reach for my cock beneath the water. Her grip is tentative at first, shy almost. I place a hand over hers, moving her to where I want her and squeezing. Every nerve ending in my body ignites. Keeping my hand over hers, I guide her into a languid rhythm.

Her features knit into an expression of sheer concentration which only makes her more fucking alluring. 'Is that okay?' she asks as she pumps my length.

'It's more than okay, sweetheart. It's fucking perfect.' I raise my hips and lift my cock out of the water so she can see exactly what she's doing to me.

'You're huge.' Her eyes are wider than dinner plates. She watches transfixed as precum leaks from my tip. The sight of her balancing on my thighs, working my cock so perfectly with her dainty hands, sets the pressure building in my balls.

'You're so good at that. I'm so close to coming all over your hands,' I warn her in a gritty tone. My muscles are tight from holding back with everything I've got.

Fire blazes over every inch of my skin and I'm teetering on the edge of oblivion. She arches higher over me, so her breasts are just inches above my cock and her hands. 'Come for me,' she whispers like a plea or a prayer, and I'm gone, spiralling over the edge.

An animalistic moan rumbles from my ribcage. My hips jerk upwards. Cum propels all over her breasts and her stomach. It's the most stunning sight I've ever seen.

A grin of sheer pleasure splits her lips. Her hand travels to her breasts as she dips a finger in the sticky liquid clinging to her skin. When she brings it to her mouth and licks, I realise I might just be looking at my future wife.

Which is fucking terrifying, considering up until roughly ten seconds ago, the thought of tying myself to someone forever isn't one I've ever been comfortable with.

Chapter Thirty-One
SCARLETT

After our impromptu hot tub shenanigans, I expected James to disappear back into his office. Instead, to my surprise, he orders sushi takeout and insists Rosa and Tim join us in the dining room. It almost feels like a double date.

'You made friends, then?' Rosa's gaze bounces between James and me as she loads up Tim's plate with a pile of sashimi. Even when she's not working, she can't seem to help serving others.

'You could say that.' James sniggers, his hand reaching for mine beneath the table and squeezing it tightly. Heat suffuses my skin.

'I'm still not happy about the pole situation.' I try to scowl, but no matter how hard I force my features, they won't obey. A carefree beam rules in its place instead.

I'm happy.

Being with James brings me so much happiness.

The way his thumb brushes over my wrist brings me happiness.

The way his eyes continuously stray to mine brings me happiness.

'You must be tired?' James says, as Rosa gets up to clear the dishes away.

'Not too tired.' Desire spikes inside my soul again but it must radiate from me like a beacon.

He chuckles, and leans into my ear. 'Oh no, lady. Don't give me those come-to-bed-eyes.'

'Why not? Are you tired, old man?' I goad.

'Not especially, but I skipped work this afternoon in order to make you come, and I need to go to my desk for another hour or so before bed.'

I pout. 'I could wait up for you?'

'Get some sleep, princess, you'll need it for tomorrow.' He stands, places a tender kiss on my forehead and excuses himself, striding across the room towards the door.

I swallow my disappointment.

Our relationship is pretend. But with every passing day, it's beginning to feel very real. Does he feel it too?

I watch as he strides towards the door, a heavy sense of longing curls in my core. As if he feels it, he pauses, his fingers resting on the door handle. He turns slowly, and shoots me a wide smile.

'Laters, baby,' he mouths and suddenly I'm grinning like a schoolgirl again.

The next morning, I'm sipping my second cup of coffee in the sitting room, when I hear his footsteps approaching from along the hallway.

I hold my breath, waiting to see if he'll come and find me. Three seconds later, he sticks his head around the door.

'Good morning.' His eyes roam over my outfit, a cashmere jumper dress and tan leather knee-high boots, selected this morning with him in mind.

'Morning.' He looks utterly edible in a Ralph Lauren polo shirt and navy slacks.

'Coffee?' I glance at the pot Rosa has left on the table at my side.

He hesitates for a second, then strides in. 'I was due to meet Caelon twenty minutes ago, but what's twenty more?' He shrugs, crosses the room and drops a kiss on my lips. My stomach somersaults.

Yep, definitely feeling less pretend by the day.

I bite back a grin, top up my coffee cup and hand it to him.

His eyes land on mine as he places his lips to the lipstick mark around the rim and drinks.

'What are you and Caelon up to?'

'Going to look at an old manor house in County Meath. Caelon thinks it has potential. He's looking to expand his chain of boutique hotels.' Frown lines indent James's forehead. 'It's going to take up most of my day, by the time we get there and have a look around.'

'And you resent having to do that on a Saturday?' I glance at him quizzically.

The man is a workaholic, so I wouldn't have thought he'd have minded a Saturday business trip if it meant expanding the Beckett empire.

'I don't usually.' His eyes flash to the bare skin between the junction of my boots and the hem of my dress. 'But I'd far rather spend the day here with you.' Warmth spreads through my chest. 'At least we have tonight,' he says, pushing the cup back towards me.

'Where are we going?' I place my lips on the crimson stain again and sip.

'Dinner. You'll love it, I promise.' He prises the cup from my hands and drinks again.

Who knew sharing a coffee could be so intimate?

I spend the day working on my dissertation. James returns home around four o'clock. His voice floats from the hallway up the stairs.

'Matteo, make it special. I want to spoil her,' he says.

Excitement zings up my spine.

I have no idea who Matteo is but if it's me he wants to spoil, I am here for it. Here for a good time, not for a long time. Avery's carefree attitude might finally be rubbing off on me.

I fling open the walk-in wardrobe, musing over my killer collection of dresses, before settling on an Alexander McQueen bow-embellished midi in a shade of ice blue. Martha, from the boutique, swore it emphasised my eyes. Given the slit up the left side that ends almost indecently, I'm pretty sure James isn't going to be interested in my eyes.

I have no idea where we're going, but given we're supposed to be putting on a convincing show of our whirlwind romance, I'm guessing it'll be somewhere very public.

I'm adding the finishing touches to my makeup when my phone pings.

Avery.

> Drinks for your birthday next weekend?
> Dying to hear how it's going with Ireland's most eligible billionaire.

I bet she is.

. . .

I don't normally celebrate my birthday. It's never been the same since my mother passed, but Avery always insists we mark it.

> Can we do lunch instead? We have a charity ball next weekend.

Three dots appear instantly.

> Lunch it is then, Cinderella! A ball sounds fancy! Remember, if you lose your shoe at midnight, you're drunk. The real question is, will you lose your panties?

An evil laugh splutters from my chest.

> Who says I haven't already?

> DETAILS!!!

> Soon.

> I'm ALL for kinky fun with the billionaire, but be careful, babes! Whatever you do, don't fall in love with him. A man like that will break your heart as fast as look at you. He's so hot he's on fire.

I know better than anyone what happens when you play with fire. You get burnt. Yet I can't seem to stay away. I force away the negativity threatening like a black cloud over my head. I'm going out with my fake boyfriend with benefits, and I'm determined to enjoy it.

Chapter Thirty-Two
SCARLETT

A knock sounds at my door. I slide on a pair of Jimmy Choo silver patent stilettos and strut across the room to answer it. James is standing outside, wearing a navy tailored suit paired with a crisp, white slim-fitting shirt which clings to his torso and leaves nothing to the imagination.

A flashback of yesterday in the jacuzzi sets a hundred hummingbirds fluttering in my chest.

'You look positively edible.' He presses a tender kiss to my cheek and steps backwards into the hallway. 'Are you ready?'

'As I'll ever be.' I grab the matching clutch from my bed and spray two more squirts of the perfume on my wrists.

I assumed Tim was waiting outside, but when we step out into the crisp, cold night, a graphite grey Ferrari waits for us.

James slips his hand into mine and guides me to the passenger side. My mouth opens. Then closes again. 'This is stunning.'

'I'm glad you approve.' He opens the door for me and ushers me in. 'I ordered it when I was away a couple of weeks ago,' he announces breezily, like it's a new tie, not one of the fanciest sports cars around.

That unique, new-car scent of leather and luxury invades my lungs as I watch him strut around to the driver's side.

'I love the colour,' I say, admiring the gleaming paint in the passenger wing mirror as he starts it up.

He chuckles. 'It reminded me of your eyes.'

My head spins to the side. I can't tell if he's joking or not. Either way, the man clearly has more money than sense, but I can't help but smile anyway.

'Can you drive?'

'Sort of.' I tilt my head to study his profile. A small smile plays on his lips. 'Don't even think about making a women driver joke.'

'I wouldn't dream of it,' he laughs, and I know I hit the nail on the head.

'I started lessons before...' I trail off. 'But I didn't finish them.'

'I'll teach you, if you like.' He takes my hand in his and plants a kiss on the back of it.

'Haven't you agreed to teach me enough already?' I smirk.

'I don't think I'll ever tire of teaching you, Scarlett.' A serious expression flashes over his face.

'Where are we going?' I gaze through the window at the lantern-lined driveway.

'Somewhere you'll like, I promise.' He puts my hand back on my thigh, stroking it gently before his hands return to the steering wheel.

Fifteen minutes later, we park outside a small restaurant overlooking the beach. Waves crash against the shore in the distance. A hint of spring lingers in the air along with the briny scent of seaweed.

The restaurant doesn't look like much from the outside. As we step through the arched doorway, I realise James has stumbled upon a hidden gem. There are ten tables, each decked with a red tablecloth and a small vase with a single rose. Only one of them is set. There's no one else here. Did he hire the entire restaurant?

I expected something bigger, bolder, fancier.

But quaint, private, and personal is so much more intimate.

'Ah, Mr Beckett.' An older man in a tuxedo approaches us. 'So good to see you again,' he purrs in an authentic Italian accent.

Italian is my favourite.

A coincidence? Or is it possible Ireland's most eligible bachelor is ridiculously considerate as well as hot?

The smile playing on his lips suggests the latter.

'Thank you, Matteo. It's great to be back.' James slaps the waiter's back like he's an old friend.

Matteo.

'You brought a friend, finally.' The waiter winks at me.

'This is my girlfriend, Scarlett.' James places his palm on the small of my back as Matteo pulls the chairs out from the table for us to sit.

'Girlfriend?' The surprise is evident in every line of his weathered face. 'I think this calls for champagne.' Matteo rubs his hands together.

My stomach flips.

It's just for show. It's not real. But damn, does that word sound good falling from James's tongue.

Almost as good as, 'you're mine.'

'Actually, do you have any of the Masseto?' James thumbs open the wine menu and indicates a bottle that costs a thousand euro.

'Absolutely.' Matteo nods and swivels on his heels to fetch it.

Jesus, this place may be small and quaint but it's something else.

'There's no need for that,' I whisper.

'Trust me, there is.' James winks. 'And you thought Juliana's was the best Italian in Dublin? Wait until you taste Matteo's wife's cooking.'

James isn't wrong.

We devour course after course of practically every dish on the menu; truffle tagliani, saffron and gold leaf pasta, lobster ravioli. And the wagyu beef blows the one we had at Juliana's out of the water.

'How was your day?' James asks between mouthfuls.

'Productive. I managed to write another two thousand words of my dissertation.' I help myself to another spoonful of pasta.

'That's fantastic.' James's foot catches mine beneath the table. 'I wasn't joking about helping with your studies, if you need me.'

Oh, I need him alright, just not for those type of studies.

Our eyes connect across the table, chemistry crackling between us. 'Dirty girl,' he says with the uncanny talent of a mind reader.

'What can I say?' I shrug. 'If I'd have known how good it could be, I would have done it years ago.'

A low growl rumbles from his chest. 'Careful, sweetheart, or I'll put you over my knee.'

'You wouldn't dare.'

'Try me.' He arches a single eyebrow. 'Do you think any of those college boys are capable of making you come like I do?'

I pick up my wine glass. 'Probably not.'

'There's no probably about it, Scarlett.' He inches closer over the table. 'An attraction like ours is rare.'

'I believe you.' Heat swamps my cheeks.

His eyes twinkle. 'Had many crushes, have you?'

'There was this one guy I used to ogle in the tabloids.' I shrug. 'I used to stare at his picture and wonder what it'd be like to kiss him.'

James glowers. 'What was his name?'

I tilt my head. 'Seriously?'

His eyes light. 'Me?'

'You must have seen the articles printed about you. I used to stare at your picture in the paper and imagine what it would be like to kiss you.'

His pupils meld into his irises in a pool of dark promise. 'And now you know.' He runs a thoughtful thumb over his jawline. 'Did it live up to your expectations?'

'It was okay, I guess.' I tease.

A small scoff catches in his throat. 'Only okay?'

'Oh, alright, it was,' I pause, trying to summon the right word. 'It was...memorable.'

'Memorable,' he repeats with a smug smile. 'I can live with that.'

'Oh, come on! Half the country has a crush on you. And the other half are men. It was always going to be hot as fuck.'

'Maybe, maybe not.' A look of indifference flashes across his face. 'But I don't care about what half the country thinks. I only care about you.' He catches my hand over the table. 'Tell me, Scarlett, did you used to imagine more than just kissing me? Did you ever think of me and touch yourself?'

I press my thighs together. 'Maybe, maybe not.' I mimic his words.

'You did.' Triumph taints his tone. 'When we get home, I want you to show me exactly what you did while you were thinking about me,' he smoulders.

A tingling sensation stirs in my panties. There's something so hedonistic about hogging his attention.

'Only if you show me how you "fucked your fist twice in the shower" thinking about me.'

'Deal.' James's lips curve, revealing a flash of white.

'Perhaps then we can move on to the next lesson? I could probably squeeze in some dessert.' The memory of his seed dripping over my stomach sets my mouth flooding with saliva. I can't wait to take his big beautiful dick into it.

Laughter rumbles in his chest. 'Ever heard the saying "you need to walk before you run"?'

A pang of vulnerability strikes my chest. 'Did I do okay yesterday?'

'Oh, sweetheart, you were perfect.' His thumb tenderly strokes the pulse point on my wrist.

'You're probably used to much more experienced women.' I hold his gaze, even as I wince internally.

'Scarlett, what we did in my office and in the tub was the hottest thing I've ever done. Teaching you to enjoy your body is the most fun I've had in my life.'

'You're a great teacher.' I swallow thickly at the memory.

'Is my greedy girl horny again?' The heat of his eyes scorches my skin. There it is again. *My girl.* It sounds so real rolling from his tongue.

'What can I say? I'm making up for lost time.' It's my turn to shrug. 'You know, I really am a fast learner, if you do want to move on to the next lesson.'

His laughter floods the space between us. 'You've waited this long. What's the rush now?'

'You.' I blurt with a blush. 'I want you.' Really, it's more like a need at this stage.

'And you will have me,' he promises, 'when you're ready.'

'Why did you bring me here?'

'I wanted to spend some time with my girlfriend.'

That doesn't explain why he went to the trouble of hiring an entire restaurant specialising in my favourite cuisine.

'Come on. It's just us here.' I don't know why I'm whispering. 'We both know this is supposed to be business, whatever pleasure we throw in on top of our arrangement.' Which is why I can't understand why we aren't eating somewhere more public.

'I've never finger fucked a business partner before.' Twin fires pin me in a stare.

'And I've never been finger fucked by a teacher before.' I hold his gaze, revelling in the desire blazing in his molten eyes.

'I should hope not. But if you keep that filthy talk up, you will be again.'

'Is that a promise?' I inhale a ragged breath.

'Yes,' he grits out.

I glance around the restaurant, still looking for answers. 'But why go to all this trouble?'

'Because I want to make you happy.'

His simple admission might just be the nicest thing anyone has ever said to me.

Chapter Thirty-Three
JAMES

'Let's walk the beach,' she begs, pulling me towards the sound of crashing waves instead of towards the car.

'I thought you were horny?' I slap her ass and she squeals.

'I am, but it's been years since I walked the beach. Indulge me, please!' She links her arm through mine and nudges my ribs.

The simple pleasure she takes in the little things is so refreshing. She's so refreshing.

It's only been a few weeks but already I'm dreading the end of our arrangement. Unfortunately, like all good things, it will have to come to an end.

Scarlett's made it clear she wants to travel the world, but my life is here. I can't leave. Not with the business to run. I jokingly asked her to stay until the next acquisition and she shot me down without hesitation. Which is why I have to make the most of now.

We stroll the pavement until we find a small set of steps leading to the sand. The wind whips Scarlett's hair across her face. I reach forwards to tuck it behind her ear. She stares up at me with those doe-like eyes and something hot and tight squeezes my chest.

'Thank you for tonight.' She beams.

'Thank *you*.' I inch forwards to drop a quick kiss on her lips but I can't seem to drag myself away. My tongue invades her mouth, tasting, teasing and tickling her tongue. Her hands reach round to the nape on my neck, tugging me into her. If I get any closer, I'll consume her entirely.

Though truthfully, she's the one consuming me.

Consuming my every waking thought and invading every dream.

It would have been so easy to creep into her bed last night when I finally finished up in my office. But it was far safer to go to mine.

I might be one of the wealthiest men in the country, but the one thing I can't afford is to catch feelings for her. And sharing her bed, holding her while she slept, waking up to those huge piercing eyes, would take everything to another level. A level that's too high and too dangerous to even contemplate. Because if I fall from a height of that magnitude, it's going to hurt like hell. And I promised myself I'd never put myself in that position again.

Though truthfully, I'm already in trouble.

Because I'm supposed to be parading this woman around Dublin to convince everyone I'm finally settling down and mending my ways, but all I want to do is keep her to myself. Monopolise every minute we have together. I have to go away again next week. Sean is working on a deal to acquire a large plot of land in Switzerland and Caelon's working on the purchase of a hotel in Monaco. Both of them are insistent we have to leave immediately before someone else snaps up the opportunities.

The only opportunity I want is to spend more time with the woman I'm afraid I'm falling for.

It fucking terrifies me.

Her fingers rake through my hair and over my scalp. It feels so natural. So real. I tear my lips from hers. 'Scarlett, we need to go home now, or else it won't just be you who gets to witness the re-enactment of the shower scenario.'

Her tinkling laughter fills the air between us, and seeps under my skin, straight to the heart I forgot I owned.

'Come on then. It's probably past your bedtime anyway,' she teases.

'I guarantee, you'll be tired before I am.' I slip an arm around her shoulder and guide her back towards the car.

The house is silent when we arrive home. Tim, Rosa and the others must have gone to bed. Scarlett tugs at my hand, pulling me towards the stairs but I refuse to budge.

'Come to bed,' she beckons impatiently.

'Who said anything about bed?' I glance towards the games room. 'Let's go play.'

Realisation dawns on Scarlett's face. 'What if someone walks in?'

'Don't pretend that's not half the fun.' My hand cups the curve of her ass cheek and she moans.

'I suppose you're the boss.' She swivels in the direction of the games' room door.

'We both know that's not true.' I drink in her slender waist and the jut of her hips. 'You hold all the power here, Scarlett. You just don't know it.'

'And what power might that be exactly?' Her voice cracks as she takes a step towards me, closing the distance between us.

'The power to turn me into a man I barely recognise,' I grit out with an honesty that even I hadn't anticipated sharing.

'Well, if it's any consolation,' she sweeps a hand between us, 'this is pretty new to me, too.' I hear her swallow. 'I find myself constantly clock-watching, waiting for you to come home, and spending every hour in between imagining what I'd like to do when you arrive.'

'Ditto.' There's a wistfulness edge to my tone. 'Now, what are we waiting for?'

Our lips collide as the door crashes against the wall behind us. I guide Scarlett to the full-sized snooker table in the centre of the room, lifting her ass onto it without breaking our kiss. Her mouth devours mine like a ravenous wild animal. Her hands tug my shirt free and slide beneath it, palming the planes of my torso with an appreciative moan.

I part her legs, nudge my hips between them and slide her dress up until it's bunched around her waist. She inches her ass closer to the edge until we're dry humping like naughty teenagers. It strikes me then, that's one of the things I lov– like about her. She makes me feel young again. Playful. Her enthusiasm is infectious.

She yanks her mouth from mine. 'Maybe we could skip ahead in the lessons?'

Laughter lurches in my throat. 'No way, baby. As much as I'd love to feel your tight walls clenching my cock, I'm enjoying this way too much to rush it.' I slide a hand up her silky thighs until my fingers meet lace, then yank it off with one swift tug. She gasps as I slide her lingerie into my pocket to add to my collection.

God knows, I'll need something to keep me going while I'm away from her.

'You promised to show me how you touch yourself, so show me.' My hands slide along the smooth curves of her calves and I encircle her ankles. I lift them until her heels rest on the edge of the table and her knees fall wide open. Her pretty pussy is already glistening for me but her oval eyes are a blend of arousal and uncertainty.

'Show me, Scarlett, please.' My voice breaks with a raw need.

She rocks back on her ass cheeks and her hand drops between her legs, her eyes locked on me as I watch. She slides her fingers either side of that rosy little bud and moans. 'Is this what you want?' she asks breathily.

'Yes,' I hiss, entranced as her fingers continue stroking. 'How does it feel?'

'So good.' It's barely more than a whisper.

'Better than my fingers?' My cock is straining so hard in my pants my zipper is in serious danger of splitting open.

'It's a tough call.' Her teeth dig into that plump juicy lower lip. 'I'd need a reminder to be certain.'

'I bet you do.' As I sink a finger into her soft slick centre, her hips jolt and her back arches in pleasure. I pump her slowly as she moans, her fingers circling her clit slowly and rhythmically.

Her arousal drips from her. 'Greedy girl. One hand isn't nearly enough for you. You're soaked for me.'

'Always,' she hisses, her eyes glazing with lust. 'Take your cock out. Let me watch you.'

I yank down my zip with my left hand while my right continues to work her. I couldn't take my fingers from her if she begged me to.

Freeing my cock, I wrap my hand around it and pump. 'Look, Scarlett. Look what you do to me.'

Her eyes fall to my crotch and she hisses her approval. 'I need to feel you inside me.'

'You will, sweetheart, you will. Soon.' Though God help us both, because when I eventually do sink into her, I've got a feeling she's going to take so much more than just my body. And I'm not sure either of us is ready for that.

Her thighs clench and her head rolls backwards. My tongue is all over her skin, licking from her collarbones to the sensitive spot behind her ears. Goosebumps rip across her skin as we both battle to prolong this for as long as possible.

'I'm so close,' she whimpers, sinking her teeth into my neck.

'Come for me, baby.' I straighten my spine, watching as she shatters and shudders, teetering on the edge of oblivion.

'Come with me,' she begs, her gaze falling to my throbbing cock.

Her core clenches on my fingers in a vice-like grip as she shatters on my hand, and when she cries out my name I follow suit, spiralling into my own earth-shattering release.

She buries her face in my chest, nuzzling into me, and inhaling deeply. 'We made a mess.' She eyes the spot on her thigh where the proof of my pleasure soaks her skin.

'It was worth it.' I slide my fingers out of her centre and clean them with my tongue.

Her finger swipes across her thighs and she brings it to her mouth.

Yep, definite marriage material.

I am royally fucked.

Because while I think she's wife material, my father will never agree, not if he were to discover the truth about Scarlett's pole dancing past, at least.

'Will you come to bed with me?' The earnest vulnerability in Scarlett's tone cracks my chest wide open. 'Just for a cuddle. I promise I won't try to jump on you in the night.'

I hope I can promise the same thing. Drawing this out is getting harder with every passing second.

'Please.' Beneath that sassy exterior there's that flash of fragility again.

I couldn't refuse her if I wanted to. And the most

worrying part of all is I don't want to. This agreement was supposed to be business, but so far it's only been pleasure.

'Come on, then.' I lift her gently off the table. 'But no funny business.'

'Says the man with his trousers round his ankles and his cock in his hand.' She barely stifles her laugh. 'My room or yours?'

'Yours.' Because if I let her into my bed, I may never let her out of it.

Fooling around with my fake girlfriend was always part of my plan.

Falling for her wasn't.

Chapter Thirty-Four
SCARLETT

James is away for most of the week on business with Sean and Caelon, which is super productive for my college dissertation, and not so productive for my other "education".

Now I've had a taste of it, of him, all I can think about is more. Waking up with him on Sunday morning was the single most transcendent experience of my life, and that's saying a lot, given the fun we had in the games room the night before. And the shower that morning, too.

I'm torn between loving the way he's dragging these lessons out and loathing it. I never considered myself impatient until now, but James is like an itch I can't quite scratch. My skin pricks with a yearning I never knew existed.

I lie awake until the small hours of the morning staring at my phone, alternating between re-reading his flirtatious texts and stalking him online.

I've got it bad.

I thought I was obsessed before, but now I know what he's capable of, now I know how my name sounds on his lips when he comes, how his lips taste as they meld with mine, it's all I can think about.

When Friday finally dawns, bright and sunny, I fling back the covers and leap out of bed.

A text pings in on my phone.

Avery.

> Happy birthday babe. Hope the billionaire bought you something nice. Are we still on for lunch tomorrow?

Pah! He doesn't even know it's my birthday. The only present I want is for him to come home. This weekend is the charity ball. Hopefully afterwards we'll progress on to the next "lesson".

I fire off a quick text to Avery then bound down to the breakfast room. Rosa is well used to the sight of my tousled morning hair and cami pyjamas by now.

But she's not the source of the rustling papers I can hear. When I open the door, I see James. And he's wearing those damn grey sweats again.

It's all I can do not to throw myself at him.

His head whips up, the smile on his face crinkles the corner of his eyes. 'Good morning, angel.' He folds a newspaper and tosses it on the table.

I can't help it. I run to him. He rises, catching me in his arms as I wrap my legs around his waist. 'I wasn't expecting you back until way later,' I squeal.

He leans back to look me in the eye. 'You didn't seriously think I'd miss your birthday?'

'How did you know?'

'Never mind. Did you really think you could keep it from me?'

Rosa bustles in bearing a tray of coffee and sweet-scented pastries. She's wearing a grey trouser suit and a grin the size of the sun. Reluctantly, I slide down James's body and slip into the seat beside him.

Rosa hands me a plate of warm buttery croissants. Happy birthday is written in what looks like chocolate sauce and heart-shaped strawberries dot the edge of the plate.

'Thank you.' My eyes well with tears at the thoughtfulness of it.

'Happy birthday.' James presses a kiss to my temple.

'I got you a present,' he singsongs.

I wait until Rosa leaves the room before answering. 'The only thing I want is what's beneath those sweat pants.' My gaze falls to his crotch and he chuckles.

'Dirty girl. Did you miss me?' James's dark eyes flicker.

'Maybe.' I glance down at my tiny cotton shorts and matching cami top. If I'd have known he was home I'd have made a bit more effort.

'Only maybe?' he says, as I reach across the table towards the croissants. Deft fingers snap around my wrists, halting me. 'I missed you. Worryingly.'

A million hummingbirds soar in my stomach. 'Why is it worrying?'

'Because it's distracting. I'm not used to being... distracted.' Our eyes lock and something shifts in the air between us.

He slides a hand inside the pocket of his sweats and plucks out a tiny velvet box. My lips pop open as I stare at it.

His laughter echoes around the room. 'Don't worry, it's not...' He trails off.

Of course it's not. I feel ridiculous for even entertaining the idea that it could be a ring.

'Though if I thought you'd say yes, maybe I would have picked differently.' Amusement taints his tone.

He's joking. Of course he's joking.

'What is it?' I wet my lips.

'Open it and see.'

I reach for it tentatively, turning over the box in my fingers with wonder.

'Come on, Scarlett, the suspense is killing me.'

'You know what it is.' My eyes snap to his.

'It's your reaction I'm waiting for.' He rolls his eyes.

My fingers shake as I pop the lid off. A shiny black car key gleams up at me. 'What's this?'

'I said I'd teach you to drive, didn't I?' He shuffles closer. Close enough that his scent surrounds me. 'You're going to need a car to practise in.'

My jaw drops. 'You bought me a car?'

'You didn't think I'd teach you in the Ferrari, did you?' He grabs my hand and stands, tugging me to my feet. 'Come on, it's outside. Let me show you.'

Words fail to form on my tongue as he leads me through the hall to the front door. I barely even register the cold draught as he yanks it open.

A sleek, black sporty-looking Audi is parked in front of the steps.

'Happy birthday, princess.' Excitement exudes from his every pore. 'It's an R8.' He says it like I'm meant to know what that means.

'What do you think? Do you like it?' He slips an arm around my shoulder and ushers me out of the door. My feet are bare but I'm too shocked to care.

'It's too much.'

'It's not, trust me. I know you want to travel, but I thought while you're stuck here until graduation, you might like a bit of freedom of your own.'

'That's ridiculously thoughtful. You've given me so much. You've saved me in ways you can't even begin to comprehend.' He's put money in my bank account, bought me clothes, and taken me into his home. If I worked for him my whole life, I could never repay him.

'I've got a feeling you're the one saving me.' He turns to face me, pulling me into his chest. His hands cup the back of my arms and rub away the goosebumps. 'After my last relationship, I struggled to let anyone in.'

'Your relationship with Cynthia Van Darwin? I saw pictures of you together in the papers.'

'Yes, Cynthia was,' he pauses for a second, 'dishonest. She had a different agenda.'

My gaze falls to the floor. I haven't been fully honest, but not because I have a different agenda.

James continues obliviously. 'After we split, I wasn't myself. Not by a long shot. You've brought me back to life. I love the way you find joy in everything. It's something I could learn to do.'

His words warm my insides. 'I thought *you* were supposed to be teaching *me*.' I nuzzle into his neck and rake my fingers over his scalp.

'I'll teach you everything I know.' His pupils glint.

'Yeah, when I've learnt to crawl properly,' I joke.

'Oh, honey, I'd never make you crawl to me. *You're* the one who brings me to my knees.' He nudges me back inside. 'Get dressed. We're going for a spin.' His fingers skim the plane of my lower back.

'I'm supposed to be meeting Avery for lunch,' I admit. 'I wasn't expecting you back until later.'

James exhales a heavy breath. Frown lines crease his brow. 'I should have said I was coming home. I wanted to surprise you.'

'It's the best surprise ever.' I reach up onto my tiptoes, inching closer for a kiss. His intoxicating cologne could be bottled and sold as a female Viagra.

'I was hoping to get some alone time with you before the ball tonight.' His lips touch mine and a hit of heat sears my soul. 'If I'd have known it was your birthday when I got the invitation, I never would have agreed to go.'

'Nonsense. It'll be nice. What time does it start?' I sink back onto the soles of my feet.

'Eight o'clock. Do you have a dress?

'I have several.' I mentally rack my brain for which one would be most appropriate.

'You'll need a ballgown. I'll arrange an appointment with Martha for this afternoon. You'll need something... spectacular. You know every eye in the place will be on you, don't you? And that's before they realise you're my girlfriend.'

I love his confidence in me. But, mostly, I love being called his girlfriend.

'My parents will be there. And Caelon and Isabella. My mother is still peeved she didn't get to meet you at the nightclub. Be warned, she can be a lot.' His eyebrows raise skywards.

'A lot,' I repeat, like I know what that means. 'So what's our story? Where did we meet?'

'It's a good question.' He pauses for a second, staring into the distance. 'Let's say you interviewed for a work placement in my office.' A small smirk plays on his lips. 'I offered you the position if you agreed to go out with me. Actually, no—that could be considered as sexual harassment, and yet another excuse for the Board to sack me. Let's say I offered you the position and you agreed to accept, if *I* agreed to go out with *you*.' He sniggers and raises his hands in a silent 'voila.'

'Shit. I still need to find a four-week placement for April. It's a compulsory component of the course. It totally slipped my mind!'

'Don't worry, I've already arranged for you to do the placement in my office.' He says it like it's a done deal. 'It's the perfect cover story.'

'I...'

'I won't have some slippery CEO perving over my girlfriend.' His jaw clenches. 'I'm perfectly capable of that myself.' He takes my hand and leads me back to the dining room.

I resign myself to my fate, both the placement, and the new ballgown. There's no point arguing with him. He told me himself, he always gets what he wants. And truthfully, I *want* to work with him. If I could pick any placement in the country, it would be by his side. 'Let me know what time Martha can take me.'

'I'll tell her four o'clock. And I'll have someone there to do your hair and make-up.'

'Okay.' I drain my coffee and stand. 'I'll go get dressed.'

'Do you have to?' He tugs me downwards until my face is inches from his. 'Give me another kiss.'

'Is kissing at the breakfast table part of our arrangement?' I'm testing the boundaries and I know it, but I can't help myself. What kind of a fake boyfriend buys his fake girlfriend an Audi?

His huge hands grip my ass and yank me onto his lap. The swell of his cock presses against my crotch and it takes every bit of self-control not to shamelessly grind against him.

'This arrangement is so fucking blurred, I'm not sure what the conditions are anymore. As I said, you're not the only one getting an education.' His fingers dig into my backside. A low groan slips from his lips as his gaze falls to my cami top. My nipples harden beneath the flimsy cotton, begging for his touch. 'They say knowledge is power, but in this instance, I feel like I've stumbled on my weakness. My weakness, Scarlett, is you.'

'I don't want to be anyone's weakness,' I whisper.

James nuzzles his face against the bare skin of my collarbone and inhales deeply. His fingers slide over my spine and rest at the nape of my neck. His touch is slow and sensual, but predominantly, tender. 'The interesting thing about weaknesses is, if you can conquer them, they eventually make you stronger.'

His lips lift to catch mine and I melt into our kiss. The softness of his lips. The heat of his mouth. The way his tongue plunders and conquers.

It's not a case of if he can conquer me.

He already has.

But as he gets stronger, it'll be me who gets weaker.

My poor heart doesn't stand a chance against him. If I had any sense, I'd leave before I fall any harder. But I have a sinking sensation, it's already way too late for that.

Chapter Thirty-Five
SCARLETT

'Am I even insured to drive this?' My palms skim over the steering wheel.

'Of course you are,' James snorts, strapping my seatbelt across my chest. 'Do I strike you as a man who would do half a job?'

'Well, I don't know...' My lips lift in a teasing smile.

'Scarlett,' he drawls. 'Why do I get the feeling you're referring to something else?'

I push my foot on the accelerator and we're thrown forwards.

'And that's why we need to learn to crawl before we can walk,' he says smugly.

Remembering how to drive takes all of my concentration. Operating the Audi feels like driving a spaceship compared to the Kia I learnt in. By the time we've done a loop of the estate, I've had enough. I pull up outside the front door and park the car.

'That's it?' His voice is incredulous. 'That was barely ten minutes.'

'I know.' I shrug. 'But I'm meeting Avery, remember?' I

unclip my seat belt and reach for the door handle. 'Laters, baby,' I tease.

His hand grips mine. 'Not later. Now.' His hand cups my chin and tilts my face upwards. His lips capture mine with that same raw carnality, deepening our kiss as his hands palm over my breasts. Eventually he breaks our kiss.

'We're like a couple of teenagers making out in the car,' I pant.

'Shame you have to go meet Avery, or we could have continued this inside.' A wolflike smile lights his eyes. 'Laters, baby.' He stretches across the car and yanks the handle to open the door for me.

'Not fair,' I pout.

'I'll make it up to you tonight, I promise.' His eyes gleam. 'Happy birthday, baby.'

At eight o'clock, Tim drops me and James outside Dublin Castle. The steps are lined with a rich red carpet that runs through a floral arch erected over the outside of the majestic doors. The building's blend of medieval and Georgian architecture has nothing on the opulence of James's mansion.

Martha kitted me out in a Valentino masterpiece of couture. Comprised of an ebony silk chiffon, the dress floats around me with every step. Off-the-shoulder sleeves elegantly expose my collarbones, whilst the corset bodice lifts my breasts and nips in my waist. The A-line skirt flares from the waist to the floor with layer upon layer of chiffon creating a fluid, almost liquid movement.

The hair and make-up team that took care of me afterwards were nothing short of miracle workers. I feel like an absolute princess. Cinderella doesn't have a patch on me. But while she only had until midnight, I have until graduation to bask in this lavish lifestyle and the company of my very own Prince Charming.

Avery's warning from earlier at lunch bursts through my mind. *'I'm all for you losing your virginity with a hot billionaire, but whatever you do, don't fall in love with him, Scarlett. He'll take what he wants and break your heart when he's finished with you. Enjoy it for what it is, but don't ever forget there's an expiry date on this arrangement between you.'*

She only voiced what I already know, but it's easy to forget when James is lavishing me with attention and gifts. Either way, I'm determined to enjoy every second of the next couple of months.

I blow out a breath and any lingering trace of Avery's negativity along with it. It's important we put on a convincing show for James's parents tonight. The whole point of this arrangement is to convince James's father and the Board that our relationship is real.

A flicker of nerves ripples down my spine. I desperately want Mr and Mrs Beckett's blessing. I'll never be part of their family, so it shouldn't matter. But it matters to me.

'What's this ball in aid of again?' I whisper as we make our way through the grand hall to the ballroom. Flowers, ivory foliage, and fairy lights decorate every nook and cranny.

'It's an education initiative supporting scholarships for underprivileged youths in Ireland.' James takes my arm and links it through his.

Approval stirs in my chest. It's a cause I can fully appreciate.

'Incoming.' James's grip on my arm releases as a woman barrels into me in a cloud of expensive perfume and silk. Slim arms wrap around me and yank me into her bosom. When she finally releases me, she takes a step back, soaking up every detail from my head to my toes.

'Oh, my goodness, James, she's absolutely stunning.' Eager

eyes bounce between James and me, like she's already imagining the babies we could make.

James's mother is blonde, willowy and classically beautiful. If I had to guess, I'd put her at around fifty, but it's clear she's had some work done. There isn't a single line creasing the corners of her eyes, even as a grin splits her face open.

'Mother, this is Scarlett.' James places a palm on the base of my spine. 'Scarlett, this is my mother, Vivienne Beckett.'

'It's such a pleasure to meet you,' she coos.

'And you, Mrs Beckett.'

'Please call me Vivienne.' She swats a hand in front of her face.

'It's Scarlett's birthday today,' James announces loudly.

'Oh, happy birthday darling.' I'm yanked in for another over the top embrace. 'I hope my son is spoiling you.'

'He certainly is.' My eyes dart to James, who's watching on with amusement.

'James tells me you're studying finance at Trinity,' she gushes.

A man appears beside Vivienne. He's tall and burly and immaculately dressed in a black tuxedo. Like James, his sheer presence emits power and wealth. His dark hair is peppered with grey and his eyes are the same striking shade as James's.

'Father.' James extends his hand and shakes his dad's hand.

'This is Scarlett.' Vivienne beams at her husband. Even with the scar on his left cheek, they make one hell of a handsome couple. 'Scarlett, this is my husband, Alex.'

'So, you're the young lady keeping my boy in line.' He politely presses a kiss to each of my cheeks, but it's not nearly as warm or enthusiastic as his wife's greeting.

'Trying to.' *Though no one ever called me a lady before.* A waiter approaches with a tray of champagne. James hands one to me, then one to his mother.

'It's Scarlett's birthday.' Vivienne says to Alex and nudges his ribs.

'Many happy returns.' Alex raises his glass.

'Scarlett, you must come to the house. We'd love to have you for dinner. Oh, and it's Alex's *big* birthday in April. Put the date in your diary. All the Becketts will be there. It's the perfect opportunity to meet the family in one go, isn't it Alex?' Vivienne places a hand on her husband's chest but doesn't wait for his reply, 'and perhaps we could do lunch this week? There's a fabulous new tapas place in O'Connell Street. The owner is a friend's son. He spent the last five years training under Marco Valiente in New York, but now he's home and he's opened this gorgeous old nunnery he's had converted. You should see the interior, it's a modernist Art Deco haven. He has the most elaborate wine selection.' Vivienne barely pauses for breath. 'Oh, and Isabella, Zara and I have a weekly spa date at Eden every Friday afternoon at three o'clock. You simply must join us sometime. They do the best LED light therapy facial, sweetheart. Not that you need it, of course. Your skin is beautiful.' She brushes a hand gently over my cheek and I flinch out of habit.

James sniggers.

So this is what he meant when he said his mother was "a lot".

I don't think I need to worry about Vivienne's approval if her invitations are anything to go by. But Alexander Beckett might be a tougher cookie to crack if his sidelong stares are anything to go by.

In the main ballroom, the tables are laid with lavish displays of peonies and primroses. A band plays on the main stage but not so loudly that you can't hold a conversation. We're seated with Caelon and Isabella, and some friends of Vivienne and Alex's.

They seem like a lovely family. Every minute movement and exchange of playful banter is weighted with warmth.

'Are you enjoying yourself?' Vivienne checks as the waitresses clear away the entrees. She places a soft hand on my elbow. Her easy affection and the maternal lilt to her tone cracks my chest right open.

I miss my mother like a heart misses a beat. It was so cruel how she was taken from me. If Jack O'Connor spent every day of the rest of his miserable life rotting in prison, it still wouldn't be long enough.

My fingers automatically reach for the silver cross at the base of my throat. Martha begged me to switch the necklace for pearls or a diamond at the very least, but while I was happy for her to pick my outfit, right down to my panties, taking the necklace off wasn't up for negotiation. My mother lent it to me a couple of days before her death. When I have it with me, I feel like I still have a part of her with me. When I touch it, I'm reminded I wasn't always alone.

'Scarlett?' Concern creeps into Vivienne's honeyed voice.

'Yes. Thank you.' I blink back the tears threatening at the corners of my eyes. 'You have a beautiful family.' I glance around the table at Caelon and Isabella, Alexander and finally my eyes rest on James.

'You're part of it now.' She offers me a conspiratorial wink as her palm brushes up over the back of my arm. 'I've seen the way James looks at you. He's obsessed.'

Her words stoke a fire in my chest. A longing steals the breath from my lungs. 'Do you think?'

'I don't think.' She beams at me again. 'I know.' She turns to her husband. 'Alex, how's your caviar?'

'It appears you've made quite the impression.' James's deep baritone rumbles into my ear, his hot breath brushing my neck. 'My mother is all over you like a bad rash.'

'So far, so good. Not sure about your dad, though,' I whisper.

'He's a teddy bear under his armour. He's infinitely more controlled when it comes to keeping his emotions in check than my mother. It's something he instilled in all of us, thankfully.'

'Thankfully?'

'Because,' he leans closer and lowers his voice, 'if I hadn't mastered complete control of my emotions, you would be spread across this table with your dress up around your waist and I'd be devouring your sweet pussy while three hundred people watched.'

Fire crackles across my skin. Sharp longing tugs at my tummy. I turn my face to meet his stare. Black pupils burn back at me. 'You look positively delectable in that dress,' he purrs. 'I think it's time for your next lesson.'

Chapter Thirty-Six

SCARLETT

'Here?' I squeak.

'Perhaps not on the table, but yes, I don't see why not.' His eyes glint as my mouth falls open.

I swipe my tongue over my lower lip as a need builds deep in my core. I am so ready for my next lesson but I'd prefer it was at home so we can take our time. 'Aren't you supposed to be behaving?' I glance at Alex pointedly.

'I suppose there is that.' James reaches for his bow tie and tugs it off with a sharp flick of his wrist. He shoves his chair back as he stands and clears his throat.

'Whatever is the matter?' Vivienne's head tilts as she glances up at James.

'Scarlett and I are leaving.' He extends his hand and motions for me to take it. 'You've been monopolising her attention all night and I'd like some alone time with her before I head to New York on Monday.'

New York? It's the first I've heard of it. But then again, I'm not his girlfriend. Not really. He's not my boyfriend. He's just pretending to be, whilst simultaneously wrecking my innocence, one life-affirming lesson at a time.

'Ah, isn't that sweet?' Vivienne coos.

'It's not sweet. It's sexual,' Caelon scoffs. Isabella slaps his forearm and tuts.

'It's both,' James smirks. 'Now, if you'll excuse us.'

I turn to Vivienne, who stands and yanks me in for another over familiar embrace. 'I'll text you about the tapas restaurant. And the spa. And we'll see you for Alex's big birthday party, won't we?' Vivienne's huge eyes dart between me and James.

'You will,' James promises his mother.

I can honestly say, this is the happiest birthday I've had in a long time. And it's not over yet.

When we slip into the back of the waiting car, James stares at me with a promising gleam in his pupils. 'You look fantastic tonight, Scarlett. Every man in the place wanted you tonight. But I'm the lucky fucker who gets to take you home.'

My stomach flips.

'You never said anything about going to New York. ' My voice cracks with disappointment.

'I have to show my face in the New York office at least once every quarter. It's a shame you have college, or I'd have asked you to come with me.'

'If only,' I groan. 'I can't wait to see a bit of the world after graduation. Dublin feels so small sometimes.'

'There are so many beautiful places out there, but it takes seeing them all to appreciate that Dublin is one of them.'

It hasn't been beautiful for me. It's been a city of sorrow. Which is why I can't wait to leave it behind. 'I'll take your word for it.'

Our eyes meet and something unspoken passes between us. It's as if he wants to say something but he's holding back.

As we pull up to the gates of his mansion, I gaze at the dome-shaped room at the top of the tower. When he gave me the tour the first night, we didn't make it that far. 'What's up there?'

James cranes forward to see where I'm pointing. 'A sun room.' His eyes slide sideways. The moonlight casts shadows across his face. 'Though, I suppose it could double up as an observatory,' he muses.

The house is silent when we enter. My rose gold Gucci heels click across the marble floor as James leads me to the stairs. 'Should I get changed?' I smooth a hand over the chiffon.

'Absolutely not.' His eyes roam over my exposed collarbone. 'Give me one second.' He raises his index finger, signalling me to stay put while he darts along the corridor. When he returns, it's with a bottle of champagne tucked under his right arm and two crystal flutes in his hand.

I follow him up three flights of thick carpeted stairs and then up another set of narrower spiral steps that lead to the dome.

Moonlight floods through the floor to ceiling glass, casting a luminous glow across an L-shaped couch comprised of cream crushed suede. An inviting mountain of plump, fluffy cushions line the sofa. A deep-pile shaggy rug sits in the middle of the floor. It's one of the most opulent rooms in the house, yet somehow the cosiest.

James's chiselled features pinch together. 'You like it?'

'It's incredible.' I gaze up at the myriad of stars twinkling outside. They look almost close enough to touch. They're definitely close enough to wish upon.

'Come up here anytime. I like to read in here, when I have the time.' He places the champagne flutes on a glass-topped table next to the couch.

'What do you read?' I smirk. 'Other than Fifty Shades, that is.'

His lips curve as he twists and tugs the champagne cork

until it pops with a delicious promise. I swallow thickly. Will that be the only thing he pops tonight? Or will tonight be the night I finally ditch the dreaded V-card?

For a man who was so keen to 'touch me, taste me, and fuck me,' he's certainly been mastering a magnitude of restraint.

Why though?

It's pretty clear the attraction is mutual.

We both know where we stand.

I have my plan for after graduation and, thanks to our agreement, the means to carry it out better than I ever thought possible.

'Mostly the Financial Times.' He pours the champagne into the glasses and offers one to me.

'A man after my own heart.' At least the Financial Times doesn't leave you longing for a love that only exists between the pages of a book. Although the sensations I'm experiencing now would give any romance novel a run for its money.

He clinks his glass against mine. 'Cheers.'

'Thank you.'

'Here's to you coming all over my face,' he runs a finger over my clavicle, 'At least twice tonight.'

I almost spit my drink out.

'Sit.' He nods towards the centre of the sofa. 'I have another present for you.'

Heat suffuses my skin and desire pools low in my tummy. 'Yes, sir.' I edge backwards until my calves hit the couch.

A low hiss slides over his lips. 'Good girl.' He nods approvingly as my bum sinks into the soft mountain of pillows. 'Lift up your dress.' It's not a request. He signals for me to hand him my drink to free up my hands.

'Do you have any idea what you do to me, Scarlett?' His hips arch forwards and the strain on his suit trousers is abundantly obvious. 'Do you know how many times I've thought about your sweet little cunt since the last time I touched it?'

I swallow thickly, shaking my head. 'But it can't be as many times as I've thought about your cock. Let me taste you,' I beg.

'Dirty girl. *My* dirty girl.' A low growl reverberates around the room as I lift the layered chiffon higher. 'You forgot the first rule from our first lesson. Ladies first. I'm going to take great pleasure in reminding you.'

I swallow hard. I've never wanted anything or anyone as badly as I want him.

'Are you sure I shouldn't take this off?' I motion to layer upon layer of material. It's not practical.

'Leave it on. I want to bury my tongue in a princess tonight.'

'But what if I ruin it?' The silk scrap between my legs is already saturated.

'Don't worry. Rosa will take care of it.' A slow smirk lifts his lips. 'But she'll know exactly what you've been up to with the boss.'

'Rosa is such a dote. And stunning too.'

'She is,' James agrees with a nod.

A crazy thought pops into my head. One that twists my tummy. 'Did she and you ever..?' The words tumble out before I can stop them. I'm not sure if I want to hear the answer.

Low laughter fills the room. 'No, I never mix business with pleasure.'

'Well, what's this then?' I gesture to chiffon bunched up my waist.

'That's the million dollar question.' A flicker of a frown flits across his face for a second before he evens it out.

He drops to his knees before me, placing a hand on my inner thighs, spreading them apart. Greedy eyes drink in my ivory silk thong. 'Very virginal. Very appropriate.'

I swallow thickly, glancing down at myself and the scrap of lingerie between my legs. At his thick quads between my thighs. 'Do you like what you see?'

'No, princess.' My stomach flips at his affection. 'I don't like it, I love it. I don't know what you're doing to me, woman, but you're living in my head every damn second of every damn day. I almost transferred thirteen million euro in the wrong investment fund yesterday because all I could think about was if your pussy was wet for me.' His fingers inch upwards until they skim over the saturated silk.

My hips arch up. 'I guess you have your answer. I've been soaked for you since the first night I laid eyes on you in the club.'

With one swift tug, he rips the lingerie from between my legs and tucks them in his pocket. 'I'll put these with the others.'

'You keep my lingerie?' I don't know whether to be flattered or freaked out.

'I like to take it away on business with me. And I wank myself senseless over it, imagining my hand is your tight little channel.'

It's my turn to hiss.

'Now open your legs wider. Allow me to teach you how much pleasure I can offer with my tongue.' His palms slide beneath my ass cheeks, fingers digging into my skin as he yanks me towards the edge of the couch.

A squeal squeaks from my lips. 'No point screaming, angel. God himself can't save you from what I'm about to do to you.'

Black eyes burn into mine as his face dips between my legs and he rolls his tongue over my slit with one long languid stroke. I gasp. 'Jesus fucking Christ.'

His low chuckle rumbles against my sex. 'He can't help you either.'

His tongue slides up and down my slickness and every single nerve ending in my body sparks and ignites. I thought his fingers were capable but they have nothing on the soft slick movement of his tongue. The way his lips surround my clit as he sucks. The way he moans like he's savouring every single second, the same way I am.

My skin tingles from the tip of my hair to my curling toes.

It's so sensitive.

It's too sensitive

But it's still not enough.

His mouth halts and I mew.

'Do you like that, Scarlett?' His voice is deep and gritty and full of need.

'I don't like it, I love it.'

'Good girl.' He offers another long, slow lick. 'I love that I'm the first man to touch this pretty pussy. I love that I'm the first man to lick it. I'm going to ruin you, Scarlett, for any other man that comes after me.'

'You already have,' I pant. The thought of there ever being another man is inconceivable. Who the hell could ever compare to James Beckett? But that's not a question I can contemplate right now. Or maybe ever.

I thread my fingers through his hair, bucking like a wild animal against his face. I never knew pleasure like it existed. 'That's it, baby. Ride my face.'

His lips capture my clit again and my eyes roll back into my head.

'Watch me, Scarlett,' he demands. 'I want the image of me on my knees for you burned into your brain. I want it to haunt you every second of every day like the image of your glistening pussy is burned into mine.'

I arch off the couch as his fingers slide into my centre. His pupils gleam through the darkness as he devours and pumps and destroys me in the most decadent manner. The sensation is sublime. Overwhelming. I'm completely a slave to his touch.

My thighs tremble. The stars outside the window have nothing on the ones bursting behind my eyelids. My eyelids flutter as I battle to hang on, desperate for this not to be over yet.

'Watch,' he commands when blackness threatens to drag me over the edge.

And I do.

Our gaze meets in a stare hot enough to burn down the entire building. My fingers grasp his hair, tugging and tearing as wave after wave of release crashes through me, obliterating everything except the hot white sensation of pure pleasure wrecking me.

When I finally float back down from heaven, James is towering over me with his fingers in his mouth and the expression of a cat who got the cream.

I reach for his crotch, desperate for him to teach me how to pleasure him with my mouth. 'I want to taste you. I want to touch you. And I want to fuck you.' I toss yet another one of his sayings back in his face and he grins.

'You will, princess.' His lips curve open in an almost cruel smile. 'But not tonight.'

'Why not?' It's a battle to suppress the disappointment rising in my sternum.

'Because you're not ready.' He lowers his face between my legs again. 'And neither am I,' he admits breathily.

I'm about to ask him what he means, but then he fucks me with his fingers again and I can't remember my own name, let alone anything else.

Chapter Thirty-Seven
JAMES

I've been in New York for two long days and I'm counting every damn second until I can return home. If it wasn't for this afternoon's meeting, I could have been persuaded to cut my trip short. Especially when I opened the text Scarlett sent me this morning; a picture of her cleavage in a white blouse way too low-cut for college. She's killing me.

But sadly, here I am. Lucien Moreau is in town. I saw an opportunity, and I took it. I make a point of showing my face here every quarter, but when Killian heard Lucien's son was opening a boutique hotel in Times Square, I donated enough of Beckett's whiskey to ensure the entire city could get shit-faced on me, to capture Lucien's attention.

Naturally, he reached out and I suggested a face-to-face meeting.

The O'Connors have made an offer on the Imperial Winery Group. A generous offer. But when I've finished with Lucien, he'll be eating out of the palm of my hand. I have a reservation at the Sapphire Rooms, the most exclusive restaurant in the city. To secure a table you need to reserve six months in advance, which is why I always reserve one for each quarterly visit.

I'm going to wine and dine him. Feed him whatever horseshit he needs to hear about running the winery the way it's been run by his family for the previous four generations. Blah blah blah blah.

By the time I leave, I'll have a verbal deal agreed. By the time I get home on Friday, the paperwork should be well and truly in motion.

The Board will be content.

My father will be happy.

And I will be fucking ecstatic to get home to my not-so-fake girlfriend.

It took every modicum of willpower not to sink my cock into her pretty pink pussy in the sun room the other night. The more time I spend with her, the more I want her.

Now there's an ocean between us, I'm kicking myself so fucking hard for being so controlled. Morally, it was the right thing to do. But tell that to my weeping cock.

All my father's lectures about mastering our mouths and emotions stuck with me. He would be proud.

But that's not why I'm holding off.

I can lie to myself and pretend it's because I need to be certain Scarlett is ready. It's a big step. One I'd hate her to regret.

I can *pretend*, but the truth is, it's me that hasn't been ready.

Because after spending the last few weeks with Scarlett, I'm pretty sure when I finally sink myself into her, I'll be giving her so much more than just my cock. I'll be giving her my heart, my soul, and every damn inch of everything I am.

If it's as good as I think it will be, I might never be able to give her up. Might never be able to let her go at the end of this arrangement.

And then what?

She's only pretending to be wife material.

She doesn't want to settle down.

She wants to travel the world, not tie herself to the first guy she sleeps with. Though, what a thought...

I pluck my phone from my pocket, pacing the Upper East side office overlooking the city below. It's true what they say about New York. It's the city that never sleeps. And unfortunately, neither have I since I got here.

I type out a text to Scarlett.

> Hope you're doing your homework in my absence. And I'm not referring to your private equity essay.

Before I left, I made her promise that she'd touch herself every night while I'm away. I had an Inez twenty-four carat gold-plated vibrator delivered to the house yesterday. You can't put a price on pleasure and I'd far rather my horny little girlfriend got off in our house than go to college with soaking panties.

I swear if those college boys got even a sniff of her sexual awakening, they'd be battering each other just to sit next to her. Something sharp stabs my chest at the thought.

Minutes pass with no reply.

When my phone finally vibrates in my pocket, it's not Scarlett.

It's my father.

'Dad?'

'A fucking pole dancer? Are you out of your goddamn mind son?' He booms across the phone. I wince.

Fuck. 'She's not a pole dancer. Not anymore, at least.' I pinch the bridge of my nose.

'For fuck's sake, son. You were supposed to be repairing your reputation, not obliterating it.'

I lurch to my feet, pacing the plush, carpeted floor. 'How did you find out?'

'Does it matter?' he barks. 'End it. Now.'

My brothers would never rat me out. They'd die for me first.

Cole. It could only have come from him. He golfs at the same club as my parents. I inhale a deep breath and blow it out slowly. 'I can't, Dad.'

'What do you mean, you can't?'

I roll my lips and sigh. 'I'm in love with her.' It's the first time I've said it out loud, even to myself, but there's no denying the truth in it.

I've known for weeks. Hell, I knew she was different the first time I spoke to her, I just didn't know how different.

'You're what?' My father's tone is incredulous.

'She's like no one else I've ever met, or am ever likely to.'

He scoffs, actually scoffs. 'Look, she's a beauty, there's no denying that. I'm sure you feel like you're in love when she's balancing on your balls and stroking your ego, but James, a woman like Scarlett is not wife material.'

I flinch. He's right. She's not wife material. But not because she's from a different social background. But because she's so young. And she doesn't want to settle down. She wants to travel and see the world. I can't blame her for that. If I was any sort of man, I'd walk away and let her do exactly that. But I'm far too selfish.

'I haven't slept with her,' I admit, staring out across the New York skyline. I'd never normally dream of blurting my private life to my father but it's imperative he understands what I feel for Scarlett is so much more than lust. So much more than a quick flash in the pan.

'What?' my dad snaps.

'I love her, Dad. And I'm not going to give her up.'

'If you want to keep your position in the company, son, you don't have a choice.' He tuts. 'Look, it's not even about what I think. It's the Board. How's it going to look when it gets out that you've finally settled down with a pole dancer? They're going to dig up absolutely every dirty little secret about her. Find every man who ever fucked her before you. It'll be all over the gossip columns.'

'There's been no one else, Dad.' God, I can't believe I'm thirty-three-years-old and talking sex with my father. 'Scarlett is innocent. She took the job at the Luxor Lounge to fund her studies, that's all. She's so smart it's not even funny. She's had to claw her way where she is today, and instead of condemning her working at the club, we should be congratulating her on surviving. Alone. She's an orphan. She doesn't have the backing of a family like you and I did.'

The phone goes silent apart from my father's slow deep breaths in my ear.

'This is far from ideal,.' My dad blows out a breath. He might be ruthless but he's also hopelessly romantic deep down. 'Is this why you had her face pixelated from those photos at the club the other night? In case anyone recognised her?'

'One of the reasons.' I can't admit Scarlett has a dark traumatic past she's hiding from, not when my father is coming around to the idea that she might not be such a bad catch after all.

He sighs again. 'Look, just keep a low profile. Get this acquisition through. And keep your penis in your pants a little longer. We'll talk about this when you get home.'

'Does Mam know?' She and Scarlett got on like a house on fire. I'd hate for her to have a tarnished view of her.

It dawns on me that I'm serious about Scarlett.

Serious about getting serious with her, at least.

If she'll have me.

The memory of Rian's opening night floods my mind. Scarlett on the dancefloor with Stenson. He could probably put his life in a backpack and travel the world with her. Up sticks and go wherever the wind carries them.

I have a lot in life. I could buy practically anything I want. Except that type of freedom. Not at this point in my life, anyway. With age, comes responsibility. Ten years isn't a huge age gap, but when it comes to life experience, I've had ten years extra to see and do the things she's only dreamt of.

Unless, I find a way to show her the world, without giving up mine...

'Alright, I won't tell your mother.' Dad's stern tone brings me back to earth with a bang. 'Just get that acquisition done, and we can worry about everything else afterwards.'

'I'm on it.' I hesitate for a second. 'Thanks, Dad.'

'Don't thank me. I haven't done anything.' He clears his throat. 'I want you to be happy, son. I do. But if you're serious about Scarlett, you're going to have to spin this story very carefully.'

'I know, Dad.' I just need to make sure there's a story to spin. As it stands, it's an agreement with an expiry date.

I hang up, and open the thread of messages to Scarlett.

No reply still.

'Where are you, angel?' I stare at my screen before pulling up the CCTV cameras on my phone. The car isn't back yet. Where are they?

I open the tracking app. Having a brother who is a security freak is pretty handy at times like this. Though his paranoia appears to be contagious given the panic swirling in my gut.

The car appears to be at the college campus. I glance at the Rolex on my wrist. It's almost eight o'clock in Ireland.

What is she doing at college at this hour?

Of all the decisions I've made in my life, having those poles removed from the college gym was up there with the best.

Not fucking Scarlett the other night when she begged me is officially the worst.

I call Tim. He answers on the first ring.

'Where is she?' I pace the room, dragging my fingers through my hair hard enough to sting my scalp.

'Miss Fitzgerald is in the college library, sir.' The sound of male voices in the background does nothing to reassure me.

'And what precisely is she doing in the college library at this hour of night?' I growl. Did she even eat? Is she safe? Who is she with?

'She's studying with a— friend.' Tim's uncertainty radiates across the miles.

'Which friend?' It better not be that fucking study buddy, Shane Stenson.

The condition of our arrangement specified she was not to be seen with another man. Studying alone after hours with the college football captain, class president, and general golden boy (as I found out from Killian who investigated him for me after the incident in the nightclub) is not adhering to the terms.

But that's not what has my blood boiling.

I don't care about our stupid arrangement.

I care that she's alone with him.

That he's the one close enough to scent her exotic shampoo. To see the way her face lights when she figures out the answer to whatever question she's working on. The way her tongue darts out over her lower lip when she's puzzling over a problem.

Is he sitting next to her?

Leaning over her shoulder to see what she's working on?

I bet he is. I know what college boys are like. Hell, I was one for long enough.

They'll be packing up their books soon and he'll offer to take her for a drink or dinner. Well, that's exactly what I would do, anyway.

I saw the way Shane looked at her at Rian's opening night. I saw his dilated pupils, watched the way they were repeatedly drawn to her full luscious lips. I didn't need to hear the words he blurted out to know he's obsessed with her. It was like looking at a mirror image of myself.

An irrational surge of jealousy rips through me.

My office door opens and Amanda Anderson, the PA assigned to me for the week, peeps in. She's your typical all-American poster pin-up with blonde, bouncing hair, perfect white teeth, and breasts the size of melons.

This time last year, I wouldn't have hesitated to ask her out.

Now, I see straight past her.

I lift a finger to indicate I'm on the phone. She nods and mouths, 'Lucien Moreau is here.'

Fuck my life.

The Imperial Winery acquisition might be one of the most important deals of my life, but I'm sorely tempted to cancel the meeting and fly home. I glance at my watch. If I left now, I could be back in Ireland before breakfast.

But at what cost?

It's fucking ironic. The entire arrangement with Scarlett was to save face until I got this business deal over the line, and now I'm contemplating throwing it all down the toilet and destroying my reputation to be with a woman I'm fake dating.

Although there is nothing fake about my feelings for her.

I'm caught between a rock and a hard place.

Between my head and my heart.

Between what's right, and what feels right.

'Shane Stenson, sir. His father is—'

'I know who his fucking father is Tim.' I cut Tim off before he can continue. 'Just make sure she goes home to our house, alone. No detours. No drinks. No dinners. I'm on my way.'

'Yes, sir.'

I hang up and type out another text to Scarlett.

> You appear to have forgotten the terms of our arrangement. Looks like I'll need to remind you.

I stride back to my desk and buzz Amanda to send in Lucien. With any luck, his wife might be in town for their son's grand opening. Maybe I can gift them my table at the Sapphire Lounge.

As long as he gives a preliminary agreement to the terms of my offer.

Chapter Thirty-Eight
SCARLETT

After a restless night, I wake with a start and pull the bed sheets over my chest. The heat of James's stare burns through the soft Italian cotton like a laser.

I should probably be creeped out by my fake boyfriend watching me sleep, but there's something electrifying about it. Like he's my protector, watching over me.

He's the first person, other than my mother and Avery, to genuinely care for me. He might not have said as much, but the fact he's here, and not in New York, speaks volumes.

I thought from his texts last night that I was in trouble but I hadn't dared to hope he was angry enough to come home early.

Weak traces of sunlight spill through the curtain cracks. I squint my eyes to adjust them to the gloom. James is perched up in the high-backed velvet armchair across the room, wearing an impeccably tailored Armani suit, minus a tie, and an expression that would give the Grim Reaper a run for his money.

His hands clasp together, elbows resting on his thick, parted thighs. His eyes are so dark, they're almost black.

'You're not supposed to be home until Friday.' My voice is thick with sleep. As I sit up, the covers drop to my waist and his gaze falls to the cropped ivory cami I pulled on before falling into bed last night.

'And you're not supposed to be seen with another man until after graduation.' His voice is terrifyingly calm but his jaw is clenched so hard, he's in danger of needing emergency dental treatment.

'I wasn't seen with another man by anyone,' I quip. 'There was no one else in the library but us.'

'Is that supposed to make me feel better?' He lurches to his feet and closes the distance between us.

The scent of citrus surrounds me, seeping into my skin. His bulky frame towers over the bed and sharp arresting eyes devour every inch of my skin, like a predator waiting to pounce.

I wish he would pounce.

After last weekend, that's all I can think about. I can't concentrate on anything else, especially my dissertation even though my deadline is looming, which is why I reluctantly agreed to go to the library with Shane. Here, in the house, the scent of James lingers. I half expect him to waltz around every corner or slide into the dining room. It's distracting to the point of destruction.

'I'd say it makes you feel about as good as I felt, knowing every woman in New York was ogling you.'

A flicker of something crosses his face but before I have time to decipher it, strong hands grip my waist and pin me to the bed. His taut body presses against my torso with a promise I can only pray he'll finally deliver on.

'I told you, angel, you're mine and I'm yours, until graduation, at least. And I don't share. Nor would I ever expect you to. I'm a lot of things, Scarlett, but I'm not unfaithful.' Twin flames lick over my skin sending goosebumps firing in every direction.

'Not even to your *fake* girlfriend?' I'm testing the boundaries, but I can't help it. This thing between us feels more real than anything I've ever experienced before. Not that I have much to compare it to.

'That's my cock pressing against you, sweetheart. Does that feel fake to you? The way I want you is real. The way you live in my head is real. The way you steal the breath from my lungs every time I lay eyes on your perfect face. The way your laughter echoes around the empty walls of this house. It's always been real. I think it's time I taught you that.' He rests his body weight on his right side and uses his left hand to tear the bedcovers back. 'Are you ready?'

'I've never been more ready for anything in my life.' My breath hitches in my throat.

'You think that, but I'm not sure you know what you're signing up to.' Thick fingers trail over my stomach before sliding beneath the cami and tracing teasing, maddening circles around my nipples.

'I'm signing up for you to do whatever you like to me. I'm yours.' The truth of it hits me as my words tumble out. 'I've been yours since the minute you walked into the club. Maybe even before then.'

A low murmur of approval slips from his lips a split second before they crash against mine. His tongue invades my mouth, tasting, exploring and dancing to a rhythm that sounds like home.

Greedy fingers finally grip my nipple, pinching and rolling it. My hips arch upwards, desperately seeking the friction I crave. Palms slide over my breast before gliding lower over my hip bone and lower until his hand slides inside my panties.

'You're soaked for me, angel,' he groans, fingers sliding

between my folds. Electricity crackles through every nerve ending in my body.

'I told you I'm ready.' I part my thighs wider in a shameless invitation.

'I'll be the judge of that.' He inches lower on the bed and dips his face to my sex, tugging my thong over my thighs. 'Fuck, I've missed you.'

'Me? Or my pussy?' I tease.

'Both of you,' he murmurs before offering a slow, languid lick.

'I've missed you too,' I gasp.

'Me? Or my tongue?' Touché.

'Both of you.' Two can play his game, although we both know he's had much more experience. A nervous shiver slides down my spine.

'Don't worry, baby, I'll make it so good for you, I promise.' His pupils reflect the hunger that's rumbling inside of me. The sight of him in that killer suit, buried between my legs, will be forever imprinted on my brain.

His tongue rolls over my clit in slow, teasing strokes and my hips buck. 'James, I need you,' I pant, scraping my nails across his scalp. I haven't a clue what I'm doing, but I'm desperate for him to show me.

I want him so badly. And not just in this moment and up until I graduate, but maybe forever. For now, I'll take what I can get and worry about the wounds to my heart later.

'I love it when you cry my name. I love it when you come on my face. My hands. But I need you to come on my cock now.' He presses tiny kisses against the inside of my inner thighs. 'You're so wet for me, baby. You're ready.' He rocks up on the bed, shrugs off his suit jacket and tosses it on the floor. He stands, reaches into his pocket, produces a square silver foil and tosses it on the bed before dropping his trousers.

My throat thickens at the sight of his enormous erection straining his black boxers.

'Someone had this planned.' I swat away my nerves and readjust myself against the plump pillows.

'Sweetheart, I had this planned from the moment I met you.' A devilish smirk lifts his lips as he unbuttons his shirt, revealing his tanned, toned planes of perfection.

'Really?' I'm flattered beyond belief. How is the hottest billionaire to bless this country so into me?

It makes no sense, but I'm going to take it. Maybe it's karma. I've had so much heartache in my life, perhaps the scales are finally tipping my way.

'Well, you're not the only one with a plan.' I roll onto my side and open the bedside locker beside me.

James's jaw drops when he sees the silver packet of pills in my hand. 'You've started taking contraception?'

'Just in case.' I shrug. 'Obviously, I'm clean. You're the first man to touch me.'

'Scarlett, you have no idea how hard that sentence alone makes me.' His eyes blaze, pinning me in a possessive stare. 'There's only one problem.'

'What?' My chest constricts.

'I don't just want to be the first. I want to be the last, too.' His velvet voice is solemn.

'You don't mean that.' I freeze, hardly daring to believe my ears. 'We both know I'm not wife material. Not really. I might have the right accent, but I don't come from the right family.'

'Perhaps we should start our own family.' His Adam's apple bobs. 'I don't mean literally. Not right away, anyway, though if it happened...'

A family? Isn't that what I always wanted? His body is everything mine needs but his words— they're a balm to my soul.

'I'm clean, by the way,' he adds. 'I've always used protection, and I got tested last month just in case.' He slides his boxers over his thick thighs and I am fucking here for it.

The man could make his fortune ten-times over as a Calvin Klein model. Every hard line, every square inch of muscle, every curve and indentation of his body, begs to be licked. He stands at the side of the bed gazing at me like I'm some sort of vision when the truth is, it's him who's the vision.

Especially his weeping cock.

I'm on my knees before he knows what's happening. I have no idea what I'm doing, but the urge to lick that glistening tip is bursting my insides open. I kneel on all fours before him, the same way he's kneeled for me. Wrapping one hand around the base of his hard length, I run my tongue over the top. He tastes like sin, but his responsive moan is the sweetest prayer.

'Baby, are you trying to kill me?'

I tilt my face up to meet his stare as I wrap my lips tentatively around his cock and inch downwards, taking as much of him as I can manage. There's something so empowering about being the woman who gets to pleasure him.

'Fuck, Scarlett. This was not part of today's lesson.' His hands tenderly cup my jaw as our eyes bore into each other's. 'But it has taught me something.'

'What's that?' It's barely decipherable, but he gets the gist.

'You're not going anywhere after graduation.' His tone is final.

My stomach flips.

Could I stay here?

What about my plans to travel?

I force the thoughts away.

His fingers glide through my hair with a tenderness he

doesn't look capable of before sliding lower over my back and gripping my waist.

I squeal as he hauls me up from his cock as if I'm weightless. He places me gently onto the bed, inching his way on top of me. My trembling thighs part as his hips rest on top of mine. The tip of his cock rests at my entrance.

He brushes a stray strand of hair from my face, gazing at me like I'm the only woman in the universe. 'It's going to hurt at first, baby, but I promise it'll be worth the pain. I'll take it slowly.'

'Don't you dare.' I thrust against his tip and he moans.

'Fuck, Scarlett.' He nudges in, never taking his eyes from mine. 'Just an inch, okay? Don't be greedy. It's unbecoming.' He shoots me a wink.

I love the playful banter. The ease of our relationship. Because whether we wanted it or not, we do have one– a real one that is. I suppose it was inevitable, given the incredible chemistry between us.

He slides the tip in and my head rolls back on the pillow. My core tenses and I force my muscles to unclench.

'How does that feel?' Hot lips blaze a trail of tiny kisses along my jawline.

'It feels like more.' My pulse roars in my ears, my skin feels too tight and the weight of him on my body is too much and yet not enough, all at the same time.

'So, my little virgin likes cock.' His tongue traces the outline of my lips as he pushes in a little further. It's heaven and hell because it's too much and nowhere near enough.

'I don't like cock. I like *your* cock.'

He nudges in further. 'Thank fuck. Because it's the only cock you're ever going to get.'

He slides back, almost all the way out. 'You okay, baby?' Concern flickers in his big brown eyes.

'Never better.' It's tight. It's sore, but he's stoking bits of me I didn't even know I owned, which more than compensates for the pain.

'Good girl.' His hands glide over my hips and dip beneath my backside, arching me up to grind against him as he plunges into me. An animalistic cry pierces the air and it takes a split second for me to realise it came from my mouth. But he's in. All the way in. I'm so full of him, I feel consumed, but in the most decadent, delirious way.

His hips rock back and forth in a slow, gentle rhythm and he alternates between gazing at me like I'm a magical pink unicorn and peppering my lips with tiny affectionate kisses. I relax into him, around him, and then surrender myself to him.

Heat builds in my core and I'm so full, so complete, it's like nothing else in this world. Every muscle in my body tightens and trembles. James's hand infiltrates the space between us, his fingers caressing my clit in slow sensual circles.

I've never known pleasure like it.

His eyes are wild as he increases his pace, slamming against me in slow debilitating thrusts that touch a spot inside of me that I didn't know existed.

'Look.' His gaze moves to our middle and he inches back enough that I can see his thick length slide into me, and I'm gone.

An orgasm shudders through me in hot, blinding bursts until I shatter in his arms and on his cock, just as he requested.

Before the last decadent wave leaves my body, James follows suit, pumping me hard. His lips capture mine, devouring my lingering moans, swallowing them as they meld with his own.

Chapter Thirty-Nine
JAMES

Taking Scarlett's virginity may be the most self-indulgent thing I've ever done, but it's also the most self-sabotaging, because there's no going back from this. The plan was to ruin her for all others. The reality is, it's me who's ruined.

I knew it.

I knew I'd lose myself inside her. She's like no one I've ever met before.

I press my cheek to her chest, listening to the rapid hammering of her heart as it pumps out the same rhythm as my own. I'm in deep. So deep. She drags her fingers through my hair in soft slow strokes. I glance up. Her platinum eyes glisten.

'You okay?'

She offers a small nod. 'Never been better.'

'You're amazing.' My voice cracks with raw emotion. I'm freefalling into love with the woman I'm supposed to let go in a couple of months. I don't want her to give up on her dreams because they aren't the same as mine, but there's no way I'm letting her out of my life. Which is why I've decided to show her the world– my way.

Her lips curve wryly. 'You're the one they call Ireland's most eligible bachelor.'

'Not anymore.' I lower my hands over her hips and pinch her ass. 'You're stuck with me after that.' I roll sideways onto the pillow next to her. 'I'm giving you three minutes to recover then I want you on all fours, face down, ass up.' My cock is already hard again.

'As amazing as that sounds, I have to get up. My dissertation has to be submitted on Friday, and I've been distracted lately.' Scarlett turns on to her side to face me, presses a swift kiss on my lips, then backs off the bed.

She isn't going anywhere. Not until I've had my fill, which will be never. I'm not a cuddler, never have been, but I would happily stay in bed and cuddle Scarlett all damn day.

'Where do you think you're going?' I cradle the back of my head with my hands.

She picks up my shirt from the floor and slides her arms into it. It looks ridiculously good on her. So does my come dripping between her thighs.

'Bathroom.'

'I love seeing you like that.'

'A hot mess?' she teases.

'*My* hot mess.' I watch as she strides across to her ensuite. 'Seriously, Scar, you're stunning right now. If you have to go to college, you should go exactly like that.'

She hesitates for a split second. 'I suppose I don't have to go. I don't have any lectures today, but I was going to go to the college library. I can't concentrate here.'

'It's the most peaceful place on this earth, trust me,' I swing my legs over the edge of the bed and hoist myself up.

'You'd know.' There's a trace of envy in her tone as her eyes travel across my torso and ending up on my dick. 'It's not the peace that's the problem, it's you. I can't think straight when I'm near you.'

'It's because you need to come again, baby. Let me take care of that for you, then I'll help with your dissertation.'

She pauses in the bathroom door, leaning against the wooden frame. Her glossy dark hair is tousled in that just-fucked way and my cock is harder than steel watching her. She's like that first drug-induced high. One shot is never going to be enough.

'Don't you have meetings to go to?' She eyes me curiously.

'I cancelled them.'

'All of them?' Her mouth drops open.

'All of them,' I confirm. 'I'm going to run us a bath. You're probably sore, are you?'

'Surprisingly not. Though James Junior has a lot to thank for that.' Her laughter floats across the room.

'James Junior?' My jaw ticks. 'Who the fuck is that?'

She stalks towards the bed and heads for the bedside drawers. She opens the top one and pulls out the gold-plated vibrator I sent her.

'You named it after me?' I cough.

'It was your cock I was dreaming of while I was pumping myself with it.'

'Now that is something I'd love to see.'

'No chance. Not when the real thing is here and ready.' She tosses it back in the drawer and slams it shut.

'Come here.' I beckon her over with my index finger and what I hope are come-to bed eyes.

She shifts her weight from one foot to the other, eyeing me with slight trepidation. 'I didn't clean up yet.'

'I like you dirty. Come and sit on my cock.' I wrap my hand around the base and pump.

Her tongue swipes her lower lip and I know I've won. 'We've got all day to finish your dissertation, but right now, I want your thighs either side of me, and your perfect cunt rocking on my cock.'

A low hiss slips from her lips. 'You have a filthy mouth, Mr Beckett.' With two strides she's in front of me, standing between my legs. She climbs onto my lap, wrapping her legs around my back, and I guide her onto my length, which she takes inch-by-life-affirming-inch.

'You say it like it's a bad thing, yet here you are,' I tell her, digging my fingers into her ass cheeks and guiding her into a slow, sensual rhythm. 'Your body was made for mine.'

'I'd have to agree with you.' The shirt falls open, exposing her beautiful breasts. My mouth captures her right nipple and her fingers dig into my shoulders as she grinds herself harder against me, finding her confidence and her own rhythm.

Her chest heaves with ragged breaths. The mews and moans she makes set my heart racing. I trail my tongue upwards, over her clavicle and up over her long, elegant neck. She angles her face down, her expression one of sheer ecstasy.

'If you ever go to the library, or anywhere else with Shane Stenson again, I'm going to pin you on the table and fuck you in front of him, just so he's in no doubt who you belong to, okay?' Her eyes widen and her core clenches my cock in a vice-like grip.

'You'd like that, wouldn't you? If I tied him to a chair and made him watch as I ate your pussy, then fucked you into next week?'

Our eyes lock and I know she's imagining the scene in her head. 'You'd like to be watched, wouldn't you?' I graze my knuckles over her sweat-sheened skin until my hand is between us. I circle her clit with my thumb and her head rolls back. 'And I thought you were a good girl.'

She moans my name as her nails scratch across my back. 'I don't mind if the entire world watches us. But I'm the only man who will ever touch you, Scarlett.'

'Yes,' she cries, tightening and clenching my cock as her

orgasm rips through her. I'm seconds behind her, soaring into the most decadent oblivion of my life.

Her hips slowly rock to a stop as we catch our breath in ragged pants. Something powerful presses against my ribcage. Something that's bursting to get out. Something that I've only ever said to one other woman before. Something that's going to change everything between us.

I cup her chin and angle her face towards me. We exchange so much more than just a look. We exchange souls. 'I love you, Scarlett.'

A single tear falls from her eye and rolls slowly over her cheek. 'I love you too. I think I have from the second I laid eyes on you.' Glittering silver pools rove over my torso before returning to my pupils. 'I felt like you were pulling me towards you with an invisible string.'

That's a pretty accurate summary given I was mentally willing her over.

I brush my thumb across her cheekbone, swipe the tear, then bring it to my lips. 'Don't cry, baby. I told you before, I'll never hurt you.'

'I know.' She nods and another tear falls. 'I can't believe you're mine. That this is my life now.'

'Well, you'd better believe it, because nothing and no one is going to get between us. Ever.' I wrap my arms around her and stand, carrying her across the room like a child. 'Let's run that bath now. It's been a big day already and it's not even nine am.'

'Tim will be waiting to take me to college.' Scarlett's hand cups her mouth.

'No, he's not. He's in his cottage with Rosa.' I smirk.

'With Rosa?' Scarlett blinks hard.

'They're married.' I'm surprised she didn't guess. Why the hell else would the two of them last out here in the sticks with no one else for company?

'No way! Why didn't anyone tell me?'

'You didn't ask.'

'We can go on double dates!' She claps her hands together and rubs them with glee.

'With the staff?' I scoff. 'Not likely.'

'Oh, come on, don't give me that crap. What about that time we all had take-out? Tim's your best friend. Don't try to deny it.'

I place Scarlett on the marble bathroom counter while I fill the tub. 'Tim's my only friend these days, apart from my brothers,' I admit. He might work for me, but he is my closest confidant outside of my family, the only man brave enough to spar with me in the gym, and the only man stupid enough to drink whiskey with me when I've already had too much. He might call me Mr Beckett in public, but it's James, or even Jim, when we're alone. Scarlett's obviously picked up on our easy friendship.

'Why?'

'I don't trust easily. I trusted Cynthia. She was dishonest. I can't stand dishonesty.'

Scarlett's teeth worry at her lower lip as she looks at me with an expression I can't quite fathom. 'What did she do?'

'She lied to me and she stole from me. From the company.'

'I see.' Scarlett glances at the floor.

'Enough about the past. Let's talk about the future.' I pour a generous amount of scented bubble bath into the tub and change the subject. 'We're going to have this bath. I'm going to devour you, and then a tonne of pancakes, dripping with maple syrup and bacon. After that, we're going to pack up your things and move them into my room.' Her eyebrows shoot skywards but I silence her with a finger until I finish. 'And then we're going to *our* library to get your dissertation done. And if it takes until three in the morning, we're going to submit it early.'

A frown creases her forehead as her fingers curl around the edge of the marble. 'Firstly, isn't that moving a bit fast? And secondly, Professor Buckley's given us until Friday.'

'On the contrary. I should have moved you into my room two months ago.' I give her a pointed look. One that leaves no room for negotiation. 'And we have other plans for Friday.' I perch on the edge of the tub as the water cascades from the taps.

'We do?' She hops off the counter to stand in front of me.

'Correct me if I'm wrong, but I believe you have a mid-term break next week, before you start your work placement?'

'That's right.'

'I'm taking you away.'

'Where?'

'It's a surprise.' I shoot her a smile.

'I was planning on spending the week preparing for the work placement. I'm determined to make a good impression on my new boss.' She smirks, tapping her foot on the opulent glossy tiles.

I wrap my hands around the back of her legs, stroking her smooth, silky skin. 'You already did. In fact, he's about to offer you a permanent position after graduation, given the initiative you demonstrated earlier.' I nod towards the packet of pills on the bedside table.

'Where are we going?' Her voice hitches.

'Don't you want a surprise?'

'I hate surprises,' she admits. 'They're usually more shocking than surprising.'

'Another thing we have in common.' My lips curve upwards. 'We're going to Paris.'

'No way! Seriously?' Her palms clutch the space over her heart. 'But what about work?'

'I told Chantel I'm taking a few days off.' I shrug, like it's nothing, even though I haven't taken a holiday in... well, forever. But I do plan on tying up some important business while I'm there.

'Are you sure about this? It seems that I'm getting so much more out of this relationship than you are.' Her earnest expression squeezes something in my sternum. She wears her heart on her sleeve. It's one of the things I love about her.

'You give me more than anyone ever gave me in my life. This relationship thing is new to both of us, but I don't make decisions lightly. I didn't get to where I am today by hesitating. I know what I want and I'm not afraid to pursue it.'

'I thought I was your weakness.'

'My weakness is when we're apart. Together, we're strong.'

'There are things you don't know about me. Things I'm not supposed to tell anyone.' She sucks on the inside of her cheek.

I pull her body flush against mine. 'You can tell me anything, Scarlett. Your secrets are safe with me. I'll keep them with my own.'

She exhales a heavy breath. 'I'll tell you everything, but not now. I don't want to tarnish the best day of my life with the trauma of the past.'

'It's your call, sweetheart. I'm ready to listen whenever you're ready to talk. You're not alone anymore. Whatever trauma you endured is behind you. You're with me now. I won't let anything or anyone hurt you again.

'Your family will probably hate me.'

'Don't be daft.' Yesterday's conversation with my father forces itself to the front of my mind. He wasn't exactly thrilled to find out about Scarlett's previous occupation as a pole dancer. Surely, there can't be anything worse than that lurking in her past?

I can't have her face pixelated out of the papers forever, and the second I stop, whatever, or whoever, she's been hiding from will be exposed. Not to mention the several hundred men who could potentially recognise her from the club.

It's inevitable. Wealth, or the prospect of it, makes people do stupid things, like selling stories.

When we announce our engagement, it will be the biggest story to hit the tabloids in decades.

And it is *when*, not if.

Because Scarlett is going to be my wife.

She just doesn't know it yet.

Chapter Forty
SCARLETT

James's room is the size of an entire penthouse. The navy décor is dark and masculine, but it suits his personality. Rosa rearranged his walk-in wardrobe to accommodate my clothing with a big fat smile on her face.

We submitted my dissertation then spent the weekend alternating between having filthy sex, eating nachos, and binge-watching *Emily in Paris* in preparation for the trip. Well, I binge-watched. The only thing James watched was my face every time he slid his hand between my legs. It was exceptionally distracting, in the most delicious way.

Now we're forty-thousand-feet in the air somewhere over Europe.

I've never been inside a private plane before. In fact, apart from a couple of trips to Spain to visit my mother's family when I was a kid, I've hardly been abroad before. Which is why I've always been so determined to see the world.

Not in my wildest dreams did I imagine I'd be seeing it with my billionaire boyfriend.

It's all so surreal.

I glance around the cabin, soaking in every detail to relay to Avery. Rich wood veneers and gold accents line the walls. The lights are controlled with integrated touch panels. There's a state-of-the-art entertainment system with a retractable ultra HD screen and surround sound speakers. A built-in bar with a wine chiller, crystal glassware, and every type of whiskey Becketts has ever produced. A high-gloss lacquer dining table doubles up as a conference table in the space behind us, while we sit on cream, custom leather seats sipping chilled champagne.

'What do you think?' James eyes me over the rim of his champagne flute and drops a hand into my lap.

'It's like I've been transported to a parallel universe.' It's a lot. A little overwhelming, to be honest.

'How about I show you the bedroom? Then I can really take you to a parallel universe.' He waggles his eyebrows at me.

'You're insatiable,' I scold, slapping the back of his hand playfully and eyeing the cabin crew.

'Says the woman who kept me up all night.' He growls at the memory. 'I'm surprised you can walk today.'

I let out a playful huff. 'What's up old man? Can't keep up?'

'Is that a challenge?' His eyes twinkle. 'Because I believe I told you I don't care who watches, as long as they don't touch. So help me, Scarlett, if you want me to fuck you right here in front of the cabin crew, believe me, I will.'

Heat pools in my belly and lower, but I move the discussion to a safer topic instead of acting on my body's needs. 'I still can't believe we're going to Paris.'

James tips his glass against mine. 'Slainte! To Paris.' In navy slacks and a crisp white shirt and suit jacket, he looks positively edible.

His lips curve upwards.

'Slainte! You know, if I didn't love you already, I definitely would after this.'

'Thanks.' He arches a wry eyebrow. 'I think.'

'You spoil me.'

'This is just the beginning, sweetheart.' He takes my hand in his. 'If you let me, I'll show you the world. I refuse to hold you back from travelling, or anything else you want after graduation but,' wistful eyes home in on me, 'I can't lose you.'

My chest tightens.

The plan had always been to leave Dublin.

To see the world.

Then eventually find a place I could call home.

But my new home isn't a place, it's a person.

I guess two out of three isn't bad.

I swallow thickly, drowning in his dilating pupils. 'You won't lose me. I couldn't leave if I tried. But after graduation, I need to get a job. One that doesn't involve you paying me to pretend to be in love with you.'

'You don't need to get a job,' James says softly.

'I do. Do you think I worked my butt off to get into Trinity, and spent four years with my head buried in the books, to not use my degree? I *want* to work.'

'Work for me,' he purrs.

'I couldn't.' I shake my head.

'Why not?' His eyebrows furrow together.

'Because everyone would think you only gave me the job because we're fucking.'

He glowers. 'We might be "fucking", but one day we'll be family. And what will it matter anyway?'

Family.

The one word that should mean so much but, in reality, has meant very little to me. Until now.

'I'll think about it.' More like, I'll see what my other options are.

He tuts. 'You're the only undergraduate to turn down a six-figure salary before you've even graduated. Don't let your pride make you fall. Take our relationship out of the situation. A finance position in a global company would look amazing on your CV. Not that it matters, because the only way you'll be leaving is to have our babies.'

A pang of longing pulls at a string inside. 'Babies?' I thought when he said it the other day, it was just in the heat of the moment. I've never dared to hope before. To think too far into the future, other than surviving the wrath of the O'Connors and passing my exams.

'Yes, Scarlett, babies. Not now, but some day. Maybe in a decade I'll be ready to share your attention with another human.' He offers a wry smile. 'I know things are moving quickly but I know what I want, and it's you. I'm all in Scarlett. The question is, are you?'

I swallow again. 'I'm all in with you, but seriously, I need to think about the job. Living together, working together, sleeping together, it might be too much. And besides, you might change your mind after the intern placement. I could be crap.'

'Don't be ridiculous. You have more drive and determination than anyone I know. Look how far you've come on your own.'

A memory of my mother hits me like a hammer.

Would she approve of James Beckett?

I think so.

'Let's talk about something else.' I drop a hand to his knee. I'll tell him everything, but not now. I'm not ready. Not when the truth has the potential to cause my life to implode so spectacularly. Not when, for the first time in a long time, everything feels right in the world.

. . .

It's dark when we land at Charles de Gaulle Airport. A sleek, black limo is waiting to take us to our hotel. I refuse the champagne the driver offers purely because I want to remember every single second of the journey without a fuzzy head.

My heart hammers in my chest as I get my first glimpse of the Eiffel Tower. The iconic structure sparkles against the navy night sky, illuminated by thousands of golden lights that cast a warm, welcoming glow. It's a breathtaking sight. Elegant. I can't believe I'm actually here.

A few minutes later, the driver drops us on the Avenue Montaigne outside the Hotel Plaza Athenee. Its classic Haussmann-style façade provides a majestic appearance, accentuated by signature red awnings and matching geranium-filled window boxes, contrasting against the creamy white of the building. Each room appears to have a wrought iron balcony. I can't wait to see what it's like inside.

'What do you think?' James pulls me into his chest.

'I can't believe this is my life. I feel like Emily,' I squeal, clapping a hand over my mouth.

'Well, if that daft fucking chef turns up looking for you, I'll throw him into the Seine,' James tuts.

'I knew you were watching it really!' I slap his chest playfully.

'I wasn't watching it. I was watching *you* watch it.'

'Do I look like Gogglebox to you?' I grab his hand and tug him towards the entrance, which is adorned with multi-coloured exotic flowers. The glass doors are flanked by two doormen, dressed in top hats and morning suits.

'I'd watch you watching paint dry if it meant I could slip my hand inside your panties,' he murmurs into my ear.

'Let's find our room.' Now I know what I've been missing all these years, I have a lot of making up to do.

I link my arm through James's and we stride into the

grand lobby. It's a haven of Parisian sophistication. I never want to leave. Marble floors gleam under the soft glow of the chandeliers. Elegant antique furnishings dot the space. Lavish crystal vases overflow with fresh white flowers.

We're greeted by the manager. 'Mr Beckett, how lovely to see you again.' That accent! If James's glare is anything to go on, I think I actually swooned.

Whoops.

They exchange pleasantries while my eyes roam over the artwork adorning the walls, landscapes of the city and the river.

The manager shows us to the lift. 'Allow me to show you to the penthouse.'

I should have guessed.

We ride the glass and chrome lift to the top floor while the manager asks about our dinner plans.

'We're eating out tonight,' James informs him. It's news to me. Maybe we will run into Gabriel after all!

'This is yours.' The manager flashes a key card over the door and opens it for us. 'You have your own dedicated butler. Buzz if you need anything at all.'

James places a hand on my back and ushers me inside.

My jaw drops at the floor-to-ceiling windows offering breath-taking views of the Paris skyline, including a direct view of the Eiffel Tower. I gravitate to the window, barely registering the opulent, soft cream and gold décor.

I suck in a long slow breath, gazing out at the cityscape. 'I think this might just be the most magnificent view I've ever seen.'

'Really?' James's deep baritone booms from behind me a split second before the sound of metal unzipping bleeds into my ears.

My lips stretch into a wide smile as I slowly turn around. My pulse spikes at the sight in front of me. James has slipped out of his suit jacket, rolled his shirt sleeves up and lowered his boxers enough to treat me to an entirely different view.

'Okay,' I concede, my eyes roaming all over my boyfriend. 'It's the second most magnificent.'

'That's more like it.' He wraps his hand around the base of his cock. 'Jesus, Scarlett, look what you do to me. You have me in this state all the fucking time. If I could spend forever with you, it still wouldn't be long enough.'

I stride across the plush carpet. 'We're barely here an hour and the most romantic city in the world has gotten under your skin.'

'No, Scarlett, you've gotten under my skin. So damn far, I swear you've breached my soul.'

'The feeling is mutual,' I murmur, replacing his hand with my own.

'You know, if you worked for me, we'd have a legitimate reason to make trips like this all the time. You wouldn't be a slave to someone else's hours or schedule.'

'Do you always get what you want Mr Beckett?' I run a finger over his torso, gliding over the smooth planes of muscle beneath.

'Always.' His eyes latch onto mine with a devilish glint. 'And I don't mind playing dirty.'

'Show me how dirty you play.' I push him back towards the bed with a smirk. 'Then show me this city like you promised.'

Chapter Forty-One
SCARLETT

Paris is every girl's dream. Last night, when we finally finished dining on each other, we ate in the restaurant on the top floor of the Eiffel Tower. James hired an entire floor overlooking the city below. A violinist serenaded us as one of the country's highest-acclaimed chefs served us course after course of sumptuous delicacies. Between the stunning scenery, the food, but most of all, the company, it was the most magical night of my life.

Today, we've spent the day strolling the city, posing in front of the Arc de Triomphe, and devouring croissants and crepes in discreet French cafés on street corners.

'Oh my goodness.' My feet come to an abrupt stop outside the window of the Dior store on the Avenue Montaigne. I could stare at the expensive, elegant haute couture all afternoon. The fabric seems to float from the mannequins.

'Let's go in.' James nudges me towards the entrance.

'No way. I was just looking.' I take a step back. 'This might be your world, but it's not mine.' I tear my eyes away from the window to look at him. Even here, in "holiday mode", he looks every bit the playboy billionaire in a pair of designer jeans and a polo shirt that presses indecently against his pecs.

I look down at myself, eyeing my own holiday wear, slim fitting jeans and pale blouse. My clothes definitely don't radiate the wealth in the way James's do.

'It is now.' He wraps an arm over my shoulder and attempts to steer me towards the sliding doors, but my feet root firmly to the spot.

'What's up?' he asks when I refuse to budge.

'I just can't believe this is real.' A lump forms in my throat. 'I've never had anyone treat me the way you do. I've never had anyone care about me like this. I still don't trust that it's going to last and that maybe I'll wake up one day and this will all have been a dream.'

'I don't *care* about you. I *love* you.' He pulls me into his torso and tilts my chin up, forcing me to meet his eyes.

'And it terrifies me,' I admit. 'Love didn't last for my mother. If anything, love killed her.'

'You know you can talk to me about it, whenever you're ready.' His hand moves to the back of my head, cradling it tenderly as people bustle by, oblivious to the moment we're sharing. 'I can't undo all the pain you've endured, but I promise it stops here. I told you I'll never hurt you. I'll protect you with my life.'

'But what if you get tired of me? Bored of this relationship? What if I give you my heart and you smash it into a trillion pieces? I don't think I could survive that.' That's the crux of it.

'It's never going to happen.' He presses a kiss on my temple. 'You're not the only one with trust issues. But we'll work through them together.'

'I want to tell you. I really do.' I grab his hands and pull them to my chest as I stare into his dark, soulful eyes, willing him to believe me. 'But I can't. It's...complicated. I'm not allowed to tell you, or anyone about it.'

James frowns. 'Not allowed?'

I turn my gaze away. 'Legally,' I say. 'You'd have to promise not to breathe a word of it to anyone.'

'Of course,' he gasps. 'Whatever it is, you can tell me. I'd never betray your trust.'

'When we get home, I'll tell you everything.' It's time. 'But I warn you, it's ugly.'

'Nothing you can say will change the way I feel about you.' His promise soothes my soul and I slump into him, every bit of tension seeping from my shoulders.

'I'd be lying if I said I wasn't utterly intrigued but if you really won't tell me until we get home, we should make the most of Paris. Let's burn some plastic. You need a new dress for tonight.'

'I do?' My eyes veer to the black silk masterpiece in the window.

'Well, you can't go on a private yacht dressed like that,' he smirks.

'A private yacht?'

'So you can experience the city in the most magical way.' He drags me inside the store before I can put up any further resistance.

The report in the tabloids about James's scandalous behaviour on a yacht flashes through my mind. I push back the green-eyed monster and replay his "I love you" instead. 'I thought you might take me to the Moulin Rouge. Maybe they'll let me dance.'

A low growl rumbles in my ear. 'I'm the only man who gets to see you dance from now on.'

'But you took away my pole,' I joke. The truth is, I miss it.

'I miss the exercise. I miss testing the strength of my body and losing myself in the music and movement.'

'But now you have a new pole,' he grunts with a sparkle in his eye as he slaps my ass playfully.

'True, although it's not quite the same size as the last one.' I stifle a laugh as he bites out another growl.

'Careful, or I'll be forced to remind you exactly how big it is.' He blows a gentle stream of air over my neck. A tingle cascades down my spine. 'Now, let's go buy you that dress.'

Inside we're treated to a glass of champagne while James insists on buying everything I glance at. A crystal-studded clutch, three two-piece suits, three new blouses, and a slim-fitting pencil skirt which he insists I wear to his office on Monday.

'Can we get these bagged up and sent directly to Ireland?' he asks the sales assistant as he hands over his credit card. 'All except this.' His palm grazes over the black backless masterpiece that had originally caught my eye in the window.

As we walk out of the store and back into the Parisian sun, he says, 'Wear this tonight. And don't even think about putting on any panties.'

The yacht, La Lumiere, shimmers under the moonlight as we cruise past Paris's most iconic sights. The Louvre, The Grand Palais, and Notre-Dame.

A myriad of stars glitter in the navy sky . I can't be certain if the goosebumps rippling over my skin are a product of the cool evening temperature, or the proximity of James.

'Where is everyone?' I glance around the enormous deck furnished with a firepit, a designer sofa, and two armchairs upholstered in the finest fabrics. It's every bit as opulent as the hotel suite.

We were welcomed by a smartly dressed crew who gave us a brief tour and a chilled bottle of Bollinger.

'I told them not to bother us with food for a while.' James looks absolutely edible in a jet-black tuxedo that showcases his broad shoulders to perfection, and the tie I bought him for Valentine's Day.

He tears his eyes from the riverbank to glance at the chunky silver watch on his wrist.

'Aren't you hungry?' I wet my lips, contemplating an entirely different hunger burning deep inside of me, one which my lack of lingerie isn't helping.

'Oh, I am starving, Scarlett.' His eyes darken. 'Just not for food.' He nudges me back onto the plush, cushioned couch and prises the glass of champagne from my hand, placing it on the composite edge of the firepit.

I glance around the deck towards the river bank. People flood the city admiring the sights. 'Shouldn't we go inside? Into the cabin?'

He eyes the hundreds of silhouettes in the streets. 'No. Let them watch.'

Heat builds between my legs at the mere idea, but sense wins out. 'We can't.'

'We can and we will.' An inferno scorches my skin. 'We both know you want them to see.' He slides into the space next to me, and slips his hand beneath my dress, inching his fingers sensually along my inner thigh.

'Isn't this how you got into this mess in the first place?' I arch an eyebrow at him through the moonlight, but I don't halt his hand as it inches higher, nudging my thighs wider apart.

'I wouldn't call this current situation a mess, exactly.' His lips curl up in devilish smile. 'Unless you're referring to this?' He swipes a finger through the slickness coating my entrance. 'Don't worry baby, I'm going to clean it up for you.' He drops to his knees, kneeling between mine, and lowers his face between my legs.

'James, what if someone sees us?' My protest is feeble. Because I can deny it all I like, but James is right. After years of hiding who I am, where I've been and what I want, I want the world to see me. Doing something so indecent in public does things to me. And my boyfriend knows that better than anyone.

'We're just two tourists.' He pushes my dress up higher. 'As far as anyone else is concerned, I could be on my knees to propose. It is the city of lovers, after all.'

The thought only serves to soak me further.

Firm hands grip my backside and tug me towards the edge of the couch. His face dips and his tongue swipes through my sex with such expertise I couldn't stop him if this was being televised on a sixty-foot screen for the entire population of France to watch. Every nerve ending in my body is on fire.

I part my legs further, offering myself to him, and feel his smile against my flesh. 'Good girl. Just so you know, sweetheart, someday soon, I will be on my knees for you for another reason.' He rocks back on his heels and pins me in a meaningful stare.

He's planning on proposing?

My stomach soars.

It's a battle not to squeal out loud.

'Look around at all the people. Anyone of them could glance over and see me worshipping my future wife.' He slides two fingers deep in my core and I moan. 'They can look. But I'm the only man who gets to touch you like this. It's my hand, my tongue, and my cock you come on.' His words are unravelling me faster than a spinning wheel.

'I'm close,' I whisper, feeling the flutters building in my core. 'I need you inside me. I need you to fill me up.' I barely recognise this brazen version of myself as the virgin that stepped out on the stage at the Luxor Lounge, but I like her. Like that I finally have the courage to speak up for what I want. That I no longer feel the need to hide.

'Whatever you want, baby.' His head angles down again and he offers one more long languid lick before rising from his knees. 'Come with me.' He places a hand on my hip and steers me towards the back of the deck, pressing me against the side of the yacht's waist-high wall.

I rest my elbows on the edge, gazing at the bridge as he nudges the back of my dress up and the chill air hits my ass cheeks. The sweet sound of his buckle undoing is swiftly followed by the sensation of his rock hard cock nudging at my entrance.

His chin rests on my shoulder and his arms wrap around my waist as he inches into me. 'Fuck, you feel so good, Scarlett.' His breath hitches as he fills me so completely. It's not just my body that's full, it's my heart and my soul. They're overflowing with him.

I arch my torso further forwards and he slides deeper, forcing a feral cry from my lips. 'You feel amazing.'

'Look around you. Soak it in.' His palms press over the backs of my hands resting on my stomach, his fingers entwining with mine. He trails a tongue across the side of my neck and fireworks explode beneath my skin.

My breasts are so full, so heavy with longing, while my clit throbs for more friction. 'James, I need...'

Before I've even finished the sentence, his hand slips beneath the front of my dress. His fingers find my clit and circle it slowly. Within seconds, I'm teetering over the edge of oblivion, my orgasm ripping through me so powerfully, it's debilitating. My legs shudder and shake as the world as I know it rocks beneath me.

James follows, seconds behind me, his final few pumps drawing out every last ounce of pleasure from my body.

Next time he asks me to work for him, the answer will be yes.

The next time he's on his knees for me, the answer will be yes,

Because there is nothing in this world this man won't do for me, and it's time I trusted him and reciprocated. Even if it means baring so much more than my body to him.

Chapter Forty-Two
JAMES

Lucien Moreau was only too keen to host us when I mentioned I was bringing my girlfriend to Paris. The paperwork for the acquisition is with our legal team, but there's no harm in checking the quality of the vineyards personally, before I sign the final documents.

We land in Marseille just before midday.

'Are you okay?' I ask Scarlett, as we disembark the jet.

She waits until we both have two feet on the ground before swivelling round and answering. 'I was devastated to leave Paris,' she says, 'but look at this.' She sweeps a hand around the scenic countryside. Rolling lavender fields and ancient olive groves span as far as the eye can see. It's quintessentially spring in Provence. 'This is something else.' She whistles lowly, her silver eyes soaking up every tiny detail. My heart swells in my chest.

I've never felt a love like it.

When I look at her, I feel like I've come home.

Maybe because what I see is a reflection of my own soul. I've been living my life. Doing what I was born to do, working hard and playing harder, but I'm beginning to realise that maybe I wasn't really living it. Maybe I was simply going through the motions?

She's technically no longer a virgin yet she still radiates an innocence that's my utter undoing. There is nothing in this world I wouldn't do for her. She takes such joy in the small things, like the caviar breakfast earlier, the Chanel dress she bought with my credit card today, even her eagerness to impress when I introduced her to my family.

Scarlett wears her heart on her sleeve and it's so fucking refreshing.

The urge to corrupt her and care for her are destined to permanently duel inside of my soul.

'It's not nearly as beautiful as you.' I press a kiss to her lips, marvelling as the midday sun illuminates her flawless skin.

'Corny— much?' She arches onto her tiptoes and inhales the side of my neck like she's snorting up a drug.

'I'm not corny. I'm horny. It's different.' I slap her backside and she squeals. 'I thought if I butter you up, you might let me fuck you again later.'

'You don't need to butter me up.' She presses her hips against mine in an open invitation.

'Well, in that case, what are we waiting for? Lucien sent a car. Let's get the tour of the vineyards over so we can get to the good stuff.'

Forty minutes later, I spot a sign for Chateau Éclatant, the largest of one of five of the Imperial Wine Group's vineyards, and the place Lucien calls home, for now, at least.

Chateau Éclatant is renowned for its exquisite range of wines. The rosés are some of the most delicate and aromatic in the world, the whites are supposed to be crisp and refreshing and the reds, robust and elegant. I'm looking forward to sampling them all.

As our chauffeur takes a right turn, a traditional-looking chateau comes into view.

'You're buying this?' Scarlett turns to me, open mouthed.

'Not me personally. Beckett's is technically the buyer and will be its new owner. There are five vineyards altogether, each with properties like this on them. The plan is to construct a number of luxury hotels, the details of which we'll leave to Sean. It's going to be perfect. This acquisition is going to benefit the group in so many ways, while also giving our distillery an edge over our competitors.' I purse my lips together thinking of the O'Connors. Slippery fuckers.

They tried to outbid us, but thankfully Lucien proved to be a man of his word and stood by our agreement. By next week, the paperwork will be complete and this will be all mine. Well, Beckett's at least.

I cast my eyes over the grounds. The spring sunshine bathes the entire estate in a golden light. Ancient stone walls, remnants of a time long past, encircle portions of the vineyard, probably to protect the precious vines. Between the rows, ragged clumps of wildflowers add splashes of colour.

'It's so ruggedly beautiful,' Scarlett says breathily.

We come to a stop outside the chateau.

It's half the size of my house in Dublin, but it has a certain charm. Lavender bushes flank the driveway, their scent brushing my nostrils as the chauffeur opens the door for us.

A large wooden front door swings open and Lucien appears, clutching a glass of red wine in his hand. Maybe if he hadn't been drinking his profits, and making bad investments along the way, he might not have been in the position where he had to sell. Oh well, his loss is our gain.

The rumour is that, regardless of how many generations

of the Moreaus have owned the family business, his wife is more than happy to part with it. As a native New Yorker, she's desperate to get back to her roots, especially now her son has established a business there.

'Bonjour! It's five o'clock somewhere, non?' Lucien lifts his glass in a toast as I help Scarlett out the car. She looks positively delectable in a cream linen dress that stops an inch above her knees. Her tanned, toned calves are accentuated by heeled wedges. She looks every bit the billionaire's wife. And I can't wait to make her precisely that.

'Amen to that.' It's the kind of axiom that keeps the whiskey—and apparently wine—corporations in business.

I introduce Scarlett as I wrap an arm around her shoulders and we take the steps together.

Scarlett extends her hand but instead of shaking it, Lucien brings it to his lips and presses a lingering kiss on the back of it.

'My darling, it is a pleasure to meet you.' His hazel eyes rove all over her as she offers a polite smile. 'I'll greet you the French way.' The cheeky cunt actually presses his weathered lips to my wife-to-be's cheek. And then again on the other one.

A growl rumbles in my chest. 'Thank fuck we're not French. It's safer for everyone.'

Laughter rolls from Lucien.

I fire him a potent glare and he stops abruptly. 'Let me give you the tour,' he says, ushering us inside. We step into a hallway which boasts high ceilings, exposed beams and terracotta tiled floors. It's exactly as I imagined it.

Lucien gives us both a glass of wine for the tour. We start in a grand salon with an enormous fireplace. Scarlett's eyes glaze as she stares at the ashes like she's seeing something that isn't there.

I place a hand on her lower back and she jumps. 'Are you okay?'

'Yes. Sorry.' Her fingers play with the cross around her neck that she refuses to remove. I make a mental note to ask her about it as Lucien leads us to the next room, a formal dining room, half the size of my own. It's quaint, but I kind of like it. Judging by Scarlett's coos, she does too.

Perhaps, I'll keep this as a holiday home for us. There's no point being the oldest Beckett if I can't have first dibs on the company's acquisitions.

Lucien shows us to our room to freshen up and tells us to make ourselves at home, encouraging us to take a look around the grounds on our own. The walls are painted a sunshine yellow and there's a balcony offering stunning views of the sprawling estate.

'He's quite a character,' Scarlett says, opening her suitcase.

The memory of him kissing her sets my jaw tense. 'He's either brave or stupid.'

'Oh relax, the man is old enough to be my father,' she scolds.

'We both know you don't mind an age gap.' I arch my eyebrows pointedly.

'There's an *older* man and an *old* man.' She tuts, changing into a pair of flat pumps.

'I don't like people touching what's mine.' I cross the room and place my hands on her hips. She tilts her face up, reaches on her tiptoes and kisses my lips.

I trace a finger along her jawline, then lower over her long elegant neck. 'When I first saw you dance, all I could think about was getting you on your knees for me, but the truth is, it's you who brings me to my knees. There isn't anything I wouldn't do for you.' I lower my fingers to the silky soft skin on her chest and inch them between her breasts.

'Are you love birds okay in there?' Lucien's voice travels from along the corridor.

'We would be if you'd leave me long enough to bury myself in my woman,' I hiss.

This is why, traditionally, I don't stay in other people's houses. But with no hotels within forty miles, it was a matter of practicality, as well as politeness.

'We're fine. Just coming,' Scarlett singsongs back loudly as I scowl. 'Where are your manners?' she whispers to me.

'That was what I suspected.' Lucien chuckles. Dirty old man.

'Where are *his* manners?' My thumb jerks towards the door and our host's echoing laughter.

I suppose I can put up with him for a night, given what I'm getting at the end of it.

The grounds are far more impressive than the chateau. The lawn is beautifully manicured. There's a modest swimming pool surrounded by several sun loungers to the rear of the property, and wrought-iron table and chairs in the middle of a terracotta patio. There's even a hidden gazebo among the trees.

As we walk, Lucien tells us about the different varieties of grapes and sustainable farming practices in passionate detail as we walk through the vineyards. His knowledge is incredible, surpassed only by his exuberance.

The winery itself is state of the art. By the time we've sampled several of the grape varieties, I no longer care how long Lucien's eyes linger on Scarlett, because my hand never leaves her arm, or her ass, or her hip. If he wants to watch, I've already demonstrated to half of Paris that I'm okay with that.

An unfamiliar feeling fills my chest. It's so rare, it takes a few moments for me to identify it. Contentment? I haven't taken a proper break from the office in years. Even in Dubai, at New Year, I was a slave to the never-ending emails and phone calls.

The stillness of the vineyard, the scenery, and the wine, all has a part to play. As does the time we spent in Paris. And the fact I diverted all my emails and calls to Chantel and warned her not to bother me unless someone was dying.

But the truth is, the warm, peaceful feeling filling my chest is predominantly because of Scarlett.

My father will accept her for who she is. Former pole dancer or not. He'll have to. Because I wasn't joking about getting down on one knee. Sooner rather than later.

Her eyes shift to mine as we stroll back towards the chateau.

'Please, join me on the terrace for another glass of wine,' Lucien insists. 'It's rare the weather is so warm this early in the year. It would be a shame not to make the most of it.'

As much as I'd like to decline, Scarlett's face lights up. Something twists in my chest. This is a novelty for her, soaking up the Provencal countryside. The sensation of the sun beating down on her shoulders.

It's easy to forget that she's struggled for years. That she's not accustomed to this type of lifestyle. But I'm going to make sure she becomes accustomed to it– and quickly.

Lucien is persistent. 'Indulge me. Make an old man happy, have another drink,' he winks at Scarlett.

She glances at me with those huge doe-like eyes and my heart inflates like a helium balloon.

'Of course, if you wish, Scarlett.'

A black BMW is parked to the left of the chateau. It wasn't there before. Lucien's wife? Or the chef perhaps?

Lucien chatters incessantly as we round the side of the building towards the glistening pool and padded sun loungers. 'Perhaps you could get married here, oui?'

Scarlett's eyes flash, as a flush of colour splashes her

cheeks. I'll marry her wherever the hell she wants, once she agrees to spend her life with me. I squeeze her hand and she squeezes mine back in an unspoken exchange.

The soft tinkling of female laughter floats through the air. It's coming from beside the pool.

'Ah, my amour is home,' Lucien grins and beckons us around the back of the building.

A woman in her fifties sits on one of the wrought-iron chairs tucked beneath a matching table. Her short, blonde hair is spiked up into a stylish fashion, while oversized sunglasses hide the top half of her face. Her lips are painted a bright shade of pink that matches the floral pattern on her floaty summer dress.

There's no denying Madame Moreau is an attractive woman for her age.

The guy sitting opposite her certainly seems to think so, given the way his hand lingers on her knee. He has his back to us, but I can see he's wearing a sharp black suit that cuts across his shoulders like it was made for them. His thick dark hair gleams in the sun.

An uneasy sensation snakes into my gut.

I appreciate that the French are more liberal, but if I caught some man with his hand on my wife's knee, he'd lose it. Painfully.

Madame Moreau rises as we come into view. 'Lucien, darling.' She opens her arms to him like they've been apart for weeks not hours. So dramatic. I fight my threatening eye roll .

'Our new owner is here.' She gestures to the man in the suit and my head snaps up so fast I risk whiplash.

Frown lines crease Lucien's forehead as his eyes narrow, darting between the stranger in the suit and me.

Ever so slowly, and with a confidence that borders on arrogance, the dark-haired man stands and turns around. A coldness glints in his blue, piercing eyes. The smile lifting his lips isn't fooling any of us.

Declan O'Connor. In the flesh.

Fuck.

'Is he one of your brothers?' Lucien cocks his head.

'No,' Scarlett says in a tone I've never heard her use before. 'He's one of mine.'

Chapter Forty-Three
SCARLETT

Time stands still. Even beneath the heat of the Provencal sun, a coldness akin to death seeps into my bones. My heart beats so hard it feels like it's going to burst right out of my chest.

The prospect of this moment has haunted my worst nightmares for years and stolen so much joy from my life. And all that time, fear of facing this man has held me hostage in my own home.

Just when I dared to try and be happy, here he is, my stepbrother, determined to destroy me, just like he always promised he would.

Our last conversation forces itself to the forefront of my mind. I remember every word like it was yesterday. Probably because I've replayed it in my head every day since.

'You've taken our father away from us,' he roared in my face, the stench of alcohol on his breath stinging my eyes.

'At least he's still breathing. Which is more than I can say for my mother.' My voice broke as the harsh reality hit me. It was the precise moment it truly dawned on me that I'd never see her again. Never hear her sweet voice again. Never feel a love like hers again.

'*It was an accident,*' Declan boomed, banging a clenched fist on the old oak table where we'd shared so many dinners. The noise shook me to the core. Violence was intrinsically woven into his genes. He was forever thumping around, punching walls and banging doors. Is it any wonder I jump even at the prettiest fireworks, or the slightest slamming of a car door?

If I'd placed any value on my life, I'd have shut up. Declan's temper was notorious at the best of times, but that night, the night the jury convicted Jack O'Connor of manslaughter, Declan looked ready to blow. I think a part of me wanted him to.

After all, what did I have left?

My mother was gone and all that remained were the monsters I called my stepbrothers.

They weren't supposed to be within a hundred feet of the house, which is why I'd snuck out of Eleanor's, the teacher who took me in. I wanted something of my mother's to remember her by. Her necklace.

But the O'Connors always believed they were above the law.

Which is precisely why I testified against their father.

'*He set the distillery on fire deliberately,*' I argued.

'*She wasn't supposed to be there.*' Declan's face was practically purple with rage, as Michael, Keith, John and Joseph flanked his sides.

'*But she was, and now she's dead.*' I folded my arms across my chest with a defiance , not caring if he killed me there and then. Part of me was already dead.

'*And you will be too, if you don't retract your testimonial,*' Declan had hissed, towering over me.

John placed a hand on Declan's shoulder in a silent warning. He might be the youngest of the five brothers but he's always been the sharpest.

'Leave it, Dec. Unless you want to be in the cell next to Dad.' John shot me a sympathetic look over Declan's shoulder.

Declan's parting shot had stayed with me. *'If I ever see you again, I swear I'll kill you with my bare hands.'*

Unlike Declan, John was just a kid when our parents got married. We shared the same memories of our parents laughing. Kissing when they thought none of us were watching.

It didn't last long.

I've learnt since that nothing really does. Not unless it's in a romance novel.

Which is why the feelings I have for James Beckett terrify me.

But not as much as the horror on his face right now.

'What the actual fuck, Scarlett?' James bites out, a vein throbbing furiously in his neck.

Sensing the seriousness of the situation, Madame Moreau steps away from Declan and reaches for her husband.

As if he can save her. Declan always used to carry a weapon wherever he went. I doubt he's changed over the years.

'It's been a while, Scarlett.' Declan steps forwards, his lips curving into a cruel smile. He unbuttons his suit jacket and sticks a hand languidly into his trouser pocket. 'Our father said to pass on his regards. He's up for parole. Good behaviour and all that.' The threat is clear.

'He's not my father. And you're no longer my brother.' It takes everything I have to control the tremor in my voice.

Laughter rips through the air, low and callous and calculated. 'It's a fucking good job.' His eyes slant to James, who is watching our exchange with an expression that could slice through ice. 'If I was, I'd have to kill this prick for fucking my little sister.'

James launches himself at Declan, but Lucien and I grab his arms to hold him back. 'Don't,' I beg. 'It's what he wants.'

Declan thrives on violence. Always has. Always will.

'What I want is for him to rescind his bid on the Imperial Winery Group and walk away from the Moreaus.' Declan's steely eyes level at James.

'It's never going to happen.' James's tone is adamant. He smooths a hand over the front of his shirt as he composes himself.

'Never say never.' Declan's tongue clicks against the roof of his mouth as his hand reaches inside his suit jacket. 'I can be very persuasive.'

My stomach bottoms out.

My chest is too tight.

I can't breathe.

Can't speak.

Can't even pretend to be okay.

I always knew this would happen. That he'd come for me. But I never expected it would be here, not like this. And now it looks like he's hitting two birds with one stone.

Or one gun.

But when he pulls his hand out of the inside of his jacket, it's not a pistol he's clutching. It's a lighter. O'Connors favourite weapon. I flinch. My shoulders are rigid. Every breath is a struggle.

Declan reaches into his pocket again, this time extracting a thick brown cigar. The type my stepfather used to smoke in celebration when he'd cut his latest deal. 'Surely we can work something out. I've made it clear how much we want this.' He glances to the chateau and the rolling vineyards beyond. 'And how far we're willing to go to get it.'

I have no idea what he's up to, or why he wants this land, but I'd bet everything it's not for the vineyards. Or not *just* the vineyards. It'll be a front for drug trafficking. Or worse.

'It's not up for negotiation,' James spits, folding his arms across his chest as the Moreaus and I wait with bated breath.

'Everything is up for negotiation. Isn't that right, sis?' Declan's thumb clicks down on the lighter and a tiny flame sparks a thousand horrific imaginings of the night my mother died.

I wasn't there, but I saw the news footage of the distillery burning with her trapped inside. I've cried a river of tears imagining what she must have gone through. The pain. The fear. I've lived it with her over and over in my mind. And while she's hopefully at peace now, I've never found that luxury in this life. Not until I found James at least.

And I'm pretty certain after Declan's shocking revelation, he'll want nothing more to do with me. It's bad enough I didn't tell him I'm an O'Connor at heart. It's worse that I never told him.

I'm no better than Cynthia Van Darwin.

'She was dishonest. I can't stand dishonesty.'

I didn't lie exactly, but I certainly omitted the truth. And the only thing I stole is his heart.

James's throat bobs and I hear him swallow. His narrow eyes are dangerously dark, except from the torrid gold flecks dancing around the edge of his irises.

Declan's thumb snaps down on the lighter again and I jump.

Then something kindles in James's stare.

Something clicks.

It's as if all the half-truths, all the things I couldn't say, but alluded to, every single one of my quirks or triggers become clear with that one tiny flicker of fire.

'Get out of here.' James's voice leaves no room for debate. 'Get out of here, and I might let you live to see another day.'

'Clearly, you need time to think about this.' Declan brings the cigar to his lips, holding it between his teeth as he lights it. He inhales deeply. 'I'll give you a week.'

James scoffs. 'Or what? The paperwork is already

complete. The Imperial Winery Group belongs to Beckett Enterprises.'

It's stretching the truth, but not by a million miles.

'Uncomplete it.' Declan blows out a ring of smoke. The scent weaves into my lungs and nausea rises in my chest. 'Or I'll start picking off the Becketts one by one.'

A shudder shakes my entire body.

Declan nods at the Moreaus, bidding them a polite goodbye, and a cruel smile cracks his face as he breezes away as if he didn't just threaten to kill everyone.

Lucien wraps his arms around his wife. 'We picked a good time to get out of the industry.'

Mrs Moreau looks as shocked as I feel. 'I'm going inside to cool down.' She fans herself with her hand as she excuses herself.

'I'll go with you.' Lucien forces a lighter tone but it's clear from his expression he's shaken. 'Dinner will be served at eight.'

'We won't be staying.' James doesn't so much as glance at him.

'There's no need to rush off. He said a week.' Lucien is like an open book. His eyes blink several times and then refocus as if he's mentally calculating how to get himself out of here in less time.

James doesn't dignify him with a response as Lucien offers a sympathetic glance over his shoulder and disappears around the side of the chateau.

I feel the weight of my boyfriend's stare long before I meet his eye. 'You and I have a lot to discuss.'

My heart sinks, torn between relief that Declan has gone, for now, and the terror of having to admit the truth.

'I think you'd better tell me everything,' he says. 'Start talking.'

Chapter Forty-Four
JAMES

I lead Scarlett to the wrought-iron table where Declan and Mrs Moreau had been sitting. The revving of a diesel engine fading into the distance signals Declan's departure and the only remaining sound is the gentle rustling of the vines and the light whispers of the breeze through the neighbouring olive trees.

It's amazing how quickly such beauty can be tarnished.

I don't doubt Declan meant what he said.

A week.

Is it any coincidence my father's seventieth birthday ball is exactly a week away?

We're going home tonight. If we're at war again, I need to prepare my brothers. Although were we ever not at war?

'My mother took a job in the distillery when I was just a child. She was a widow, young and naïve. Jack O'Connor took a fancy to her. Lavished her with his attention and gifts. Everyone knew his reputation, but he said he loved her. And he promised her the world.' Scarlett's silver eyes brim with tears. 'But, he took it from her instead.' She shakes her head.

Her hands clasp on her lap, fingers woven together so tightly the tips turn white.

'In public, Jack treated my mother like a queen. She wore the best clothes, drove the nicest cars, and they sent me to the best school in Dublin. But behind closed doors, he was always yelling at her. Belittling her. He stopped her from seeing her friends. She was trying to get out. To get us both out.' Scarlett's eyes drift out over the horizon, blankly.

Whatever she's looking at, it isn't the same view I can see. 'The O'Connors were struggling financially. While Jack liked to spend money, he didn't invest it wisely. Fortunately, my mother had secretly stashed a bit away and hidden it at the distillery.'

She sucks in a breath. 'I can't prove Jack knew she was in there when he torched the place, but somehow, deep down, I know it's true. I couldn't let him get away with it. He killed my mother and I'll never forgive him for that, which is why I was determined to testify against him in court.'

'What?' Jack O'Connor is the biggest lunatic out of the whole family. Given his reputation, I'm surprised Scarlett's still alive to tell the tale.

The man killed his own wife. Scarlett's mother.

My chest cracks open for the woman in front of me. The one I love so ferociously, but I realise now, know so little about.

It all makes sense now.

Scarlett's fear of fire.

Why she's been locked away most of her adult life.

Why she hasn't let a man close enough to touch her. What I once thought was a blessing, was truly the worst curse, for her anyway.

'The court gave me anonymity, so my name was never reported in any of the papers,' she explains.

Of course. I would have remembered otherwise. After all, Scarlett's face isn't one I'd easily forget. It's no wonder she insisted on not appearing in any photographs of the two of us together. She was terrified the O'Connors would come after her. And now, thanks to me, they know exactly where to find her.

'I was a minor.' Giant, pear-shaped tears spill over her pretty face. 'So my name was protected.'

'What happened? Did they put you into care?' Oh, Jesus. Just when I thought it couldn't get any worse.

'Thankfully, one of my teachers took me in and hid me from the rest of the family.' She nods. 'When I turned eighteen, a couple of weeks after the trial, I got a job in a pub in Temple Bar and they let me stay in a room above it.'

'I'm surprised you didn't just leave the country. What if they'd come looking for you? I know what the O'Connors are like.' My guts twist at the thought of a world where Scarlett doesn't exist. I reach out and swipe a thumb across her cheek and instinctively bring it to my lips.

My head is spinning.

So many questions. Questions I'm not sure I want the answers to.

'My mother wanted me to get an education. A good one, so I'd have the choices in life that she never did. I was– no I *am* determined to make her proud.' She lifts her gaze. 'I'd already applied for my scholarship to Trinity and received the acceptance offer shortly after my eighteenth birthday. None of them knew about it.' She shrugs. 'I figured I could hide in plain sight, in the one place they'd assume I'd surely leave.'

It doesn't bear thinking about.

I want to kill every single one of those O'Connors for what they've done to her, but that doesn't quell the shock that I've been sleeping with the enemy.

She's one of them.

Or *was* at least.

If not by blood, then by marriage.

She lied to me.

Or at the very least omitted the truth.

'Why didn't you tell me before?' I pin her with a stare, keeping my voice as level as I can while adrenaline courses through my body.

'After the trial, I was given a new identity. Nathan, the detective in charge of the investigation, is the only person who knows who I am and where I am.'

'Nathan?' The man I've spent way too many nights wondering about.

She nods, gripping the cross around her neck again, running her finger over its sharp edges.

I wish she'd told me the truth. I hate that she lied to me. I get it, but I hate it. Hate the thought that I don't really know her at all. 'I asked you once before if Scarlett was your real name.'

'I never lied about that. Scarlett is the name my mother gave me. Fitzgerald is my mother's maiden name. She changed it to Maguire when she married my father and kept his name when he died. It felt right that I should take her name when she died. I've only been to her grave a handful of times. I'm terrified they'll spot me there, and of someone making the connection between us. But by taking her name, I felt like a part of her is always with me. And I suppose I have this.' She holds out the chain around her neck. 'She lent it to me. A few days before she died. While I have it around my neck, I feel like I have a piece of her with me. It brings me a small sense of comfort.'

'It all makes sense now.' It's why Killian couldn't find much information about Scarlett Fitzgerald. He was searching for a girl who died along with her mother.

'I know there's been bad blood between your family and the O'Connors for years, but I'm not one of them. I never was. They're my enemy as much as yours. Maybe even more so.'

She's right. I know she is.

But try telling that to the rest of my family.

And the Board.

My father will likely have another heart attack when he finds out.

If I were to marry a pole dancer and the former stepsister of our biggest rivals, who incidentally are connected to the biggest crime syndicate this country has ever seen, it would be the scandal of the century. But then again, I've never been one to shy away from scandal.

Being associated with an O'Connor will wreck me.

Fuck, it already has.

Because if I walk away from her, I will have nothing.

I reach across the table and take Scarlett's hand. She glances up from beneath those long back, lashes, weighted with unshed tears. Vulnerability etches into every line of her face.

'I'm sorry I didn't tell you.' Her fingers weave between mine. 'I couldn't.'

'No, angel, I'm sorry.' I bring her hand to my mouth and pepper tiny kisses over the back of it. 'I'm sorry you had to go through all of this alone. I'm sorry about your mother. And I'm so sorry I didn't know.' I pull her lithe frame into my arms and sit her on my lap as if she were a child, cradling the back of her head as she nuzzles into my chest. The familiar scent of her shampoo invades my senses and suddenly I just want to be at home with her. Our home. Surrounded by our protection staff. Because if anything should ever happen to her, I'd never forgive myself.

'I'll never let anything happen to you, Scarlett.' I rock her back and forth as harrowing sobs wrack her body, emotions that she's probably had to bottle up for years just to survive. 'This doesn't change anything. But no more secrets.'

She lifts her head to meet my eyes. 'You forgive me?'

'There's nothing to forgive. You've been through so much. Shut yourself away for years, but yet you let me in. Let me get close to you. Your feelings for me overrode your biggest fears. And that means everything to me.'

Concern creases the corner of her eyes. 'But what about your family?'

'I'm not going to lie to you, it's not going to be easy.' I inhale a deep breath. 'But they're your family now. Whether they like it or not. You're going to be my wife one day. And I don't care if they fire me as CEO or if the Imperial Winery Group acquisition doesn't go through.'

Her lips pop open. 'But that's everything you've been working for. Everything you've been fighting for since we met.'

'No, angel, everything I've been fighting for is you. Even if the person I was fighting was mostly myself.' I brush her hair back from her forehead with a tender sweep. 'I didn't intend on falling in love with you. You're not the only one who doesn't trust easily. But I'm in too deep to ever go back. A life without you in it isn't a life at all. We'll face this together, whatever the consequences.'

Chapter Forty-Five
JAMES

I've never been as happy to get home. At least in Dublin I have my brothers and our security teams, and I can protect Scarlett from anything and anyone who might contemplate harming her. She's never further than the next room away. The only way either of us can sleep at the moment is in each other's arms, and even then, she often wakes with night terrors.

Is it any fucking wonder given everything she's been through?

Her work placement in my office is both a blessing and a curse. I'm so grateful to have her in my direct line of sight, but when she's strutting around in pencils skirts and stilettos all damn day, it's a distraction I don't need.

Twice today, I've had to bend her over my desk, and it's barely even midday.

A knock sounds on my office door. 'Come in.'

Chantel enters, her ponytail swishing as she stalks in. 'I thought I ought to warn you, your father's on the way up. He's just stormed into the building, and according to the girls on reception, there's actual steam pluming from his ears.'

Oh fuck.

I could do without his wrath on top of having to deal with Declan O'Connor.

I glance at Scarlett who is poring over the final figures for the Imperial Winery Group acquisition. Her lips purse and vulnerability flickers across her face. 'Chantel, grab an early lunch and take Scarlett with you.'

Chantel beams. 'Sure.'

'Go to Azure. Put it on the company credit card. Take your time and don't rush back.' My father is neither quick to anger, nor is he quick to calm. It was only a matter of time before he found out what happened in Provence. No doubt he's about to bollock me for not telling him, but I didn't want to give him another heart attack.

'Azure? Seriously?' Chantel claps her hands together. 'An early birthday present?'

'No, just my treat.' I send flowers every year, but with all that she does for me, she deserves a hell of a lot more.

Scarlett closes a file on the desk and stands. 'You sure you don't want me to stay?'

'I can deal with my father, but take the stairs. I don't want you running into him.' He's still not sold on the idea of me dating a former pole dancer, so I'm pretty certain he won't be thrilled that she's now working for me. He'll get used to it, in time. He'll have to. But if he's already stressed about the O'Connors, I don't want to poke an angry bear.

Chantel beckons Scarlett towards the door, not even attempting to hide her glee at this sudden turn of events. 'Lunch in Dublin's most exclusive restaurant awaits. It's only right we wash it down with a fancy bottle of Gavi.'

Scarlett hesitates as she rounds the corner of my desk, like she's debating whether to kiss me goodbye. I lurch forwards and press my lips to hers, to save her from making the decision.

'Gross,' Chantel mutters.

I tear my mouth from Scarlett's. 'Take Tim and two other security guys. Don't go anywhere but Azure. I'll come and find you when I'm done here.'

Scarlett nods and follows Chantel out of the office without further protest.

I tap my desk with my pen, listening as the lift doors ping open at the far end of the corridor. Thunderous marching feet approach and the office door swings open so hard, it bangs against the inside wall.

'Come in, why don't you?' My sarcasm is lost on my father as he storms into my office. As usual, he's wearing a smart, tailored suit, even though he's supposed to be retired.

'What the fuck are you thinking, son? Jack O'Connor's fucking daughter. You are literally sleeping with the enemy! If her deranged brothers don't kill you, you'll be lucky if she doesn't stab you herself while you sleep!' His face is a deep shade of violet, his features scrunched with disgust.

Fuck.

'I can explain.' I raise my hand, attempting to quell my father's temper before the blood vessel throbbing in his head actually bursts.

'You'd better have a good explanation,' he booms incredulously, 'because as far as I can see, there is no fucking explanation for this abomination! Bad enough that she's a pole dancer, but for fuck's sake, son, an O'Connor? Look at this.' He points to the deep scar on his face. 'Even if they weren't our business rivals, you know they're involved with the biggest organised crime syndicate in the country. They are dangerous fuckers. I heard what happened in Provence. Lucien Moreau called me and told me everything, how Declan turned up and had the gall to threaten my entire family.'

'I'm dealing with it.'

'And dropped the bombshell that that tart you're supposedly dating is related to them.' The vein in my father's temple continues to pulse furiously.

'She's not a tart and she's not an O'Connor.' My gaze narrows. If he'd just stop ranting and listen for a second, I could explain.

'I said find a suitable wife, not an unscrupulous one. This is yet another scandal, an abomination. And on top of all that, it's a death wish.' He bangs a fist on the desk. 'End it. Now,' he roars and stalks out of my office, slamming the door behind him.

I'll do no such thing.

In fact, I'll make sure the whole damn world knows Scarlett's not an O'Connor.

And there's only one way to do it. I grab my suit jacket from the back of the chair and set out towards Grafton Street.

I'm going to officially make her a Beckett.

Chapter Forty-Six

SCARLETT

It's hard to pretend everything is normal when it feels like a ticking time bomb is perched beneath the balls of my feet. Seeing Declan again has dredged up a lot of long-buried emotions. I'm struggling to process. The thought of Jack O'Connor getting parole haunts my nights and plagues my days.

The only saving grace is the timing. In James's office, I'm safe. He hasn't let me out of his sight. When he's not educating me on the financial aspects of the business, he's educating me on all sorts of kinky desk sex.

My cheeks are permanently flushed. Despite the threat hanging over us, maybe even in spite of it, nothing has changed between James and me. If anything, our bond has only grown stronger. He's seen all of me, even the ugliest parts, and he still accepts me.

We're the talk of the building, so Chantel revealed over lunch the other day when James's father turned up out of the blue. But James doesn't seem to give a flying fuck. The Board are apparently delighted now the acquisition is almost officially through.

The fact that James is involved in a serious relationship with a fourth-year finance student from Trinity is apparently a good thing.

Well, as long as they don't find out that particular finance student is a former pole dancer, the stepdaughter of one of the country's most dangerous criminals, and who's regularly getting banged rotten on a Beckett work placement...

I gather Alexander Beckett heard the news and is none too happy about it. Understatement of the century.

James promises he'll come round, but I'm not so sure. It's a bit like Romeo and Juliet, except James didn't know I was Juliet until he was already invested. Plus, I'm not planning on drinking any poison. In fact, if I thought I could get away with slipping some Declan's way, I'd do it myself.

How are we going to spin it when word gets out? Because it will, eventually. James assures me he'll take care of everything. And I believe him. Trust is earned, not freely given, and James has earned mine implicitly over the past few months.

So far, the O'Connors haven't made good on their threats, but security has significantly increased since we arrived home from France. Killian's men flank the mansion night and day and accompany us to his office. I can't even go to the toilet without having someone outside the door to make sure nothing untoward happens!

Above anyone, I know how necessary it is when dealing with the O'Connors, how real the threat hanging over James and his family, and over me, now Declan knows exactly where I am.

James has met with his brothers every evening this week. I gather they have a plan. They've all been informed of the situation and of my past. Unlike their father, they don't seem to be holding it against me.

It's Friday night and James is still holed up in the office in the house. He's not due to finish until past ten o'clock. Sean, Caelon and Killian left half an hour ago. Rian is the last to leave. Even his usual carefree demeanour has been replaced with a sombre one.

'I'm sorry about this,' I blurt as we meet in the hall on his way out.

'It's not you they came after. The O'Connors would find any excuse for trouble.' Rian shakes his head. 'Why don't you go up and see James. He could do with cheering up.' Rian nods towards James's' office and strides off towards the front door.

'Wait,' I call before I can stop myself. He swivels slowly on his heels with a curious expression pinching his features.

'Just be careful, okay? I know how dangerous the O'Connors can be.'

'I can take care of myself,' Rian assures me with a tight smile.

I only hope he's right.

As I stalk towards James's office, my stilettos click on the marble. They're not the most comfortable shoes, but I've decided to at least try to look like a billionaire's girlfriend, even if I still don't feel it on the inside.

Two suited security guards flank the door, but step aside as I approach and knock tentatively.

'Can I come in?' I nudge the door open a crack and I'm immediately hit with his unique scent, and the smell of the leather upholstery.

'Of course,' his deep, gravelly voice sends the best type of shivers down my spine.

Dim evening sunlight streams through the sash windows, illuminating every shadow on his face. Dark circles linger beneath his eyes as he beckons me to his desk.

He's still wearing a tailored suit and crisp, white shirt. He looks every bit the billionaire CEO behind his vast wooden desk. 'Hop up here and let me see you.' Given the hungry look gleaming in his pupils, maybe he isn't as tired as he looks.

Those deep, dark eyes roam over the black pencil dress I'm wearing. It seemed appropriate for my work placement. Judging by his expression, he agrees.

I cross the thick plush carpet but I don't sit. It's not that I don't want him. I do. More so than ever, but my feet are itchy.

I need to burn off some of this nervous energy that's been hovering over me since I came face to face with my past.

'I was thinking of popping out to meet Avery. I haven't seen her properly in weeks, other than for a quick lunch on campus, and I'm starting to feel like a caged animal.'

'You can't be serious.' He stiffens in his chair, his back straighter than a steel pole. And I should know. 'You heard what Declan said. He's going to start picking the Becketts off one by one.' He grimaces.

'I'm not a Beckett,' I remind him, trying to lighten the mood.

'You're about to be. Sooner than you think, if I get my way.'

My stomach somersaults, and it has more to do with his words, than his palms slowly sliding up the back of my legs.

'Are you serious?' The words come out as barely more than a whisper.

'I've never been more serious about anything in my life. It took me thirty-three years to find you. I'm not going to risk losing you now. You, of all people, know how dangerous those fuckers are. Dangerous and deranged.' His fingers inch higher on my thighs until they hit the top of my lace hold-ups. A low growl rumbles in his chest. 'Are you sure the O'Connors didn't send you here to kill me slowly with outfits like this?'

'Don't even mention that name. Please. I can't joke about them. Not now, not ever. Any developments?'

I don't know why I'm asking. I'm not sure I truly want an answer.

'I'm sorry, sweetheart. Bad joke. We're working on it. The Imperial Wine acquisition is hours away from completion. I refuse to submit to Declan's demands, or anyone else's. Well, anyone but you, that is.' Ebony eyes slide towards mine. 'We're going to bring the O'Connors down once and for all.'

'What do you mean, "bring them down"?'

James raises an eyebrow, his pupils steely with determination.

'You're not going to...' I can't even bring myself to finish the sentence. Surely, he isn't suggesting meeting violence with violence. As much as I hate the O'Connors, Jack and Declan in particular for everything they've done, there has to be another way. I've seen enough brutality to last a lifetime. Where does it end?

James shakes his head. 'I would, if it came to it. I'd wring their necks with my bare hands if it meant keeping my family safe. But no, we Becketts operate differently. We stay on the right side of the law, where possible, at least. There are other ways and means of taking people down.'

Another shiver slides down my spine. This one is far from sexual.

'I'm worried,' I admit, arching forwards and raking my fingers through his cropped dark hair.

'I won't let anything happen to you.' his hand catches mine and he pulls it to his lips.

'I'm not worried about me. I'm worried about you.' I exhale slowly. 'I've already lost my mother to them. I couldn't bear to lose you as well.'

'You won't. Not to them. But tomorrow is promised to none of us, which is why we need to make the most of today.' He forces a smile. 'What we need is a distraction from all of this stress. Come with me, I have a present for you.' He rises, taking my hands in his and guides me to the door.

'Not another one.' I've barely used the last present he gave me. My driving lessons have taken a backseat to all my other "learning". Driving him is exponentially more thrilling than driving any car. Even an Audi R8.

The security guards immediately fall into step behind us as we step out of the office.

'I don't need a present. You've given me more than I can ever repay.' I glance down at my outfit and at the eye-wateringly expensive Jimmy Choos on my feet.

'Nonsense. I love spoiling you.' James takes my hand and leads me along the corridor towards his personal gym. I've been in there a couple of times, mostly to perve on him lifting weights, watching in awe as the slick sweat coats his skin.

But instead of taking the door on the right into the gym, he veers me towards a door on the left.

'Wait here,' he tells the security guards, before nudging me inside the thick panelled door.

I take a tentative step into the darkness. Unlike the rest of the house, this room has no windows. James steps in behind me and closes the door with a definitive click before flicking the light switch on.

Millions of tiny stars cascade across the ceiling and bounce over the four walls. My eyes adjust to the dimness and home in on a stage in the centre of the room. It's an elevated circular black marble platform, not a million miles different to the ones in the Luxor Lounge.

The best part? There's a gleaming steel pole in the middle of it. 'Is this for me?'

'I'm pretty sure we're both going to reap the benefits.'

He shrugs, a smirk curling his lips upwards. 'You wanted exercise?' James sweeps a hand towards the stage. 'Be my guest.'

I don't need telling twice.

It's not the most traditional gift in the world, but it's the most thoughtful one I've ever received. Dancing is my escape from the real world. Its familiarity is my solace. And James knows above anyone, after years of laying low, I crave being seen.

I'm truly touched. Not by the expense or trouble that he's gone to, but by the fact he sees my soul. Knows what I need, and does everything he can to meet those needs.

My fingers reach around to the back of his neck, pulling his face down until his lips touch mine. He deepens the kiss, his palms sliding over my backside and wrenching my hips towards his.

It takes all my willpower to tear myself away. 'Let's play a game. Heaven knows we could both do with some fun,' I suggest.

'What kind of game?' he purrs, exposing straight, white teeth.

'Pretend we're strangers. I'll dance for you. And you have to try to persuade me to have sex with you. Call it role play, if you like.'

James's eyes glint with approval. 'I warn you, Scarlett, it won't be much of a game. I can be very persuasive.'

'And I quite believe it.' My lips quirk. 'But I haven't danced in weeks and I'm going to revel in having your undivided attention for as long as I can physically hold out.'

'I have a secret weapon,' he warns.

'I'm pretty sure it's not that secret. I, and copious amounts of other women, have seen it before.' Desire curls in my core as I tear my eyes from James's crotch to scan the vicinity. Tiny, subtly positioned speakers dot the room.

There's a small bar to the left stocked with James's own whiskey.

'I wasn't referring to my cock, but now you've brought it up, excuse the pun,' he eyes the bulge in his suit trousers with a wicked grin, 'you're the only woman who will ever see it again.'

'I'd better be. Now, get a drink and put on some music while I get ready.'

'If you insist.' He slaps my ass before striding towards the bar. Within seconds, a low sensual beat echoes through the air. 'You know, I thought I was teaching you, Scarlett, but you're teaching me more than I ever could have dreamt of.'

'Like what?' I inch myself onto the stage, eternally grateful for the stockings and heels I selected earlier.

'That no matter how many times I think I'm getting to know you, there's always another layer to peel back.' His head whips up as my dress slides to the floor. 'Case in point.' Enormous pupils rake over my lingerie, a transparent, lace balconette bra and matching thong, which is so sheer it leaves absolutely nothing to the imagination.

James's mouth drops open and I grin. This is going to be so fucking hot.

He finally manages to drag his jaw from the floor to pour two neat whiskeys as I kick my dress off the stage.

James settles into the only armchair in the room— centre stage. Lounging against the black leather, swirling his crystal tumbler in his right hand, he looks every bit the billionaire playboy he was the night we met.

But I am far from the same woman. My confidence has grown in leaps and bounds. Thanks to him. And it's time he reaped the rewards of it.

The air crackles with the promise of pure hedonistic pleasure. I throw a leg around the cool, chrome pole and hoist myself up. My biceps burn, but in the most life-affirming way.

I drag my pelvis against the pole as I climb higher and higher until I'm two-thirds of the way up.

James's pupils blaze as I slowly part my legs in the splits. He hisses his approval and satisfaction sizzles in my stomach and lower. I propel myself around the pole several times, revelling in the sensation of flying through the air before gliding down in slow seductive increments, until both heels are on the floor.

James stands, takes a swig of his whiskey, and places it on the edge of the stage. Reaching into his pocket, he plucks out a wedge of hundred euro notes and throws them at the stage. 'Take your lingerie off,' his voice is weighted with a want that mirrors my own.

I pause for a second, wetting my lips. 'Yes, sir.'

His answering grin implies he thinks he has this in the bag. He seems to have temporarily forgotten I'm a survivor.

Though truthfully, there's no surviving those dark, decadent eyes for long.

It's my turn to grin. 'You can look, sir, but you can't touch. It's forbidden.' I glance at the door, as if I had a boss who might care.

James clenches his jaw but I don't miss the way his pupils gleam. He's enjoying this game every bit as much as I am.

I reach around and unhook my bra, keeping my eyes latched onto his, revelling in every micro twitch of his face as he battles to remain composed.

When it falls to the floor with a soft thud, a low moan rumbles from James's throat. 'Fucking beautiful,' he murmurs. 'Now show me that pretty pussy,' he urges, taking a step closer to the stage.

Chapter Forty-Seven

SCARLETT

His face is inches away from my stomach.

He pulls out another wad of notes from the inside of his suit pocket and tosses them onto the stage. My fingers dip beneath my waistband and push the lace down over my thighs, inch by inch. His lips roll, like he's biting something back.

When I finally step out of the thong, he grabs it and pulls it to his face, inhaling deeply.

'Fuck, Scarlett, your panties are drenched. How about you let me help you out with that?' He beckons me forwards with that index finger like he did the very first night we met.

'You must think I'm easy, Mr Beckett.' I arch an eyebrow at him. 'I assure you, I'm not that kind of girl.'

'One lick,' he pleads, dipping his face so he's mere millimetres away from the very sensitive spot that's silently screaming for his touch. 'One tiny little taste.'

'I can't. Even if I want to.' I glance at the door pointedly.

James takes a step back from the stage and every fibre of my body silently screams in protest. He falls back into the chair. 'In that case, you'd better dance for me again.'

I grab the pole, raising my leg around it high enough to give him a clear view of my sex.

'Not there,' he grits out. 'I want a lap dance.'

Wetness pools between my legs. 'Yes, sir.'

I step down from the stage and close the distance between us. Naked apart from the stockings and my stilettos, I sway my hips in front of his face in time to the slow, sensual beat. His gaze blazes a trail over my breasts, along my stomach, and then lower.

His Adam's apple bobs as I hover over his lap and roll my body until it almost brushes against him. So close, yet so damn far. His fingers casually thrum against the arm of the leather chair, but his eyes are molten lava. He can try to hide it, but he is wild with desire.

The urge to see how far I can push him rises like a riptide.

I shimmy closer to his face, close enough that his stubble grazes my thigh. His fingers tap the leather harder. I nudge them away with my shoe and put my patent black heel in their place, offering an unrestricted view of exactly how turned on I am.

His tongue darts out to wet his lips and his fingers adjust his collar. I continue to roll and sway and torment him.

'Scarlett,' his voice is primal. 'So help me God if you don't let me devour you this second.'

I pretend to think about it, playing my role to a tee.

My gaze flicks to the door, then back to his chiselled face. 'Okay, sir.'

His hands grip my ass cheeks as he lunges forwards. His tongue is between my legs in seconds, sliding from my entrance up to my clit and back down again. My hips arch forwards as he fucks me with his tongue. Every single cell in my body crackles with need as my thighs tremble and tighten. White hot light builds between my eyes, but before I can explode, he stops.

I look down to find those teasing eyes glinting up at me. 'Dance.' He squeezes my ass before tearing his hands away.

Oh, this is war.

I blow out a frustrated blast of air and he actually laughs.

We'll see who has the last laugh.

Lowering my trembling legs, I hover just above the rock solid bulge in his trousers. Two can play his game. I drop into his lap and he hisses.

'Oops, sorry, I slipped.' I grind myself against his enormous erection, not giving a flying fuck that I'm destroying his trousers with my arousal. He deserves it after bringing me to the brink like that and leaving me hanging.

His head rolls back against the leather as I grind a few more times before sliding backwards over his quads until I'm standing. I swivel on my heels, turn my back to him, spread my legs and slowly reach towards my toes, giving him a full view of the junction between my thighs.

It's his turn to blow out a frustrated breath, and my turn to laugh.

I have a clear view of him between my legs as he inclines forwards in the chair, even if my torso is upside down. His eyes burn with a clear intention.

'You want me to see you, Scarlett?' His voice is rough and gravelly. 'I see you. And I fucking love you.' Strong hands curl around my inner thighs as he buries his tongue between my legs from behind.

The sensation as he devours me has me rocking on my feet. This time, when my legs tremble, he supports the weight of them as my orgasm consumes me with a soul-shattering ecstasy.

I shove my fist in my mouth, biting hard to muffle the cries of pure primal pleasure.

His mouth finally slows to a stop and his hands release

me. I hoist myself upright and turn to face him. He licks his glistening lips with a smug little smile.

But the game isn't over yet.

In fact, it's far from over.

His right hand reaches for his belt, and within seconds his huge cock springs free. It's magnificent. 'Sit on my cock, Scarlett.' He grips the base of it and pumps it until the head is glistening.

'I'm not supposed to.' I glance at the door again. I'm enjoying our game too much for it to be over yet. 'What if someone walks in?'

His eyes darken with delight. 'If they walk in, they'll have to watch, and we both know what that does to you.'

Hot, potent desire strikes my stomach.

'I have a good mind to call those two security guards in here right now to see you like this, naked and dripping— a fucking vision.'

I glance at the door once more. It's one thing having strangers in the distance watch us on a private yacht in Paris, and entirely another to let the staff observe at close quarters. He wouldn't, would he?

'The problem is, if they saw this vision,' his hand gestures to my breasts, where my nipples are like bullets and a hot need is building in my core again, 'they'd want to touch you. And I refuse to share.' His fingers dance over the arm of the chair again. 'How about we make sure they hear you, instead?'

James Beckett knows exactly what to say to turn me on.

I step forwards and lower myself into his lap until I'm straddling him, a leg draped over each arm of the chair so we both have a clear view as his tip rests at my entrance.

'Just an inch.' I eye him.

His jaw clenches. 'Fine. Just an inch,' he agrees, his pupils are enormous as they glint through the dimness. He nudges inside me, then stills.

'There's your inch,' he says defiantly. 'How does it feel?'

'It feels like more,' I admit, clenching around his cock.

He grins. 'That's my greedy girl.' He pushes in another inch. 'You love my cock, Scarlett, don't you?'

'I adore it.'

'Good, because it's the only one you're ever going to feel inside you.' His fingers trail up my torso and cup my breasts, squeezing and weighing them in his hands.

His words are my undoing. He is the only man I've ever wanted inside of me.

I swallow thickly. I can't hold on anymore. Can't play this game a second longer. I need him.

'Game's over,' I whisper, attempting to wriggle further down his length, but he halts me, dropping his hands to my hips.

'Game's not over, Scarlett. Not until I say so.' He flashes me a wolfish smile. 'You might have started it, but I'm going to finish it.'

'What have I done?' I groan, but his teasing only serves to soak me further.

'It's your turn to persuade me to have sex with you,' he says.

'But technically, you already are.' I clench his tip in demonstration.

'Scarlett, if you're going to be part of the Beckett Enterprise, you need to think more ruthlessly.' His fingers sweep from my hips to my stomach and lower. His thumb gently swipes over my clit.

'Ruthlessly,' I repeat, barely able to see straight with lust, the promise of intense, addictive, carnal pleasure goading me on the horizon, just millimetres out of my reach.

'Ask yourself what the other person wants. Then decide if you're willing to give it to them, in order to get what you want.' Amusement glimmers in James's eyes, as he watches on while he wrecks me.

'What do you want?' I pant.

'I want you to marry me.' His thumb stills to a stop, and he reaches into his jacket pocket. An enormous solitaire glitters in the palm of his hand. 'Marry me, Scarlett, and I'll give you every inch of me. Everything that I am. Everything that I own. Just say yes.'

My heart swells so large in my chest, it feels as if it's going to explode. My hand cups my mouth, and I feel my eyes widen.

It's quick, but it feels so right.

James is it for me.

He's everything.

'Yes.' I nod, our eyes locking. 'It was always going to be yes.' He slides the ring onto the fourth finger of my left hand at the same time as his thick length glides into me.

Our lips lock as I ride him hard. Strong hands grip my hips and drive me harder until both of us cry out hard enough to be heard in Paris.

Chapter Forty-Eight
JAMES

I had every intention of making my proposal a million times more romantic than a role play scenario in Scarlett's new pole dancing room last night, but with everything hanging over us, wasting a single second seems imprudent.

Scarlett needs to know how much she means to me, but so does my father, the O'Connors, and the rest of the world. Which is why I plan to announce our engagement tonight at my father's lavish birthday ball in front of every single person I know.

It'll be a triple celebration to mark my father's birthday, my engagement and the acquisition officially going through in the early hours of the morning. Chantel has already tipped off the press that something big is brewing , and I fully expect the story of my engagement to be plastered over the front page of every newspaper in the country. Except this time, I have no intention of asking any of the editors to pixelate Scarlett's face.

She's not in hiding anymore. She's going to be my wife. And if anyone wants to hunt her down and harm her, they'll have to get through me first.

By morning, the O'Connors and anyone else who threatens us, will have learnt that the Becketts never surrender.

I pace the outdoor patio area. The April sunshine is unseasonably warm. Scarlett bobs in the deep end of the hexagonal infinity pool overlooking the Irish Sea. She's gazing out across the landscape like she's seeing it for the first time. I hope it's finally settling in that this is hers as much as it is mine, now.

As soon as Declan O'Connor is safely behind bars with his father, and we have Scarlett's graduation behind us, I'm whisking her away to see the world.

I didn't realise what I was yearning for, but now I've found it, I intend on spending the rest of my life making her happy.

My phone rings in my pocket. Hopefully Killian with the confirmation I've been waiting for.

I pluck it from my pocket and glance at the screen. Mother. She's probably calling to remind me about tonight. As if I could forget.

'Darling, just reminding you not to be late tonight,' my mother coos down the phone.

'As if I would. I'm looking forward to it.'

'You are?' Doubt fills my mother's voice.

'Yes, Scarlett and I have an announcement.'

'You do?' Her voice shoots up ten octaves. 'I wasn't sure if you were still together.'

'Well, we are. Did Dad tell you she's related to the O'Connors?' No point beating about the bush.

'He did.' My mother is unusually sombre.

'She's not really related to them. Her mother was married to Jack. She's had nothing to do with them for years.'

'You don't have to explain yourself to me, son. As far as I'm concerned, you're old enough to make your own decisions. As long as you're sure. But you know this is going to cause one hell of a scandal.'

'You of all people know I don't care about scandal, Mother. I care about her. I'm in love with her.'

My mother squeals and I hold the phone a foot away from my ear while she gets it out of her system.

'Calm down. You'll deafen me.'

'Sorry, I'm just so excited for you. I can't believe it.'

Rosa appears at the sliding doors at the rear of the house. 'An Avery Williams is here to see Scarlett,' she says quietly.

'What a surprise!' Scarlett beams at Rosa. 'Send her out, please'

I couldn't allow Scarlett to go out with Avery, not until Killian confirms our plan for Declan O'Connor has been executed, but I did arrange for Avery to come here.

'Is that Scarlett I can hear in the background?' Approval taints my mother's tone.

'It is. She's moved in.' Satisfaction rumbles through my ribcage.

'What?' My mother's joy is probably audible in County Cork. I only wish my father felt the same way. I haven't heard from him since his outburst in my office earlier in the week. He may actually keel over when he hears I've asked Scarlett to be my wife.

'I hope it's what I think it is!' my mother coos.

'We'll see you at eight.'

'Don't worry about your father. Leave him to me. You know he's a teddy bear underneath that grizzly exterior.'

I'm not convinced.

I end the call before she can ask any further questions.

Avery appears at the door wearing more clothes than I've ever seen her wearing before. Wide eyes scan the area in awe before homing in on her best friend in the pool.

'Avery!' Scarlett beams at her friend. 'I can lend you swimwear if you want to get in?'

'No need! I'm wearing some.' She lifts her top and I look away, regardless of the fact all the patrons of the Luxor Lounge have seen it before.

I won't be seeing it again though.

I've cancelled my membership. I refuse to give Christopher Cole another cent. It's bad enough what he tried to do to Scarlett, but then, it turns out, he was the one who ratted her out to my father.

And besides, I've signed me and my fiancée up to another type of club. One where we can explore all our kinks, safely, anonymously, and in total luxury. I can't wait to take her there and see what other desires she might have hiding beneath that innocent exterior.

'Hurry up.' Scarlett lifts her hand out of the water, motioning for her friend to get in. The sun dances from the five-carat diamond, the penetrative rays refracting and sending a spectrum of vibrant colours dispersing over the surface of the water.

'Holy fucking shit balls!' Avery screeches. 'Is that a rock on your left hand or an engagement ring?' Her jaw almost hits the floor as she scrambles out her clothes.

With as much grace as an elephant, she dive bombs into the deep end next to Scarlett. Water cascades in every direction. I glance down at my Gucci loafers and shake my head.

Scarlett's answering laughter fills the air like the sweetest melody. My heart swells in my chest.

Avery bursts up from beneath the surface and squeals with delight for her friend as Rosa reappears with a chilled bottle of Bollinger and two champagne flutes.

'I can't believe it!' Avery shrieks, snatching Scarlett's hand and thrusting it under her nose. 'Oh. My. God.'

'Will you be my bridesmaid?' Scarlett drops her hand to Avery's bare shoulder.

'Hell, yes!' Avery whoops, yanking Scarlett into a bear hug that pulls them both under the water for a brief second.

'Easy,' I warn playfully. 'That's my wife you're almost drowning.'

'Don't worry, Beckett. I won't let anything happen to her,' Avery promises. 'You're not the only one who adores her.'

'So when is the wedding? And where is it? And most importantly, who's the best man?' Avery glances between us, bobbing around like an excited Labrador. 'You know as bridesmaid, it will be my official duty to shag the best man. Please make sure he's hot and rich and has a massive...'

'Okay, Avery, I get the gist.' I raise my hand up. I've heard enough.

Rosa snorts as she places the champagne at the side of the pool.

'We haven't decided on any of those things just yet,' Scarlett's eyes shift sidewards, 'but we will soon. We don't want to wait.'

'I don't blame you.' Avery waggles her eyebrows.

My phone rings again, saving me from suffering anymore girl talk. I squint at the screen. Killian. I swipe as I stride purposefully back into the house.

'Is it done?' I demand. I'm desperate to put this whole mess behind us. It kills me that I couldn't be there, that I couldn't handle the O'Connors personally. But my priority is Scarlett. I'm utterly unprepared to leave her side for even a second until I'm certain those mad fuckers are behind bars.

'It's done,' he confirms.

Relief crusades through my veins.

'Declan's in custody. I filled the boot of his car with half a million euros worth of cocaine and a shedload of firearms I found in his warehouse. The coppers set up a road block exactly where I tipped them off. You should have seen his face when the guards slapped the handcuffs on him. He was murderous.'

'No surprises there.' I stalk through the house, admiring all the little touches Scarlett has put in place since she moved in. I love how the scent of her perfume lingers in the corridors. 'What about the others?' I ask, desperate to know what's happened to the rest of the O'Connor clan.

'Keith is out of the country on business. He'd be a fool to try to make it back through customs now. If he's not arrested, he'll at least be brought in for questioning. The other brothers headed southbound towards Cork. There's an alert out for them at all Irish airports and ports. If they leave the country, we'll know about it.'

'As the saying goes, keep your friends close and your enemies closer. I want to know if there's any sign of retaliation looming. Hopefully with Declan and their father behind bars, they won't be stupid enough to try anything.'

'All O'Connor assets have been frozen. Even if they have the balls to try, they don't have the cash to carry out their weekly shopping, let alone pay their usual heavies.'

'And what about the old man? Declan said he was up for parole?' Out of all of them, he's the one who concerns me most. His vendetta with this family has always been personal, but now Scarlett is one of us, he has twice as many reasons to come after us. She is the reason he's rotting behind bars, after all.

'There's no chance of the old man getting out. I paid a hefty sum to make sure of it.' Killian's tone is curt but I detect a hint of relief in it.

'So basically, you're telling me everything is under control.'

'It is. But just in case, I've ordered a full security detail at the ball tonight.'

That's why he's the best in the business.

'Good. I've invited the press, and you know what Dad's parties can be like—they can be wild enough without a poor retaliation attempt from the O'Connors.'

'See you tonight,' I say, hanging up the phone.

The whole world is about to find out that Ireland's most eligible bachelor is no longer a bachelor, and my father is about to find out that if he won't accept Scarlett, I will happily resign as CEO of the Beckett empire and spend the rest of my life running the vineyards in Provence.

Chapter Forty-Nine
JAMES

I stride back out to the pool and call Scarlett out of the water.

'Oh, can I not just have her to myself for five minutes, Beckett?' Avery splashes water in my direction. If I wasn't in such a euphoric mood, it might piss me off.

'This will only take a minute.'

'That's what they all say.' Avery splutters at her own joke as Scarlett hauls herself out of the water. In a tiny, crimson bikini, she'd give the Baywatch cast a run for their money.

'Is everything okay?' Concern weighs heavy in her tone.

'Everything's perfect. Declan is behind bars, Jack's had his parole rejected, and there's no sign of the other O'Connor boys. The threat is over. The past is behind us.' My lips curl upwards. 'Now, it's time to concentrate on the future.'

Scarlett's cherry-coloured lips pop open. 'But how?'

'Killian dealt with it, his way.' I shrug. 'Ask me no questions and I'll tell you no lies.'

She launches herself into my arms, wrapping her legs around my waist and peppering kisses all across my jaw.

She's dripping wet, and not in the way I like her to be.

'You know I'm usually all about your wet pussy grinding against me, sweetheart, but this is taking things to another level.'

'Sorry!' she slides down my body, leaving half the swimming pool contents after her.

'Don't be.' I take her hand in mine and bring it to my lips. 'I love you.'

'I love you too. I'm so glad it's over.'

'Me too. Now we can start a new beginning.' My gaze falls to the diamond on her finger and a sublime sense of satisfaction rolls through my stomach. 'Have fun with your friend. I'm going to get ready for tonight.'

The Shelbourne is one of Dublin's most exclusive hotels. It's elegant, timeless, and sophisticated.

It's the perfect place to introduce my future wife to the world.

Hopefully, the lavishness of tonight's ball will overshadow speculation about Scarlett's past and her identity as a former pole dancer.

Her association with the O'Connors should remain hearsay, if that, thanks to the efforts that were made to maintain her anonymity after the court case against Jack, not to mention the fictional past Killian has constructed for her and dripped liberally around the internet. If anyone from her past attempts to sell a story about her true identity to the press, I will be notified. I've made certain of it.

I have no idea what the Board will make of my engagement, but I don't really give a flying fuck what Julian Jones, or the investors, think about my relationship status.

Honestly, deep down, a small part of me actually wants to be fired.

At least then I'll have the freedom to show Scarlett the

world without the pressure of having to rush back to work between each trip. And I've made enough shrewd investments not to have to work another day in my life.

'Are you ready?' I turn to Scarlett as Tim opens the car door for us.

'As I'll ever be.' Her teeth dig into her lower lip nervously.

'Don't.' I brush my thumb over her mouth. 'If anyone's going to ruin your lipstick tonight, it'll be me.'

'Promises, promises.' Her crimson lips lift and her eyes flash with desire as she slips her dainty hand into mine.

'You look beautiful.' My eyes rove over the ivory silk clinging to her curves in all the right places. It nips in at her waist before sensually kicking out over her hips in layers that extend to just below her knees. Her shapely calves are accentuated by rose gold satin heels and tiny straps that fasten round her ankles.

'Have you got any panties on underneath there?' I ask as I help her out of the car when we arrive at the Shelborne .

'If you're good, I might let you find out later,' she quips. Tim barks out a laugh, which he masks as a cough.

Killian's men flank the hotel, replacing the usual doormen. They usher us into an opulent hallway. Scarlett halts beneath an elaborate chandelier, and inhales a large breath.

'Don't be nervous. My family is your family now.' I place a hand on the base of her spine and she inclines into my side like she's seeking protection.

Unbelievable.

The woman can stand in a courtroom and testify against one of the country's most notorious criminals, yet she shies away from a Beckett family ball. 'Come on, I've got you.'

We follow the sound of brass and woodwind instruments to the ballroom. Trust my mother to have booked big band jazz. She loves to dance. At least that's something she and Scarlett have in common.

The ballroom is packed. The tables are arranged at the far end of the room to allow space for a full-sized dancefloor. The place is decked out like it's for a wedding. There's not a helium balloon in sight, but there are enough fresh flowers to fill a football field.

Three of the most respectable journalists I know hover at the back of the room with their cameras and microphones at the ready.

Every head turns as Scarlett and I stroll in, fashionably late.

My mother is the first to greet us, pulling us both into her bosom. 'Finally!' She arches back, her eyes darting between us. 'I saw the news. Congratulations on the acquisition. Who would have thought we'd have a winery in the family?' Given the glassy look in her eyes, my mother looks as though she's spent the afternoon in a winery.

'Happy birthday, Dad.' I extend my hand. He hesitates for a split second before taking it in his own, his pupils darting between Scarlett and me.

'The winery isn't the only thing I've acquired this week.' I drop my father's hand and drape my arm around Scarlett's bare shoulders.

My mother's mouth drops as her gaze falls to Scarlett's left hand. 'Oh. My. Goodness.' Her squeal is enough to attract the attention of the whole room.

I guess there's no time like the present to do what I came here to do. A waiter approaches with a tray of champagne. I take two glasses and hand one to Scarlett. She smiles gratefully.

I tap my watch against my glass. 'Ladies and gentlemen, friends and family, and... the Board.' My pointed tone elicits a small giggle, followed by what sounds like a hundred hushes, as everyone is eager to hear what I have to say.

'Thank you so much for joining us this evening to celebrate the birthday of the best man I know.' I turn to my father, whose cheeks are blushing a deep shade of crimson. Unlike my mother, he despises being the centre of attention. He's about as keen on having a ball thrown in his honour as he is on O'Connor's whiskey.

'Happy birthday, Dad.' A round of applause ensues and I take a moment to glance around at the faces of everyone I hold dear. Killian, Sean and Rian flank our mother, each of them clutching a whiskey, which I bet my life is Beckett's Gold. My grandmother, aunts and uncles flock forwards, necks craning to get a better view.

When the applause finally subsides, I clear my throat.

'We Becketts have a lot to celebrate tonight. Most of you have probably seen or heard the news this evening. Beckett corporation has successfully acquired the Imperial Winery Group.'

My sister Zara stands beside Chantel, who gives me the double thumbs up.

Julian Jones is at the front of the crowd, trussed up like a penguin, holding a glass of red wine the same shade as his large, porous nose. Maybe he's dressed to impress Sylvia DeLacy, the vice chairperson. He looks at her like she's the last cream cake in the bakery. His expression towards me, however, is decidedly less appreciative.

When the applause subsides again, I tug Scarlett forwards and place my hands on her shoulders. 'And if all that isn't enough to celebrate, I made a personal acquisition this week, too. Ladies and gentlemen, some of you have already met my girlfriend, Scarlett Fitzgerald, but please allow me to introduce the future Mrs Beckett.'

Chapter Fifty
SCARLETT

There's a stunned silence for about three seconds, which feels like three hours. Vivienne Beckett, my future mother-in-law is the first to squeal her excitement. She lunges for my left hand, drawing it up to her face and twisting it to catch the light. 'Oh my goodness! What a beautiful ring! Congratulations to both of you!'

Suddenly, cameras flash from every corner of the room. I'm bombarded with hugs and kisses and congratulations from absolute strangers.

It's a lot.

But James doesn't leave my side, and his hand doesn't leave my hip as we're pulled in every direction, answering the same questions over and over again.

When did it happen?

Where did it happen?

Was I surprised?

We should have been more prepared. Should have invented a story. Because we can't very well say he asked me to marry him when we were in the middle of the hottest sex of our lives.

Thankfully, James fends off the questions with a wry laugh and, 'Buy Okay magazine and you'll get all the answers there. We have an official engagement shoot next week.'

It's hard to discern if he's joking or not.

The bubbles keep flowing, the congratulations keep rowing in. From everyone except Alexander Beckett.

A bell sounds signalling dinner is about to be served and our guests begin to scurry towards the tables at the far end of the room. Gorgeous orchid centrepieces dot each table alongside giant church candles. The high-backed chairs are lined with ivory covers, complete with huge pastel pink bows tied around them.

'Come on. Let's go eat.' James lowers his lips to my ear, his hot breath fanning over my neck. 'You're going to need the fuel for when we get home.'

'I can't wait.' Not just because the urge to have him inside me is overwhelming, but because the urge to be alone with him in the comfort of each other's company is equally as enticing.

When I think back to how intimidating I found him just a few short months ago, it's like we were two different people. Which I guess we were. He's softened. I've got stronger– at least I think I have. I used to pretend to be strong on the outside, while cowering away from life on the inside, whereas now, I am stronger on the inside because for the first time in years, I know I'm not alone anymore.

James sees me.

He understands me.

But most of all, he accepts me. Even the ugliest parts of me.

I just hope I can convince his father to accept me.

James might be okay with the tension between him and his father, but I'm not. Not if it's because of me. Just like he didn't want me to miss out on things that are important in my life, like seeing my friend, I don't want him to miss out on things that are important in his life, like his family.

I just need to convince Alexander Beckett I'm not some money grabbing daughter of his enemy.

How though?

Time is probably the only answer.

As we approach the tables, I spot the tiny place cards in front of each space. Each table sits ten. James and I are seated with his parents, his four brothers, and his sister, Zara, who looks adorable in a pink, tiered flapper dress and matching headpiece.

We slip into our seats. I glance at the place card beside me. Alexander Beckett. My stomach somersaults.

James rests his hand on my thigh beneath the table and offers a reassuring squeeze. The man is so in tune with me, it's frightening.

Alexander hesitates, his weathered hand hovering on the back of his chair like he'd rather do anything but pull it out and sit down.

I suck in a breath and turn towards him. 'Please, sit Mr Beckett. I'd like to get to know you better.'

His silver eyebrows dart upwards, but surprisingly, he lowers his bulky frame into the chair.

Waiters circle each table, offering red and white wine. Between the blanket of chatter in the room and the glass of bubbly, I summon the bravery to grab the bull by the horns.

'I know you don't approve of me, but I love your son. I'll do my best to make him happy. To be a good wife.'

'I don't doubt you will.' Alexander raises his wine glass to his lips and takes a sip. 'It's not you, personally. I mean, you're not the wife I envisioned for him,' he pauses and the unspoken words *pole dancer* float invisibly through the air, 'and your family are—'

I stop him before he can go any further. 'My family are

dead. My mother passed tragically at the hands of a man I have reason to despise more than you ever will.'

'That may be so but didn't he raise you?' Alexander's voice is barely audible.

'I raised myself at St Jude's boarding school.'

James stiffens beside me as he listens to every word. 'Father,' his voice is a warning, 'this isn't the time or the place.'

'I think it's exactly the time and the place.' Alexander stares at his son defiantly. 'Why not get it all out in the open. You don't usually mind flashing your private bits. That's what got you in this predicament in the first place.'

'I wouldn't call my engagement a predicament. I'd call it a privilege.' James's voice drops to a dangerously low hiss.

Vivienne is cooing over Zara obliviously beside us, and Caelon and Rian are deep in conversation about whether the lamb chops might be more succulent than the steak.

The only other person who seems to be paying any attention to the conversation is James's brother, Killian, who seems to miss nothing, but says little. Which is why he surprises me when he leans across the table and opens his mouth.

'Dad,' he says in a languid drawl. Alexander and James both glance up. 'Do you remember the underage witness from O'Connor's trial?'

Alexander pauses, running his thumb over his jawline, a mannerism I've watched James do a hundred times. He purses his lips, then his head twists and is eyes collide with mine. Realisation dawns in his pupils.

'You.'

'She lost her mother to that bastard. But she also lost her own life in the process. She's been alone for years. She surrendered her identity to stay alive. Had to sever contact with her mother's remaining family for her own safety and theirs,' James says. 'The least you can do is accept her into ours, even if you're not ecstatic about it. She's going to be my wife.'

'Here, here.' Killian raises his glass.

Alexander has the grace to look at the floor.

'I'll resign as CEO if it's going to be a problem for you, Dad.' James snakes his arm around my waist.

'You'd really resign from the position you fought so hard to keep?' Deep lines furrow Alexander's forehead.

'I'd do anything for Scarlett.' His fingers flex on my hip.

Alexander pauses, a thoughtful expression across his face. 'Well, perhaps you've learnt something at long last.'

'Excuse me?' James inches forwards.

'With big talk like that, you might just be husband material yet. I never thought I'd see the day.' The corners of Alex's eyes soften slightly. 'Looks like Scarlett may be a good influence on you after all.'

'I know it'll take time, but I hope we can form a friendship. Despite your previous beliefs, I never really had a father. I wouldn't mind having one now.'

Alexander slowly raises his eyes. 'Congratulations on your engagement. Welcome to the family.' He stands and signals for me to do the same. I toss my napkin onto the table. My heart hammers like a drum in my chest as I look to James. He smiles and jerks his head towards Alexander, who is waiting with his arms open.

My mouth pops in surprise as he pulls me in for a hug that lasts several seconds longer than I'm comfortable with, but I guess he's used to Vivienne Beckett and her overenthusiastic PDAs.

'Easy, Dad.' James's tone is jovial but his warning is genuine.

'Perhaps we should start again?' Alexander says as he releases me.

'Absolutely.' My cheeks burn as I sit back in my chair. I'm not sure if it's the emotion or the champagne.

'Where's Isabella?' James asks Caelon.

'She'll be here later. She's sorting the kids out. They're going through a really clingy phase right now and they won't even let the nanny put them to bed. It has to be Isa.' Caelon winks at James. 'You guys will know all about it soon enough.' He nods towards the ring on my finger.

'Here's hoping,' I blurt before I can stop myself.

James's eyebrows arch. 'Hoped I might get you to myself for a while first.'

'You know, I knew I liked you.' Alexander actually winks at me. Winks! 'Vivienne and I have been begging for more grandchildren for years.'

'What's this about more grandchildren?' Vivienne's head whips from Zara to us.

'Oh Jesus, can we at least get married first?' James rolls his eyes but his smile suggests he's not entirely averse to the idea of starting a family.

A family of my own.

Of our own.

My fingers reach instinctively for my throat and stroke the silver cross. I'm not sure I believe in heaven but if there is one, my mother is there.

James calls me angel, but truthfully, it's him who's heaven sent. And I'm pretty sure I know who sent him my way. I have an angel watching over me. It's the only explanation.

Because I morphed from having nothing to having everything.

And best of all, I have him. The man I wanted long before I ever met him.

My eyes slide towards my fiancé . Our eyes lock in an unspoken exchange.

I love you.
I love you too.

EPILOGUE
Graduation

Scarlett

With its gilded tapestry and walls of mahogany shelving, the majestic library at Trinity College is the perfect venue for graduation.

When my name is called, I stride across the polished stage to collect my degree. The spotlight shines down on my black graduation cap and gown, and I feel the weight of every eye in the room on me.

My fiancé sits in the front row, with all his siblings and my future mother and father-in-law. They're clapping and cheering like I've scored the winning point in an all-Ireland final in the last few seconds of a game.

Eleanor and Nathan perch in the row behind them. Eleanor's eyes crinkle as she shoots me a wide smile. Nathan shifts in his seat and adjusts his tie. From his sideward glances at my former teacher, I gather it's her proximity that has him hot under the collar and not the May sunshine.

Everyone I know and care about is here.

Even my mother.

I feel it with every fibre of my body. A comforting warmth surrounds me like a caress. A sensation you'd have to feel to believe, but I know it's her, and I know she's proud of me.

Euphoric tears threaten the whites of my eyes but I blink them back and beam at the dean as he shakes my hand vigorously. 'Congratulations,' he booms, handing me a tightly bound scroll. My degree.

An ear-splitting wolf-whistle pierces the air and I don't need to look around to see who it came from.

I take a tiny bow, allowing my gaze to settle on James. He jumps to his feet, his hands clapping hard enough to burn. In a navy tailored suit and a slim-fitting white shirt, he looks every bit as gorgeous as the first night I met him.

His eyes bore into mine like twin flames. 'I'm so proud of you,' he mouths as a triumphant smile splits my lips wide open.

I had no idea it was possible to be this happy.

To be this content.

To feel so alive.

My engagement ring glints on my finger as I exit the stage. We've set the date. New Year's Eve. James insisted we start the new year as man and wife. We're looking at venues in the Caribbean and planning a month-long honeymoon around the States afterwards.

James is adamant he's going to show me the world—his way.

Avery is beside herself at the prospect of a luxury trip away with the Beckett brothers.

I weave past my fellow students, back towards my family. I'm met with hugs and handshakes and more love than I could ever have dreamt of.

Finally, James throws his arms around me, lifts me into the air, and swings me around like I'm a doll. 'Congratulations, wifey.'

'I'm not your wife yet,' I remind him, nuzzling into his neck, even if he has updated his contact info in my phone from boyfriend to husband.

'Semantics.' He peppers a trail of kisses along my jaw. 'Are you ready for your graduation party?'

'As I'll ever be.'

James has hired an events management company to set up a marquee at our house and invited his entire family over to celebrate. He's hired Matteo and his wife to provide the catering, and my mouth is already watering at the prospect.

'Meet us at the house,' James calls to his family. 'We'll be right behind you.'

As we're exiting the library, we walk straight into Shane Stenson. He's barely said two words to me since the opening night at Rian's club.

'Congratulations,' he says, beaming, and for a second I think he's about to kiss me, but instead, he extends a hand.

'The same to you.' I mean it, genuinely. Shane is a decent guy, but he was never going to be my guy.

A tiny growl rumbles from behind me.

'Where are you celebrating tonight?' Shane asks, his gaze drifting between James and me.

'At home, with our family.' James steps forward and drops an arm around my shoulder.

'Cool. Enjoy.' Shane switches his attention to James. 'Take care of her.'

'I always do.' James hesitates for a split second then extends a hand 'Congratulations on your degree.'

Shane's blue eyes light up. 'Thanks.'

'See you around.' I raise my hand to wave as James nudges me away.

'You won't,' he mutters into my ear.

I roll my eyes. 'It's nice to be nice. Look at you, shaking his hand. You're getting soft in your old age.'

Suddenly, I'm pinned against a corridor wall by a powerful set of hips with my wrists pinned above my head. 'Is that any way to speak to your fiancé?' James's thumbs trace over my pulse points and my veins flood with a searing heat. 'Does that feel soft to you?' He thrusts between my legs, and my skin flushes with arousal.

'Take me home,' I beg, 'to our bedroom, not the party.'

His lips curve upwards as he releases his grip on my wrists and slips his arms around my waist instead. 'We have somewhere we need to go first.'

'Where?'

'You'll see.' He takes me by the hand and leads me outside. The humidity is unusually high with the sun stuck behind heavy, low-hanging clouds.

Tim is waiting outside. 'Home?' he asks, opening the car door.

'St. Mary's cemetery first.' James's tone is sombre.

'St. Mary's?' I repeat.

'I thought you might like to pay your mother a visit.' He shifts from one foot to the other. 'If you want to, that is,' he adds with some uncertainty. It's the first time since we've met that I recall him looking uncertain about anything.

'Of course I want to. It's one of the most thoughtful suggestions ever.' I slide into the back of the car, and he slips in beside me. He takes my hand in his and squeezes it tightly.

We arrive at the cemetery twenty minutes later. I dread to think what kind of state my mother's headstone is in, but now the O'Connors have been taken care of, I can visit more often and maintain it better.

Tim slows to a stop at the wrought-iron gates. 'Do you

want me to accompany you?' he asks with a respectful bow of his head.

'We're fine, thank you.' James motions for Tim to get back in the car.

We stroll through the weaving, overgrown pathway in silence until we reach the far end of the grounds. I stop still in my tracks as I see my mother's headstone ahead. The original drab grey headstone has been replaced with white marble and is overflowing with yellow and orange tulips.

My eyes fill with tears as I crouch to the floor, placing my palm on the cold stone. 'You did this?'

'Of course.' James kneels next to me. 'I wanted to pay homage to the woman who brought you into this world. We can come as often as you like. It's safe now,' James says quietly. Declan and Jack are still behind bars, and the rest of the O'Connor brothers have fled the country. I can visit my mother in peace, without looking over my shoulder.

'Thank you.' It's the best graduation gift ever.

The clouds drift apart and the brightest blue cracks of sky appear overhead. My eyelids flutter closed and I tilt my chin upwards. The sun appears bright and strong and kisses my face with a comforting warmth, and I just know she's watching over us.

We sit on the grass, me between James's legs, my back resting on his chest, until our backsides go numb and our stomachs rumble.

I twist my head to glance at James, admiring the way the sunlight glints in his glossy dark hair. 'We have a party to go to.'

'We sure do.' He stands, dusts the grass from his suit trousers, and helps me to my feet. On the few occasions I've dared to visit before, I've been smothered with a sense of sadness, but not today. Now I know I can come back anytime. Now I have James.

I kiss my fingertips and touch them to the marble. 'We'll visit again soon, Mam.'

James and I leave the cemetery, with our fingers entwined. We don't speak. We don't need to.

When we get back to the house, the party is in full swing. The pool area is decked out in giant rose gold balloons. A DJ has set up by the pool, and the soft beats of tropical house music pulsate through the air. Waitresses circulate with exotic, fruity cocktails and bottles of Bollinger.

Alexander Beckett is lounging by the pool in a pair of dress shorts and a pale blue shirt. Finally, he appears to be embracing his retirement. Vivienne has kicked off her Christian Louboutins, her floral dress swaying in the gentle breeze, and she bops along barefoot to the music with Zara and Rian.

Sean and Caelon are lounging on rattan recliners by the firepit, beers in hand. They raise their bottles as they spot me and James stepping out onto the deck.

Chantel is here, wearing a hot pink summer dress. She's dancing with a gorgeous little boy who I assume is her son, Miles, who I've heard so much about.

I spot Avery at the far end of the pool. In a Grecian-style white maxi dress, that's so sheer it's practically see-through, she could pass for a Greek goddess. If the way Killian is staring at her is anything to go by, he agrees. For a man who doesn't say much, he certainly seems to be engrossed in conversation with her.

Before I can go over to them, Eleanor catches my arm.

'I'm so proud of you, Scarlett.' Her head tilts to the side as she pats the back of my arm. 'Look at all you have achieved.'

'Thank you.' I glance around. 'Where's Nathan?'

'He just got called away on an emergency,' she tuts. 'Hopefully he'll make it back later.'

I lean in closer and whisper, 'Are you two...?'

Her eyebrows wing up. 'No, we're just friends.' She scurries away before I can interrogate her further.

Yeah, and I'm the Queen of Sheba.

Watch this space.

James appears next to me with two glasses of champagne. 'Congratulations again, my love.' He clinks his glass against mine as his ebony eyes twinkle. 'Did you think about my proposal yet?'

I glance pointedly at the enormous diamond glittering on my left hand.

'Not that one.' His lips brush over my temple. 'The other one. Work for me. You'd be a huge asset to Beckett Enterprises. We'd be lucky to have you.'

'Okay.' I shrug.

'Okay, as in yes?' His voice jumps two octaves.

'But only if I can keep the desk where I did my work placement. I became quite fond of it.' Well, fond of the memories it stirs.

'I wouldn't have you anywhere else but by my side.'

'That's settled then.' As much as I wanted to be independent, I've been alone too long. If James wants me with him at work and home, then I'm there. The family business is where I belong.

I am Scarlett Beckett-to-be, after all.

Caelon

'Come on, Isa, pick up the phone. Pick up the phone. Where are you?'

The soles of my shoes thwack against the opulent marble flooring of my brother James's mansion.

My wife is not one to miss a party.

Ever.

Especially not the lavish, extravagant graduation party my brother is hosting for his new fiancée.

A shrill ring echoes through my ear and a chill slides down my spine. I glance at my sleek, silver TAG Heuer watch, a gift from Isa on our wedding day. Ten years next week.

Though I've loved her for a lot longer.

The first moment I set eyes on Isabella Harte, I knew she had irretrievably stolen my heart. Every inch of her was perfect, from her wavy, waist-long hair to her twinkling emerald eyes.

Fast forward fifteen years and we have two fantastic, but mischievous, children. A stunning home. Enough money in the bank to last several opulent lifetimes. The only thing I don't have right now is her.

Where is she? Perhaps the kids are playing up. Sometimes I swear they can sense it when we're planning to escape for the night.

I pluck my phone from my pocket to call her again, but the second I touch it, it vibrates with an incoming call.

Thank God.

My eyes dart to the bright screen,

But it's not Isa's name lighting it up.

Unknown number.

An icy terror squeezes my chest as I swipe to answer. Every single atom in my body screams at me that something terrible has happened. Something unthinkable. My throat thickens. My mouth dries. My chest rises in uneven ragged pants, yet my voice remains neutral.

'Caelon Beckett?' A deep voice rumbles in my ear.

'That depends who's asking.'

'Detective Nathan Sterling. We met earlier. At Scarlett's graduation.' He clears his throat, allowing time for the significance of his introduction to sink in.

'What's happened?' My stomach bottoms out. Nausea

rises in my stomach as the steak I had for dinner threatens to reappear up my thorax. Does this have something to do with why he was called away the moment he arrived at the party?

It can't be good.

'I'm afraid there's been an accident.' Nathan's words hit me like a bullet to the chest.

'What kind of an accident?'

'A road traffic accident.'

Oh, please God, not Isa.

'Is it serious?' I swallow a hard lump in my throat, my imagination playing a slideshow of all the worst possible scenarios in my head.

'It would be better if we could discuss this in person.' The grim edge to his voice tells me all I need to know. It is Isa.

'It's my wife, isn't it?' I gasp. 'Please tell me she's okay.' Tears prick my eyes as I cling to the desperate hope that Isabella is going to walk in the door right now with some hilarious tale of how our children tried to stop her leaving the house tonight.

I imagine her stepping into the lobby. She's wearing the violet silk dress that was laid out on the bed earlier. It clings to her curves before falling in waves to the floor. Her gorgeous, glossy hair is piled up in an updo. Her eyes sparkle as they meet mine and she flashes that half smile she reserves just for me. The one that says I love everything about you.

I love you, Isabella. So fucking much it hurts.

'I know the drill,' I growl, 'You're supposed to break bad news in person, but fuck your police protocol. All of my family are here with me. Just tell me what happened.'

The detective clears his throat. 'There was a head-on collision. Three people were fatally injured. I'm so sorry, but Isabella was one of them.'

No. No. No. No. No.

All the oxygen whooshes from my lungs as I spin towards the intricate wooden panelling lining the wall and smash my fist through it. The cry that pierces the hall is so animalistic it takes a second to register it came from my throat.

The phone slips from my hand, smashing against the marble floor into a trillion tiny shards, along with my heart.

Pain engulfs me.

Pain, and rage, and the urge to punish someone.

Because there's no way this was an accident. No fucking way. James assured us the business with the O'Connors was dealt with, but a fatal head-on collision is too much of a coincidence after the stunt Killian pulled on the O'Connors last month.

And they will pay for this.

Slowly and painfully...

REDEEM ME-

Beckett Brothers book 2... Preorder Caelon's story here.... Redeem Me...

IVY

I'm the queen of handling tiny tyrants—I've been nannying since the era of bedtime bribery. But there's no guidebook for living with Dublin's most notorious grump and widower—my brother's brooding best friend.

Mr. Tall, Dark, and Tortured isn't just a challenge; he's a full-blown occupational hazard.

Under his icy shell, a fierce fire burns. Every fleeting touch ignites an attraction so intense it's impossible to fight.

He's broken.

And I want to fix him.

But who will fix me afterward?

Because if my brother discovers our forbidden fling, it won't just be fireworks—it'll be an inferno the size of hell.

And that's before Caelon's shadowy past comes blazing back into our lives...

CAELON

I live for two things: my kids and a relentless pursuit of revenge for the love of my life.

Tragically, I'm failing at both.

Then Ivy Winters, my best friend's sassy little sister, blazes into my world in search of a job and a fresh start. And while she's babysitting my children, I'm stuck with a promise to her brother to keep an eye on her.

But Ivy defies my rules.

Challenges me at every turn.

And somehow, she manages to ignite a spark that threatens to melt the ice surrounding my heart.

But just as I start to see the possibility of a life beyond my pain, the past comes knocking, demanding its due.

Now, I'm faced with the ultimate choice: revenge or redemption...

Click here for a super spicy bonus epilogue set in the 'new club' James and Scarlett join!

https://dl.bookfunnel.com/1tcmv0d6hp

ACKNOWLEDGMENTS

Thank you so much for reading *Wreck Me*. I hope you enjoyed Scarlett & James' story. I can't wait to bring you Caelon & Ivy!

I need to say a massive thank you to my beta readers, Jennifer Brooks-Brown, Kathy Mercure, and Katy Pyle. Your feedback, help, support, and encouragement mean the world to me. I'm so glad we found each other! I hope I get the chance to hug you all in person one day.

A massive thank you to my bookish besties, Sara Madderson and Margaret Amatt. I don't know what I'd do without both of you.

Thanks to all the fabulous members of my Facebook reader group, Lyndsey's Book Lushes. I appreciate your friendship and support, and I love our daily check-ins, the inappropriate memes, and just hanging out with you all. If you want to join us, we'd love to have you. https://www.facebook.com/groups/530398645913222

Last but not least, thank you to my endlessly patient husband who told me in no uncertain terms that this book wrecked him!

If you enjoyed Wreck me, please consider leaving review on Amazon, Goodreads & Book Bub.

Click here for a super spicy bonus epilogue set in the 'new club' James and Scarlett join!

https://dl.bookfunnel.com/1tcmvod6hp

ALSO BY L A GALLAGHER

REDEEM ME

IVY

I'm the queen of handling tiny tyrants—I've been nannying since the era of bedtime bribery. But there's no guidebook for living with Dublin's most notorious grump and widower—my brother's brooding best friend.

Mr. Tall, Dark, and Tortured isn't just a challenge; he's a full-blown occupational hazard.

Under his icy shell, a fierce fire burns. Every fleeting touch ignites an attraction so intense it's impossible to fight.

He's broken.

And I want to fix him.

But who will fix me afterward?

Because if my brother discovers our forbidden fling, it won't just be fireworks—it'll be an inferno the size of hell.

And that's before Caelon's shadowy past comes blazing back into our lives...

CAELON

I live for two things: my kids and a relentless pursuit of revenge for the love of my life.

Tragically, I'm failing at both.

Then Ivy Winters, my best friend's sassy little sister, blazes into my world in search of a job and a fresh start. And while she's babysitting my children, I'm stuck with a promise to her brother to keep an eye on her.

But Ivy defies my rules.

Challenges me at every turn.

And somehow, she manages to ignite a spark that threatens to melt the ice surrounding my heart.

But just as I start to see the possibility of a life beyond my pain, the past comes knocking, demanding its due.

Now, I'm faced with the ultimate choice: revenge or redemption...

Redeem Me... click here to learn more.

ABOUT THE AUTHOR

L A Gallagher writes swoon-worth contemporary romance featuring billionaire bad-boys, blush-inducing steam, and copious amounts of glamour.

Come hang out at her Facebook reader group Lyndsey's Book Lushes to find out more! https://www.facebook.com/groups/530398645913222

Made in the USA
Monee, IL
15 August 2024